MONOCOLO

also by Theodore Taylor

THE STALKER

MONOCOLO

A NOVEL BY

Theodore Taylor

DONALD I. FINE, INC.
New York

Library of Congress Cataloging-in-Publication Data
Taylor, Theodore, 1922–
Monocolo : a novel / by Theodore Taylor.
p. cm.
ISBN 1-55611-165-7
I. Title.
PS3570.A9549M6   1989
813'.54—dc20   89-45517
CIP

Manufactured in the United States of America
10   9   8   7   6   5   4   3   2   1

DESIGNED BY IRVING PERKINS ASSOCIATES

For Pat and Tom Killoran
With Love

The Book of Bocor defines "jumbi" as an *evil spirit* . . .

To kill an evil spirit drive a gilded splinter into its heart.

—THE BOOK OF BOCOR, PARIS, 1827.

To kill a jumbi shoot it six times with lead bullets.

—DETECTIVE LIEUTENANT LABURNUM HOTCHKISS
ST. THOMAS POLICE DEPARTMENT, 1987.

BOOK ONE

PART I
Las Vegas

1.

SUNDAY NIGHT, JANUARY 28, 1979—Epperson "Fingers" Watts, Jr., wide receiver for the Oakland Raiders, was saying, "Now, here's a good-looking piece of thigh," as he inserted it into the full-color erotic jigsaw puzzle. Well, he thought it looked like a piece of thigh, up near the hipbone. Female thigh, he believed. Smooth enough, ivory flesh tone.

"And here's a man's foot," said Mavis O'Connor, smiling over at him. "Isn't this fun?"

Yes, it surely was.

She'd said she wanted to play a game before they went off to bed, something stimulating. Epp didn't think he needed much of that. He was already stimulated just looking at Mavis.

"Yeah," he said, and laughed. The laugh was as much cough and grunt as laugh.

They were at O'Connor's glass-top table in front of her rain-spattered picture window on the tenth floor of the Bay Vista condos, in Alameda. San Francisco and the bridges, visible most nights across the way, were wiped out by the Pacific storm front that extended south to the Mexican border. So said the FM, which was providing silken Sarah Vaughn as well as a weather report.

The rain did give a cozy, closed-in feeling to Mavis's apartment. All it lacked was lazy flames and a dog asleep on an Oriental rug by a fireplace. The expensive rug was there. It was one of those white-on-white apartments. White drapes, white rug, white couch. Epp had never seen so much white, including Mavis, in an apartment.

Looking around for an adjoining piece of female thigh in the curlicue pile on the glasstop, Epp asked, "Where did you ever get this?"

"Specialty shop on Broadway, in the city. Nineteen ninety-five.

Or you take your own negative over there and they blow it up to ten and a half by thirteen, mount it on heavy cardboard and then jigsaw it. That's thirty-five. I haven't done that as yet."

She would, in time, he guessed. Something unique. "What else will they think of? Porno jigsaw puzzles?"

"I knew you'd say that." Mavis looked up and smiled, using her thumb and forefinger to pincer part of a man's leg.

Mavis was a dark-haired water-rights lawyer, apparently doing very well for herself. Only one floor above her was the penthouse. About thirty, Epp estimated when she'd opened the door. Nice slim body under the red caftan, he also estimated. She was wearing Bombay sandals. Nose a little too large, she was not so much pretty as striking. Mideast rather than Irish. Brown eyes.

Spotting what had to be part of a breast he began searching for the other half. "You collect football players?" he asked casually, without looking at her.

"A few. They have nice bodies, like yours."

"Only the wide receivers and running backs. Not the linemen."

"Not the linemen," Mavis agreed. "I like speed and agility. I'm a real fan, Epp. Watched every game last season. Watched every catch you made."

"Did you, now? The one I hang my hat on was against the Chiefs in the fourth quarter, first game. Kenny threw that one on a wire. I went up five feet, I swear, got my fingertips on it. Still don't know how I caught it, even after looking at the film ten times."

Mavis said, "I don't know how you caught it, either. They'd put in four defensive backs."

This was shaping up as an exceptionally fine evening. The lady knew her football; outright said she wanted to go to bed; had this crazy puzzle going. Fun and games on a wintry night.

She'd cooked curried breast of chicken in wine, white grapes spread over it; broccoli with cheese sauce; whole midget carrots; poached pears for dessert. Rather than go out and get all wet, we'll eat here, she said. No choices.

That was great with him, anyway. Home-cooked meal for a change. Elegant apartment. What more could he ask for? Coffee and Grand Marnier at the table. In addition to knowing her football, she knew how to live. Epp was learning how to do that, at long last. Live the sweet life.

George Williams, a running back who'd gone home to Anahuac, Texas, after the Raiders lost out in the play-offs, had arranged the date. Mavis wasn't at all a groupie, George had said. Just a fan who goes to extra lengths to be nice to football people.

"You two'll get along just fine," he'd said.

So far, GW was absolutely right, Epp thought, trying to locate the woman's upper arm. Mavis was doing the guy. They were working the puzzle outside-in. The usual way, Epp remembered from childhood.

Mavis's long fingers were poised with a cruciform of an erect penis. "You said you were leaving in the morning for Vegas."

Epp nodded. "Yep. Our publicity man has a Stardust connection and got me comped for two days. I'll see the show, shoot a little craps, then go on to Philadelphia."

"Driving?"

"I need wheels back there. Papa's in Philly."

"That's right, you were born there. I read that in *Raider Profiles*."

"No, that's wrong. I was born down in the islands. St. Croix. But left there when I was a kid."

"You like Vegas?"

"I've only been there once, passing through."

They finished the puzzle about nine o'clock, Epp saying, "God-almighty, look at that position."

Amusement in her eyes and smile, Mavis said, "You want to try it?"

Rain was still blotting out San Francisco.

Same night, almost same time, Jin Lee was about to die in a sewing loft at Ninth and Wall in downtown L.A., and his whole slender body, clad in a white shirt, dark pants and black cloth slippers, rather like what most people wore to the electric chair, was rattling, doing a Saint Vitus dance.

Even his wide-eyed head was bobbing as he stared at the stocky man in the Brooks Brothers gray topcoat and snappy gray Borsalino felt hat. The battered face beneath the brim was truly as void of feeling as the eyes of a frozen piglet.

Jin, who was forty-six but looked much younger, really too young to have to join his celestial ancestors on this drizzly Sunday night, pleaded, "I give back the money, I give it all back . . ."

"Yes, you did," quickly acknowledged Yorgos Stathos—"Yorgi Greco" in certain sub-circles in Illinois—black leather briefcase resting against the muscular calf of his left leg, also encased in premium wool. Inside the case was five hundred thousand in laundered cash, in hundreds, heroin proceeds from the Golden Triangle. Not a lot, admittedly, but money was money, L.A. or Laos.

"But you had to be asked, Jin Lee, dintcha?" said Yorgi, pulling a silenced Walther .38 out of his wide coat pocket, shooting the thief first in the bridge of his nose, then in his open mouth and finally in the hollow of his throat. The Singaporean went backward at a jerky forty-five-degree angle, splattering crimson and pieces of his head over a rack of white dresses.

To Yorgi Greco and his employers, Jin Lee was now a positive and timely lesson to the other Asian laundry boys who operated around greater L.A.—a newly deceased example of why never to steal from people you don't really know.

He picked up the heavy briefcase, hurrying out of the old four-story Sid Issac building, which was begging for a six-point Richter scale earthquake, out into the chill and wet California night, soon catching a cab to The Biltmore, which was also begging for an earthquake. All of L.A. was waiting for the big one in '79.

Up in the room, after carefully cleaning and shifting the Walther over to his suitcase for United luggage check-through to Las Vegas—there was no security check on hold luggage—Yorgi called Guido Malavasi, in Oak Park, Illinois, not a great distance from The Loop.

"Got the money," said Yorgi, without salutation or jubilation.

Guido well knew the voice, a scratchy, raspy one.

"Any problems?" Guido asked.

"Nope."

"Okay, *amico*," said Guido. "I'll tell the other party."

Four hundred fifty thousand of the recovered money to the "other party," whoever they might be. Yorgi didn't bother to ask. In fact, he didn't want to know. Ten to Guido and his father, Tony Ox; forty to Yorgi. It wasn't much of a job. A no-risk contract. Yorgi was quite satisfied with the forty. Tax-free, of course. Fly out Saturday, meet with Jin Lee Sunday. Whack him. Worked out to twenty thousand a day. Not bad at all. Better than running numbers, in fact. A lot better.

Send the money back to Oak Park by Federal Express on Monday, Guido ordered. "To me!"

Why? Yorgi wondered about that, truly puzzled by it. What was Guido's reason? Why couldn't Yorgi take it on back himself? He'd be going Wednesday. What was two days? Whatever . . . But smiling now, almost gleeful, a rare event, Yorgi said, "I'm off to Vegas in two hours. I'll say hello to Molly Bodden for you."

"Do that," said Guido, in a nearly pleasant tone. "Have fun and remember what I told you about Molly—she's a *mortaretto*."

Thinking about Molly Bodden being a firecracker, exploding, Yorgi laughed and said, "Don't worry, *amico*."

As he hung up in Oak Park, Guido Malavasi had a thoughtful look on his round dough face. Redialing to a number in Searchlight, Nevada, which wasn't too far south of Vegas, in the high desert west of Lake Mojave, Guido got Floyd Cramer, same name as the pianist, saying to him, "He's coming in tonight, staying at the Stardust. Why don't you go on up there tomorrow?"

Floyd said, "I'll be glad to do just that."

He drawled it. He was an Oklahoman from Cordell, in Washita County, currently living in a rundown mobile park in Searchlight, one of those places with thin dust on the windows and car hoods, Coors and Bud empties all around; rusting auto parts.

Tall, slack-jawed, thin-wristed, with an oversized adam's apple, he looked like he might be a Dennis Weaver tobacco chewer and wear overalls. But Floyd didn't even smoke, and he wore jeans over his polished cowboy boots; wore a crisp denim shirt, wore a Stetson, black or cream-colored. Floyd was the type that drove pickups. He had one, white Dodge '76, gun rack above his big ears. On occasion, a Steyr Mannlicher Model L occupied it. Floyd was pretty good at shooting elk, over in Wyoming.

"He'll be under the name of Joseph Carlucci. Write it down. I'll spell it."

Floyd scribbled while Guido spelled it.

"I told you what he looks like."

"Yep. Little like an ape."

"A lot like an ape."

"When do I do it?"

"Whenever you can. I fixed him up with a showgirl for Tuesday night. Molly Bodden. She's in the Stardust and likes to play roulette on her off-nights."

"Where?"

"Tropicana, Hilton, Dunes. But don't do it there, for chrissakes. Wait'll he takes her home, then pop him."

"What if she gets in the way?"

"Whack her, too."

Guido had gotten Floyd Cramer from an old friend in Oklahoma City with the following recommendation: he's a Mormon, doesn't drink, hasn't got much of a record and he's not too expensive.

The latter was the decisive factor. Guido offered him ten thousand to take out Yorgi Greco.

Floyd Cramer agreed. Pop him.

Mind off elsewhere but displaying the usual wide, set smile that matched those of the other chorus girls on the Stardust stage, Molly Bodden was going through her routine in the big finale of the second Sunday-night show, her long legs gliding, her long arms sweeping.

10

Lead in the high-kicking, fast-paced Donn Arden Parisian revue, her final near-nakedness was adequately covered by a rhinestone loin strap below the belly button. Elegantly tall, she had a near-perfect body, yet there was a young innocence about her that was drawing the looks of most males, and quite a few females, in the crowded, smoky big red room. The innocence played counterpoint to the exotic, stirring up random thoughts of sweet seduction.

Rightfully so, she was one of the few dancers ever given voice credit in the Café Continental show, ". . . Brazilian Nights, featuring Miss Molly Bodden, from the island of St. Thomas, down in the Caribbean Sea . . ."

As usual, Molly knew the eyes were out there but she had learned the trick of appearing to look into them yet over them. And, in fact, she was not conscious of her nudity. She felt as dressed as anyone in the audience. . . . This night, as she moved to the beat of the music, she was designing a long skirt to be worn a few inches above the ankle, flat-pleated all around. Perhaps with buttons all the way up one side. Partly unbuttoned, the skirt would reveal a portion of leg. Last night, through most of the two performances, she had thought about a perky red suit with a knee-top skirt and hot pink blouse. Wear it with matching red stockings and red low-heel pumps. She was always designing in her head. One day she would do it for real. . . .

Brass and drums rising to crescendo, the show was suddenly over, dancers scurrying off, Molly thinking she had, indeed, put gold buttons up one side of that long skirt.

2.

THINKING ABOUT THE NIGHT with Mavis, indeed a most challenging, fulfilling evening, promising himself he'd keep in touch with her, come back to all that white-on-white in the spring, Epp got on the road to Vegas Monday morning in time for the seven A.M. rush hour.

He took 580 out of Oakland, planning to cross over to 99 at Los Banos; then from Bakersfield 58 on into the desert and finally 15 to Vegas. Figure on arriving Tuesday.

The silver-gray Porsche with CATCHER on the plates had been fine-tuned the week before and was running smoothly, as if all the parts were bathed in premium light oil. Finally clearing heavy traffic after Livermore, he glued it on sixty-five and settled down for the long drive, wishing Mavis was sitting beside him for talk. Class lady.

Though he tried not to show it, Epp was still uncertain when he was around class ladies, especially older ones. But not more than five, six, seven years separated them, he thought. Yet she'd been instructional last night whether she knew it or not. The apartment, the food, the wine, the puzzle; the bed. Beneath that red caftan had been a superb body. No surprise there.

He wondered whether or not he could handle a white lady like Mavis O'Connor over a lengthy relationship. Would he always feel inferior as he'd felt at times last night? Would she make him feel inferior without even knowing it?

He showed the cocky Epp Watts everywhere—until he got into places like Bay Vista condos, with women like Mavis O'Connor. Likely, he was making a helluva lot more money than she'd ever make. But she already had what money couldn't buy.

12

For quite a while, Epp had felt inferior to very few men. He was expert at what he did and had as promising a career as there was in the NFL. With his flying feet, split-second reflexes that were on automatic pilot and hands that caught and held like sorghum, Epp had everything going for him Sunday afternoons from August to December; perhaps even into Super Bowl again. Sometime.

But he was thinking more about Mavis O'Connor than about football as the Porsche traveled a lot of miles south.

Also on Monday morning, comfortably settled into the Stardust to do a little gambling and date Molly Bodden, the *mortaretto*, a vacation of sorts, Yorgi decided not to ship the briefcase by Federal Express after all, no matter what Guido Malavasi had said.

That was a damn fool thing for the *sottocapo* to say, a careless thing to say.

Plane might crash; some *kooklah* could mix up the tags. He'd take it back to Oak Park personally, the safe way. Yorgi thought that Tony, the *capo*, who always vacationed in Miami Beach in January and February, would approve of that—flying the money back personally. Tony Ox never took chances with money.

In the afternoon, he called Molly Bodden at the number Guido had given him.

"Molly? Molly Bodden? Joe Carlucci!"

"Yes."

"Guido Malavasi told me to call you."

There was a pause.

"Guido, from Chicago," Yorgi reminded.

"Oh, yes . . ."

"You busy tonight?"

"I'm working tonight, but we're dark tomorrow night."

"You available for dinner, a little roulette?"

"You like roulette?" She sounded young, like Guido had said.

"No, but I hear you do."

She laughed. "It's my only vice."

Not the only one, Yorgi thought, according to Guido.

"Okay, what time do we get together?"

"Nine-thirty."

He'd been with the Malavasi family for seventeen years, first as an amateur fighter around Chicago, a brawler, no finesse, no counter-punching. Just stalking and slugging, taking a lot of punches just to get one in.

Owned by Tony Ox from the day he turned pro at eighteen, a fighter from St. Louis had broken Yorgi's jaw in three places and Tony retired him at the age of twenty-one to become a full-time enforcer. Just his looks were scary, even then—flat nose, scars in his eyebrows, cauliflower ears, all that black body fur.

By the time he was twenty-five, Yorgi was known as a man *che non porta mosca sul naso,* one who would not allow a fly to dance on the end of his nose. By the time he was thirty, the *animale* was a part-time *caporegime.* And the free-lancing began.

Yorgi's services were usually required in the Chicago area, but sometimes he went to New York or to Kansas City or out to San Francisco or Los Angeles; sometimes to Phoenix or Dallas. Sometimes as Joseph W. Carlucci, other times as Nikolas Katsanis. He was lent to other friendly mafioso now and then though they hadn't known him by name.

Told to look up Jimmy Rosenberger, publicity director at the Stardust, Epp was trying mightily to get to Vegas but sat in a funk at police headquarters, 1601 Truxton, in Bakersfield, while a methodical detective named A.D. Gleason filled out a report. The time was 9:50 P.M. and Epp was annoyed.

"That your full name, Epperson Watts?"

"Junior."

"Junior. Okay. Now, physical description."

"Why do you need that? I'm just a witness."

14

"We require it."

Epp said, "I'm six-two, weigh a hundred ninety-six, ninety-seven . . ."

"Slow down," Gleason complained.

"Gray eyes?"

"Last time I looked."

"Brownish-red hair?"

Under his breath, but barely, Epp said, "Jesus," and added, "or reddish-brown hair."

Detective Gleason, a gum chewer, asked, "Age?"

"Twenty-five."

"Occupation?" His pen took forever, as did his mouth.

"Football player."

Detective Gleason glanced up again from his report form, a little surprised. "You do look familiar."

"Oakland Raiders," said Epp.

"Yeah! Yeah, now I know who you are," Gleason said, nodding. "You're the black guy they got who isn't black, from the Caribbean?"

"Or the white guy who isn't white. I'm all screwed-up in that regard. Yeah I was born down there."

"Well, pro football player? We don't get many of them through here. We had Joe Namath come up here for a benefit when he was with the Rams. Now, your address."

"Oakland or Philadelphia?"

"You live in two places?"

"Oakland, during football season."

"Give me both." A. D. spit out a Juicy Fruit ball and put in a fresh stick.

Epp complied, with a sigh: the Oakland answering service and his papa's number in Philly.

"Okay, now the good stuff," said Gleason. "The shooting went down at six-twenty. That's what I have."

"About that time. I know I went into the store sometime after six. I went in and went straight to the icebox."

"Which is here." Gleason's pen point was touching the diagram.

"Yeah. I was bending down and getting the six-pack of Seven-Up when I heard this voice say, 'Empty the drawer.' I stood up and saw this guy with an Afro standing up at the counter, his back to me, and I figured he had a gun . . ."

"Slow down," said the detective.

Epp waited.

". . . and I said to myself, I'm not gonna be a hero, and damn if I didn't drop the six-pack. The guy with the Afro turned to look in my direction, then I heard the shots, bang, bang . . ."

"Slow," said Gleason.

Epp waited.

"What happened then?" Gleason asked.

Epp said, "You already know what happened. The stickup guy got it twice in the chest. I stayed ducked down for three or four minutes . . ."

"Anything else?"

"I finally went up to the front counter, and there was the Afro on his back, gun still in his hand, mouth wide open, blood all over his chest, the Iranian still pointing his gun at the dead guy, holding the phone in his other hand."

"He was that way when the first car arrived," said A. D. Gleason.

Epp nodded. "And you know, the son of a bitch still charged me for that six-pack of Seven-Up. If I hadn't dropped it, *he* might have been on the floor."

Gleason laughed. "You going on to Vegas tonight?"

Epp shook his head. "I've had it. I'll go tomorrow."

"You a gambler?"

"Not much of one," said Epp. "Little craps, little blackjack. Actually, I'm on my way home. Philly. My papa lives back there. I flew back to Oakland from Miami so I could take my car home. Vegas is just a stopover."

"What were you doin' in Miami?" asked Gleason.

"Dallas and Pittsburgh. Super Bowl, ten days ago." Man where were you? On Mars?

16

"You want to sign this," said Gleason, shoving the report over. "Read it first."

Epp found it hard to sleep, still seeing the guy with the Afro being blown away, pool of thick red on his chest, look of surprise on his face, tenth-of-a-second shock when he realized the Iranian had a gun, too.

Dumb bastard should have known a store like that one, neighborhood convenience in a mini-mall, wouldn't be holding a lot of cash. Maybe two hundred, three hundred. Maybe that's all the guy wanted, needed. Just enough for forty-eight hours of fix. Yeah, he must have known that when he walked in. Took his chance.

Epp had never remotely thought of doing dope, though it was all around him in Philly when he was a kid. He'd puffed a little weed in high school, a little more at Elon. But he hadn't done a suck of grass since college. Wasn't interested. Didn't do that much for him, got him laid-back more than he was already. And even the thought of kissing the horse lady, like the Afro guy was probably doing, scared him to death.

There were two mean worlds out there, and he was lucky to be in the right mean one.

What bothered him about the guy with the Afro was his age. Somewhere between twenty and thirty, and that made him close to twenty-five. Here Epp was at twenty-five, making a couple of hundred thousand a year going out to catch passes and run with a forty-dollar ball, and that guy had cashed it all in for a syringe.

The first cop to arrive pulled the sleeve of the corpse up, nodding at what he saw. Tales of the needle.

Epp kept thinking how lucky he was as the trucks on 58 rumbled on into the night.

Molly usually removed foundation and eye makeup in the Stardust dressing room after the last show but waited until she got home to do the rest. Take a long hot shower, cleanse her face thoroughly and moisturize.

Towel around her head, she sat in a faded cotton robe on a high stool in the bathroom, in front of the basin and mirror, massaging the tubed Lancome into her skin. Having gotten a letter from her mother that day—Chaktri asking if she could spare a couple of hundred—Molly was thinking of St. Thomas as her fingertips worked over the cheekbones.

Okay, she said to herself with a sigh, she'd send down two hundred on Friday. She wondered what Chaktri had done with the five hundred she'd sent at Christmas. Yet she also knew it was tough to make ends meet down there. Chaktri, a seamstress; brother Nedley still in school. Thank God the little house was clear.

Now matter how frugal she was, at this rate Molly knew it would take her ten years to get enough money to open a dress shop on Main Street in Charlotte Amalie. She'd now been at the Stardust for ten months, and as of this night her savings account had eleven hundred eighty-some dollars in it, eight hundred of which had come from roulette. Now the account would drop below a thousand again.

Looking at herself in the mirror, she said, "You got to get lucky at the wheel. You got to tell it when and where to stop. Mind over matter, Molly. Mind over matter . . ."

Epp rolled away from Bakersfield after breakfast, about eight o'clock, heading for Barstow, Baker, and the Nevada border. The weather was blue-skied and crisp, southern California's usual winter sun shining down.

"Staying Alive"—wasn't that what it was all about?—was drumming out of a Bakersfield station in stereo, filling the Porsche with sound.

He pushed the dead guy with the Afro as far away as he could get him, way out there, trying to think about Philly and Papa. Once he got home it'd be the same thing for a week or so, Papa taking him everywhere to see the same people all over again, all of Epp, Sr.'s friends; everybody at Bookbinder's, where Papa still cooked.

"My son, Epp, Junior, the star *wiiide* receiver for those mean Oakland Raiders."

His papa would be standing there beaming, grinning so hard Epp thought he might lose his false teeth.

He'd even introduced his son to the Puerto Rican pot-scrubbers in the kitchen. They couldn't understand a word of English.

He'd met all the old cronies and some of the giggling senior citizen women Epp, Sr., was playing with now that Thready was long gone. Epp got a kick out of it, knowing that Papa was bursting with pride. During the season, he'd have as many as twenty over on Sunday afternoons for beer and popcorn when the mean Raiders were on TV, leading the cheers.

The music from *Saturday Night Fever* and *Grease* followed Epp until the Bakersfield signal gave out, then Barstow came in with country, a Merle Haggard salute. That lasted almost to the Strip.

Floyd Cramer thought he spotted Joe Carlucci at a Stardust blackjack table Monday afternoon.

He went over to a house phone, keeping his eye on Carlucci, to have him paged.

He watched as Carlucci passed a bill to a drink girl to have her go answer the phone.

That's *him*, Floyd decided. He was an *ape*, hairy as a bearskin.

The girl came back to Carlucci, probably saying that no one was on the phone.

Carlucci stared up at her.

Epp checked into the Stardust about two P.M., went by Jimmy Rosenberger's office to say hello and thanks for the comp, but the publicity man wasn't on the premises. Epp left his message of gratitude for the comp with the secretary. She said Jimmy would call.

The late afternoon sun was pale and the air on the cool side this thirtieth of January, but Epp spent an hour by the pool reading the L.A. papers, then twenty minutes in the Jacuzzi.

Dinner by himself at eight. Jimmy hadn't called.

Now, at a little after nine, he was in the casino halfheartedly into craps, playing the *front line* and losing. He'd dropped sixty so far, big-bellied dice shooter a dud. Mainly due to Papa, Epp always watched his money.

A half hour later, he was back in his room, propped up in bed, intent on finishing a John D. MacDonald novel he'd started in Oakland. Travis McGee adventuring again.

So much for the bright lights of Vegas.

3.

YORGI STOOD PATIENTLY by Molly Bodden, watching her as she finished dropping twelve hundred, *his* twelve, here at the Hilton. Like Guido had said, she was making sexy little moans, throaty little ululations, doing torso-English that could inflame icicles, special pleadings to the roulette ball, coaxing it with her shoulders, urging it to drop with her head, cleavage straining. Little moans, all right, Yorgi observed, watching her blow a kiss at the white sphere that was running the groove. Moans should come with the second act, maybe the third, when her head was between his legs, not with that lousy three-quarter-inch ball. From the moment he'd rung her apartment bell, he'd had a terrific mental hard-on, a throbbing cylinder up in his brain, thinking about those long dancer legs twining around him, that pink tongue making him scream, her whole exotic body doing kinky things to him.

Nineteen tender years, Guido had sworn.

She was a shade darker than a ripe lemon. Long hair the color of a slick young sable. So young, yet she seemed to look serenely around at the world as if she owned it; was dangling it like a yo-yo.

Guido had promised Yorgi a good time after L.A., Jin Lee and the half million. This was it! *Now!* A living bonus, so to speak, a *chocolate mousse*, a *cafe au lait*.

From a lounge came echos of a group singing, "Alive, alive, oh, alive, alive, o-oh, singing cockles and mussels . . ."

Yorgi grinned. Yeah, the right music. Cockles and muscles.

He'd watched Molly undulating like an eel on stage Monday night, early and late shows, sitting there alone at his postage-stamp table, giving the maître d' twenty for a runway seat, priming himself, sipping brandy; thinking about his Jin Lee bonus. Four drinks all night. Yorgi wasn't much of a drinker because of his line of work.

This nineteen-year-old was truly fantastic, Guido had sworn. Trip around the world. Sixty-nine. Yorgi couldn't wait. Said she'd won eight hundred dollars here at the Hilton a couple of weeks back, using psychokinesis, guy from Salt Lake staking her. Yorgi didn't know what those words meant, and she explained, during dinner, that her mind influenced the ball. She played the blacks and had this compelling mystic power.

"You do?" said Yorgi, forehead bunched. "Like that ESP stuff?"

"Sort of."

Well, okay, said Yorgi, not having the faintest idea what she was talking about. And the compelling mystic power sure as hell wasn't working this night. He'd drawn off twenty-five hundred dollars of his own before putting the other party's briefcase into the Stardust vault.

She'd alternated between straight, split and street, the high odds, going nowhere.

Twelve hundred was enough.

The ball went *tock-tock-tock-tock* over the frets and slid into black six. She was on black 26, straight, for a hundred.

He murmured, "Thass it."

Molly turned a big, dazzling smile. "I tried for you, Joe." *For me, too.*

Illinois driver's license, all ID under that name. Joseph W. Carlucci. Nodding, he shrugged away the twelve hundred; grinned, thinking she looked like a teenage Lena Horne, lighter in skin, taller.

"Thass okay," he said.

Then he laid on an even wider comforting grin. But twelve hundred was enough stake on this goofy psychokinetic high-yellow split-tail sexpot.

"Where to?" he asked, as they went by the dollar slots.

One dumped for twenty, clattering hollowly, setting off a racket.

"Coffee shop. I'm an ice cream nut."

Over shoulder, that big, glittering smile beamed strongly at him, set in its pool of saffron. Almost two inches shorter than she was, he nodded and followed her happily, walking spread-legged, bullnecked-furry-beast behind the tall beauty, sniffing the expen-

22

sive perfume that trailed her. The sweet odor turned him up a notch as they went along, heads revolving as they passed, *looking at her*, frowning at him. Nothing new.

This was a surprising arrangement, thanks to Guido, who'd never seemed to like Yorgi, in Yorgi's long-held opinion.

Always before Yorgi had paid fifty to a bellhop, any place, then another two hundred, two-fifty, to a hooker. Only once had there been a problem: Dallas college hooker screaming at him, "You're ugly, you're fucking repulsive, you're a perverted ape . . ."

He'd promptly thrown her through the third-story window, glass and all, in only her panties. One of his split-second thoughtless reactions he'd more or less regretted later on. She was DOA at Parkland Memorial, also one of the last stops for John Kennedy, and Yorgi was contentedly on a plane for O'Hare about the same time, reading *The Sporting News*. That one and *Fighter's Magazine* were his two favorites. Unfortunately what the Dallas college girl hadn't known was that he was never a man to insult or be called ugly. As for perversion, that was always a matter of opinion.

"So, you're from St. Thomas, in the bee-utiful Caribbean. Never been there," said Yorgi, closer at her heels as they wound through the late-night casino crowd. "I'll pay you a visit sometime."

Purple sheath skintight, not a ripple, he wanted to grab her on the spot, palms already sweaty.

Over shoulder again: ". . . born in Trinidad but have lived on St. Thomas since childhood. My mother 'n brother are still there."

She didn't talk like a dinge from the tropic islands, down where the sun shined all day and the rain was gentle, as the Jamaica commercial said. Didn't talk like Harry Belafonte sang. *Maltilda. Day-o. Day-a-a-o.* She talked regular English.

A big sundae with a huge cherry on top was what she ordered, chocolate dripping down, scattered chips of nuts, whipped cream encircling it. It matched her, Yorgi thought, not having had anything the age of nineteen in years. God bless the changed Guido Malavasi. Yorgi had always thought that Guido was a turd-headed, spineless *porco*. Now maybe he was wrong about Tony's only, fatso son.

Licking and smacking her cherry lips, pink tongue lapping the spoon, driving him crazy, Molly said she sometimes just stood around casinos watching the roulette bowl, making mental bets. Winning, too. Just stood around watching. A roulette freak, she admitted.

Yorgi said he wasn't much for roulette. Basically a ladies game, always had been, he said. He was for craps, poker, the race and sports book. Men's games.

She smiled.

Molly knew there was a certain risk dating men like Joe Carlucci, friend of a "friend." The Carluccis always had stake money and were usually generous with it. They also liked to be seen with pretty girls. She knew that some of them had ideas about going to bed afterward, but so far she'd been able to handle that part. She'd made excuses, talked her way out of it. The dates had usually ended in the coffee shop, though sometimes there was more fuss and hassle than she needed. Still, with her larger purpose, she felt the risks were justified, went with the territory.

She was also convinced that sooner or later she would hit it big at the wheel. Go on a fifty-thousand roll: give the guy five for his stake, whatever it was, and put the rest in the Stardust safe until morning, then head for the bank. Molly constantly reminded herself of her plans for the future.

Sundae finished, she yawned and stretched. "I have to call it a night, Joe. But I've really had a good time."

Yorgi smiled at her. "I'll take you home."

"That isn't necessary, Joe. I'll catch a cab."

"No, no, no. I don't treat my ladies that way. I'm door-to-door." His smile widened.

"That's thoughtful, but it's silly. You live right across the street. I go home by cab all the time."

"Wouldn't think of it," said Yorgi, rising, going around to slide her chair out.

* * *

When Yorgi was only twenty-two, daffodils coming up in Illinois, Tony Ox told him to go visit Saul Persky, find out why Saul's grocery-clerk-and-meat-cutter's union hadn't been paying the monthly insurance premiums to Five Lakes Mutual Benefit.

"Tell Saul we're a little disappointed he hasn't kept up his insurance the last three months. Tell him we'd like a check for three thousand today an' try to keep up his payments, like a good fella," Tony Ox said.

As a new enforcer, Yorgi asked what he was supposed to do if Saul Persky didn't want to write a check.

"Up to you, Yorgi," said Tony. "I'll leave it up to you."

Fifty-nine-year-old Antonio "The Ox" Malavasi, or "Tony Bue," did resemble a *bue*, big-chested and heavy-thighed. He enjoyed being a storybook mafioso, even though he was not the major one in Illinois. Not a Giancana. He smoked a long panatello, saw Brando in *The Godfather* five times and hoped someday to be a Giancana. Guido, the son, educated at DePaul, wasn't even a pale copy of Tony Ox.

"My son, with his business administration degree, doesn't know how to administer business," said Tony, behind Guido's back.

Yorgi went along to see Saul Persky on Pershing Road, near Comiskey Park, and quoted the *capo* precisely. The family was principally involved in labor racketeering, loan sharking, numbers and prostitution. There were nineteen members.

Always mild-mannered, Saul was a bespectacled diabetic, always wearing black sleeveless sweaters October to May; said to tell Tony Ox that they were all sick and tired of paying extortion. Tell Tony the Local's council said that, all seven of them.

"Tell him we're not paying a dollar more for his phony insurance."

Yorgi said, "Okay," and left Saul's office.

Walking about a block to a hardware store, buying a rubber mallet, he returned to deck Saul with an overhand right, knocking him out, stuffing his thirty-dollar pocket handkerchief into Saul's mouth. Then used the mallet to break every bone in Saul's left hand.

A little later, Saul signed the check for the insurance arrears with his right hand. Yorgi had threatened to break that one too. He took his damp pocket handkerchief and departed.

Tony Ox was impressed with Yorgi's inventiveness and elevated him to chief enforcer two years later, as well as giving him a numbers district.

Secretly, Tony began wishing Yorgi was his son, his heir, not Guido. After a while, he wasn't so secret about it.

Guido had wanted Yorgi dead for a long time. Now it was up to Floyd Cramer.

At nine-fifteen, Floyd, driving his girlfriend's fender-dinged yellow '71 Mustang, had followed Carlucci from the Stardust to Molly Bodden's apartment house on Thirteenth, staying half a block away while the Whittlesea taxi waited for them to come down the steps, then he'd followed the cab, at another safe distance, to the Hilton.

He'd seen Carlucci again Monday in the Café Continental and he'd seen the girl as well during the show. A real beaut, he thought, hoping she wouldn't get in the way. Floyd had a soft spot for good-looking women.

By now, past midnight, parked where he could plainly see the Hilton taxi stand and doorman, he'd decided to do as the man in Oak Park said: follow them back to the girl's apartment, then wait outside for Carlucci to come down. He was betting the cab that brought them would be dismissed.

Wait for him, hit him just as he opened the door so he'd be framed in light. A Browning 9mm was nestled in the pocket of Floyd's Spanish sheepskin.

A few minutes before one he saw them walk out, jabbering, and started the Mustang, seeing the doorman beckon a cab from the line, watching them climb in, cab moving quickly to the Strip, turning north.

Traffic was light and Floyd kept a leisurely pace behind them, Volksie separating them. Then he saw the green light ahead changing to yellow and said, "Oh, fuck," as both the cab and the Volksie went on through the yellow fifty yards ahead. He pushed on the gas pedal to send the Mustang through the red.

No sooner had he cleared the intersection when he saw roof lights flashing in the rearview. "Christ," he groaned. Bastard must have been tucked in against the right-hand corner, just waiting for some late-night clown to run the light.

The Browning suddenly started to feel like stone in his coat pocket. Without moving his shoulders too much, he eased it under the passenger seat, then slowed to a stop, rolling down his window.

The two young cops came up singly, the first one staying a couple of feet behind the door jamb but leaning his head forward to say, "Good evening, sir. You aware you ran a red light?"

Floyd said cordially, "Not until I saw you behind me."

"Well, you did, sir." All young cops seemed to have been trained by the U.S. Marines. "May I see your driver's license, please?" So polite.

Floyd said to himself, Get this over with, take the ticket, go on to the girl's apartment and wait, pop Carlucci. No big deal, he thought, extending the wallet. Keep smiling, he said to himself.

"Please take the license out, sir."

Cop One passed the license to Cop Two, who took it back to the patrol car. Routine.

"It'll be a few minutes, sir," said Cop One. "You're from this area?"

"Searchlight."

"In the boonies?"

Floyd nodded, wondering how in the hell he'd know if Carlucci was up in that apartment or not. Hurry, fellows.

Cop One said, "I know a lady who has a sixty-four-and-a-half Mustang. Antique already. They only made twenty thousand on the first run."

"Is that right?" Floyd said, suddenly getting itchy. What the hell was that other cop doing back there?

"What is this one?"

"Seventy-one," said Floyd, beginning to sweat a little.

Then Cop Two walked back up, asking, "Do you own this vehicle, sir?"

"No. Belongs to my girlfriend."

"Did you know there's a bench warrant out for her arrest?"

"Jesus Christ," said Floyd, dumbfounded, "What for?"

"Failure to appear in court for two moving violations and five parking." She lived in Vegas half the time.

"I'll talk to her," said Floyd. Stupid broad, why didn't she tell him what was against the Mustang? He would have taken the truck, but thought it'd be too conspicuous around the casinos.

Cop Two came back and conferred with Cop One, then said, "Sir, could you please step out of the vehicle?"

"What for?" Floyd asked, a tic developing in his throat, a faint alarm that he might be in mud up to his navel.

Cop One said, "There's also a warrant out for your arrest. Suspicion of murder. Could you please step out of the vehicle and place your hands on the hood." Cop One had drawn his gun, Floyd noticed.

Then Floyd saw that another patrol car had pulled up behind the first one.

"There's been some kind of mistake," he drawled.

Back at Molly's apartment, a modest two-story fifties' pink stucco, twenty-unit place for showgirls to stay, seven blocks off the Strip, in the older part of town toward the sawdust joints, she was saying, in the hallway, "Well, goodnight, Joe. Thanks again."

Well, Goodnight, Joe, in a pig's ass. You my L.A. Jin Lee bonus, girl, knees to chin, my chocolate *mousse.* His foot was in the door. "Hey, arncha gonna invite me in for a nightcap?"

Stake her to twelve hundred and another hundred on lobster with forty-dollar wine and not get laid? Was she kidding? Had Guido been kidding? Think he was some *kooklah* who paid just to sit with her, stand around while she psyched the ivory ball? Thirty-five-year-old guy sit with the sexy teeny just to show off? Was that what she thought?

28

"Joe, the only thing I have is soft drinks."

Twelve hundred she just blew, some bonus, he was thinking, foot staying firm, now a knee. Maybe playing hard-to-get, being so young and tender. Kids often played funny games, he knew. Maybe she did this same thing to Guido?

"Okay, I'll have one an' we jus' talk. Okay?" he said, now smiling widely at her with his superior teeth, so good that people around Naperville asked him who was his dentist. Italian boy on East Ogden. Dr. Salerno. Yorgi had grown up around the Illinois wops and spoke their language. His barber was from Castelvetrano, around from Palermo. Yorgi was as much *guappo* as he was Greek, in some ways. He looked wop, Greek, Arab.

"Not for long, Joe. I really do have to get some sleep."

Daylight, maybe.

He had a plane to O'Hare to catch at ten-thirty. Call a cab at eight, get back to the Stardust, grab his bag, sign the half million out of the vault, check out.

Molly stood aside and he went on in, looking around, impressed. Ferns everywhere. White-painted wicker furniture. "Nice place you have."

Lots of bright colors. Some real paintings on the wall. Sewing machine. A mannequin with cloth draped over it. Full-length mirror, one-by props behind it. She didn't look at all like the type to have a sewing machine. His little sister, Ekaterini, had one and she wasn't at all like Molly Bodden.

"Very nice. Very, very nice," Yorgi said, smiling at her, nodding approval. "Very nice."

"I like it," nodded Molly, feet planted, standing with thin arms folded.

He took off his five-hundred-dollar blue blazer, dropping it on the back of the couch, and settled in. Yorgi always dressed well, dating back to his fighting days—Kuppenheimer suits, Henry Grethel ties, Arrow shirts, eight-hundred-dollar topcoats. Hats by Borsalino of Rome.

"Guido said you were only nineteen." Yorgi studied her face, thinking to catch a lie.

"Twenty next month."

"No roomies?"

Molly shook her head. "You want Calistoga natural orange, lemon, cherry, strawberry? Perrier?"

Perrier, yet? "Brandy. If you don't have that, scotch and soda."

"I said I didn't have hard stuff."

"Orange," he said with an alum face.

She went on into the kitchen and he sat down on the couch, calling out from there, "You got a boyfriend?"

"No one steady," she called back.

Winking toward the kitchen, he said, "How 'bout me bein' your boyfriend?" and grinned to himself, seeing his head in the full-length mirror. Why not? Yorgi Greco with this gorgeous creature, hand in hand, cheek to cheek, tongue to tongue, belly button to belly button.

She didn't answer.

From what he could see, the kitchen was painted red and yellow. Parrot colors. He could see she had a thing for parrot colors. Maybe being from the islands caused that. They were everywhere. They were on the mannequin. Everywhere. Maybe she did sew?

Out from the kitchen came her voice, finally. "You said you were from the Chicago area. That's a long way from Nevada."

Well, Molly, that's being diplomatic, Yorgi thought. "Naperville, 'bout thirty miles from Chicago. You go back with me, I can getcha good work."

She came out with the Calistoga natural orange, milk for herself. "What kind of work?"

"Any kind you want. I got friends in Chicago who got first-class clubs. Real high-class, like you are. Big spenders come in. Doctors, developers, iron and steel guys."

She sat down on the opposite end of the couch, tucking her legs, making sure no thigh was showing though her sheath was split. Ladylike, he saw, approving.

"No thanks, I like it here, Joe."

He kept on smiling widely at her. "Or I'd just put you up in a nice apartment. Let you decorate it. Pamper you."

He could see half her left breast hiding in the vee of the sheath and was so hard he thought he'd turn to stone. Nineteen going on thirty, eh? But she was acting like he hoped Kathy would act until she married Nikos Hajadaki. Ladylike, not showing her inner leg. The difference was that Kathy *was a lady*, not a topless dancer.

"What do I do then?"

"Wait for me to come home with roses in my hand an' take you out. To those classy places. Show you off, every night a new place."

"I don't think I'd like that kind of life."

"Well, what kind of life do you like?" Yorgi asked, betting on the answer, double or nothing. Five hundred.

"A quiet life," said Molly, eyes distant, looking off, looking into the future.

He'd won his bet, a thousand to himself.

Yorgi laughed. "Up on that stage every night, with that G-string? That's a quiet life?"

"That's not the real me out on the stage," Molly said. "Just the way I make a good living."

All these showgirls—Vegas, Reno—all had the same identical bullshit. *I'm really a good girl.*

"What is the real you?" Five-hundred-dollar hooking come with room service? Six hundred?

"Someone who is telling the truth. I'm working to save enough money to open a fashion shop down in St. Thomas, sell to all those people off the cruise ships. I design beautiful clothes, Joe. I designed what I have on and made it in this room."

"It's very nice."

"I figure three or four more years up here, then I'll go home, rent a store on Main Street and call myself Molly Bodden's." She was talking as much to herself as to him.

Yorgi shrugged. "But meantime you're not havin' much fun for nineteen."

"Enough."

"You date guys like me often?"

"Older men?"

"I'm not that old, for chrissakes. Twenty-nine. That ain't so old,"

31

he said, dropping six years. Just because he was half-bald didn't mean he was ancient. Wait'll he got in bed with her. She'd love his chest hair, snuggle it with her cheek.

"You date guys like me?" he repeated.

"Sometimes. Your friend called and said you were very nice."

Yorgi grinned, again exposing those glistening teeth against the midnight blue beard. "Now, haven't I been nice?"

Molly nodded quickly. "Yes, very nice."

"Well, why don't you come over closer?"

"You said we were just going to talk, Joe," she reminded him, rising, and excused herself to go to the bathroom.

Yorgi got up, turning the latch on the outer doorknob, dropping the two safety chains into their slots, and went over to stand in the short, narrow hallway, waiting for her to come out. The bedroom was only six or seven feet from his shining shoetips. He looked in there. A king-size. Plenty of room to do all those things Guido had said she'd done to him. Sixty-nine and so forth. Maybe they'd done it in the hotel. Yorgi had done it in cars and standing up in alleys. Even in a rowboat off Fifty-seventh Street beach.

The door opened and Molly saw that his thick, black-fuzzed arm blocked the way back to the living room. She said, "Joe, no problems, please. Time for you to go home. Thanks very much for tonight."

Her face told him she was suddenly terrified of Joe Carlucci, the way that Jin Lee had been.

Just like an old movie scene, he thought. "You let a thousand people a night look at your tits, now get in there an' get naked for me." Exactly like a scene in a flick, girl saying, "Me? Little me?"

She was staring at him, breathing shallow.

Grabbing for her, deflecting her hand, there was a sudden blur in his right eye and he felt a bee sting down the right side of his face, going down into his neck, as she twisted away and got safely back into the bathroom, locking the door.

Through it, he heard her say, "Go home, Joe, *please . . .*"

Looking down with his left eye he realized the whole front of his

32

yellow shirt was splashed with blood. He reached up to his right cheek and his hand came away covered with blood.

Good Christ, she's sliced me open, he thought.

He ran into the kitchen for a dish towel, found one that said Le Lapin on it and pressed it against the right side of his face.

He went back to the bathroom, yelling at the door, "You're *dead, you bitch.*"

Coming out, he saw himself in the full-length mirror, taking the towel away to look closer. Blood welled from the cut eyeball, more trickled down from the long cut on his cheek. He couldn't believe what he saw, what she'd done to him.

Retrieving the blazer off the couch back, he fumbled with the front-door locking system, finally getting it open, but ran back to the bathroom to shout again, "You goddamn nigger bitch, Guido tell you what I did for a living? Did he? Did he, goddamit?"

Blazer tucked under his arm, still holding the rabbit towel to his face, he went out into the street, walking west up toward Las Vegas Boulevard to catch a cab. Temperature in the low thirties, he began to shiver though it wasn't from the cold.

He finally hailed a cab, yelling, "Get me to a hospital."

The Chicano cabbie took one look at the man in the yellow shirt, blood all over him, and said, "*Si, senor.*"

4.

BUTTOCKS UP AGAINST THE BASIN, shaking all over, Molly hadn't heard the door slam but thought that Joe Carlucci was gone.

It had all happened so suddenly, so unexpectedly. Over in a second or two.

Earlier she'd guessed he might try something: the way he talked and moved, the way his eyes took her clothes off. She'd inserted the pinnacle of razor under her right index nail to use as a last resort. It had been in the bathroom for months, ever since Lucille Fernandez had visited, something Lucille had learned from Club Babalu girls on the San Juan docks, though Lucille was no hooker. They even used Krazy Glue to put on a razor tip for instant circumcision. "The guy is all ready to stick his thing in when the girl reaches down like she's cutting on a broom handle. It's bloody but it works," Lucille said.

Then she laughed. *"No mas problema."*

Now Molly knew she'd made a terrible mistake with the Italian. He'd knocked her hand back when he grabbed, so it was accidental, but how to explain that.

She now realized she'd been frightened of him from the moment she first saw him out in the hallway, guessing he was mafioso just as she'd guessed Guido was mafioso. But fat Guido had been the perfect gentleman, not touching her, not even making a verbal pass at her, just staking her at the table, content to be seen with her. He was a balled eunuch, she also guessed.

Lucille had warned her about letting strangers stake her. Howie Piaggi, the stage manager, and Jimmy Rosenberger, both had warned.

Molly waited another five minutes, still shaking, then slowly turned the knob lock and cautiously opened the bathroom door.

34

Looking out into the hallway, she saw that the front door was standing open—he'd gone—and ran to it, closing it, double-locking it, double-chaining it.

Then she stood with her back against it, heart beating wildly.

Panicked! Oh, my God, how stupid, cutting him! He'd never believe it wasn't on purpose.

Ten minutes later, Yorgi was in emergency at Humana Sunrise, young doctor on duty asking, "How did this happen to you? You might have lost your right eye. Whatever cut you came within a half inch of your jugular. I've got to numb your face up."

Shirt off, exposing all that coarse, black hair, Yorgi sat silently on the white stool, mind on an apartment across town. For a moment or two, he thought about going back to the hotel, getting the Walther and paying a short visit. But he wasn't sure about the location of the apartment.

Turning to the nurse, the doctor said, "This'll take fifteen, twenty stitches." Back to Yorgi, he asked again, "How'd this happen?"

Yorgi glanced up, blood trickling from his right eye and down his cheek. The nurse dabbed at it with gauze. There was the wild rage in his good eye focused on the questioner. "Cut myself shavin'."

This was Vegas: wise emergency-duty doctors didn't ask many questions in certain situations. Two A.M., a gorilla by the name of Joseph W. Carlucci comes in with what looks like a scalpel swipe, like someone set out to disfigure him, blind him.

"I'm not a plastic and reconstructive surgeon, but I'll do the best I can with your cheek unless you want to wait until morning. You'll wind up with a scar, either way. The plastic man might be smaller."

"Do it," snapped Yorgi, clasping and unclasping his hands, his feet almost stamping.

The young doctor knew nothing about ophthalmology; all he could see was an eye laid open. Ophthalmic surgeon Theodore Steinberg, awakened in a fashionable house off Rancho Drive, hurried over to Humana Sunrise, thinking there'd been an auto wreck.

35

Quickly examining Yorgi, shaking his head while doing it, he asked the same question, How did it happen?

"Shavin'," snarled Yorgi, wanting to bash the doctor. Someone.

"You're cut all the way through the cornea. Lens, retina, sclera, all cut. I can't save this eye, Mr. Carlucci."

"Take it, goddamit," said Yorgi, in a whipping, savage voice, thinking of the girl with the lemon skin.

Though gentle and balding, rather small, the surgeon did not intimidate easily. "I want you to understand that if I leave it in, problems may develop with the other eye. The membranes are actually very tough but with the damage done here . . ."

Yorgi roared, "Take it, I said!"

The doctor said, "All right, but you'll have to sign a paper. That's my protection in this optional procedure."

"Well, get the fucking paper," Yorgi shouted, both fists clenched on his knees, good eye aimed at Teddy Steinberg like a laser.

Teddy paid little attention to the glare and said calmly, "I'm going to plant a plastic ball in the socket, suture it in so that the prosthetic eye will have some movement."

Yorgi said, "Do what you have to do," in a voice barely heard.

The surgeon nodded and went off to prepare for the operation.

Yorgi awakened in the recovery room with an IV drip in his arm and felt up around his right eye. A bandage covered the socket with its inserted ball.

The nurse in attendance asked, "How do you feel, Mr. Carlucci?"

Yorgi glared at her like a cornered badger, ready to go for her throat. "I feel like I'm half-blind."

She had no answer for that statement.

An hour later he was wheeled from recovery to a room on the fourth floor and declined help getting from the gurney over to his bed in the ridiculous gown that exposed his fur, legs up to his shoulder blades.

"Doctor wants you to keep still," the nurse advised.

Swiveling his head, fixing her with his good eye, Yorgi asked, "When can I get out of here?"

"He'll tell you," she said, hastily departing, not wanting to tangle with Mr. Carlucci.

A few minutes later he got out of bed to go to the bathroom mirror. The eyesocket was covered with a gauze pad, and there was another bandage going down his face on the right side. He lifted that one and saw the thin red furrow down his cheek, black nubs of stitches like tiny railroad ties. She'd worked him over, all right. He looked like a disaster survivor.

Hands on the basin, he kept looking at the funny distorted face for a moment, making up his mind to take *both* her eyes, nineteen-year-old or not. Gouge them out with his thumbs, cut them out with a knife.

Floyd Cramer called Guido Malavasi from Clark County Jail at five-fifteen A.M., saying, "It didn't happen."

The phone warped Guido out of sleep and at first he couldn't put it together, despite the Oklahoma drawl. "Who is this?"

"Floyd Cramer."

"What the hell do you mean—it didn't happen."

"What I just said. You want me to say it another way?"

"Why didn't it happen?"

"I ran a red light and had complications. I'm in Clark County Jail on two counts and I think more are coming up."

"What's that got to do with me?" Guido asked, wide awake now.

"One of 'em is concealed weapon. *That's got to do with you.*"

"What do you want?"

"Money, pal. Bail and lawyer. I was working for *you.*"

"Okay. I'll wire you twenty-five hundred."

Floyd said that was a start and that he'd call again from Searchlight, if and when.

Guido got a faint but distinct whiff of blackmail all the way back to Oak Park and said to himself, "Uh, oh!"

Goodbye, Floyd Cramer.
Never heard of you, Floyd Cramer!
Let the Mormons bail you out!

Besides, Floyd Cramer hadn't done his work. Yorgi Stathos was still alive, still a threat, the apple of Tony's sharp eyes. Well, he'd try again with someone else.

Guido got out of bed and lumbered to the john.

5.

DOZING, THEN AWAKENING with a jerk at the slightest noise, Molly got up a few minutes after seven, going to the street-side window, parting the drapes carefully, scanned down for any sign of Joe Carlucci.

Early chill sun was creeping into the street.

She thought her hands had trembled all night and didn't know what to do about them. What kept coming back, almost photographically, was how he looked—oval head; dark shadow of beard; bristly hair on the back of his hands, even heavy on his stubby fingers; hair curling over his collar.

She could still hear his raspy voice through the door: "You're dead!" It went into her echo chamber. *Dead, dead, dead.*

Finally, she showered and put a robe on, going back to the street-side window several times to look out, thinking of calling the police but decided against that. Just mention *mob* in Vegas and out you go. "Addio."

She wanted some yogurt and fresh fruit but was afraid to unlock the door, go over to the mini-mart; afraid that Carlucci would be in the hallway or out by the front door. So she ate some dry cereal, washing it down with tap water. Then she paced for more than an hour, one room to another, back and forth, breath coming short, heart slamming.

She had Guido's number in Oak Park and thought about calling him, saying she'd accidentally injured his friend. By mistake. She was sorry. She'd panicked! She'd been gang-raped long ago and just plain panicked. Fear of rape was something she couldn't handle.

Could he please understand?

Please!

39

No, that wasn't a smart idea. If both men were mob, it wasn't smart at all to make that call.

She stood by the window, looking out, then closed her eyes, chin quivering . . . maybe it had been a superficial cut . . . She'd seen blood spurting before she ducked back into the bathroom . . . seen him touch his face . . .

She knew he was supposed to go back to Chicago this morning.

Maybe he *was* gone. Maybe just scratched, the blade didn't penetrate.

Maybe, maybe?

She went back into the kitchen, thinking about calling the hospitals to see if a Mr. Carlucci had been treated and was he all right? Had he been released?

Hesitating a few minutes, she began dialing. The second call was to Humana Sunrise. "I'm calling about a patient named Carlucci. C-a-r-l-u-c-c-i."

"Just a moment, please."

Molly waited, then the operator said, "I'll connect you to the floor nurse."

Molly asked about Mr. Carlucci and the nurse replied, "He's doing fine. He's resting now. Why don't you call late this afternoon."

Molly said, "I know he had an accident, but I'm not sure how serious it was."

The nurse said, "He lost an eye."

Molly almost dropped the phone.

"Hello?" said the nurse.

Molly said, "How long do you think he'll be there?"

"That's up to the doctor. Three or four days, I'd guess."

"Thank you."

Molly hung up.

Should she call Irene and ask her if it was all right to stay there a few days? Irene, another dancer, was her best friend in Vegas. But Irene had a one-bedroom place, a baby . . .

She'd wait another day.

* * *

About seven A.M., Epp placed a call to his friend Detective Sergeant Laburnum Hotchkiss on the St. Thomas force, but Laburnum wasn't in the waterfront office, Charlotte Amalie. He was over in St. John. Please tell Laburnum that Epp Watts is staying at the Stardust. Call collect.

Epp wanted him to check again on a piece of Bovoni Hill property, in one of the better sections of the island. Seller was in a bind, he'd heard last week during halftime between the Cowboys and Steelers, in the Orange Bowl. Epp had some cash on hand.

Laburnum had been his "police" escort when he returned to the islands for "Fingers Watts Day" after the '77 Super Bowl. Rookie Epp had caught two passes, one for a score. They'd gotten along famously and had kept in touch. Laburnum was a good man, a good cop and a good football fan. He enjoyed the annual thrashing and crashing on Sunday afternoon and Monday night.

Mid-morning, Yorgi was talking to his sister, Ekaterini, back in Naperville, thirty miles from Chicago via the East-West Tollway and the Eisenhower Express. Or the express Burlington commuter was just thirty-two minutes to The Loop. Yorgi liked Naperville because it was a family town and the priest at St. Athanasious, in Aurora, Father Peter Potamianos, was a fine man. Kathy attended regularly, though he didn't. Easter he went with her.

Tony had told him, "Buy in Stone Park, Melrose Park, Elmwood Park, Oak Park, be with our family," but Kathy had insisted on Naperville. She didn't want to be "with our family." Their family scared her.

"I'm in a hospital in Vegas, Kathy, so I won't be home today." She was at work at AT&T, in Lisle, so he wouldn't talk long.

"A hospital, Yorgi? What happened to you? Car wreck?" Alarm was in her sweet voice.

They were close, Ekaterini and Yorgos Stathos: their parents had been killed in a jet crash in '62, and Yorgi had practically raised Kathy. Like a daughter. He'd been a hen and brood mare to her. She was now twenty-five, a little pudgy, thick ankles; needed to lose

41

twenty pounds. But she had a pretty face, rosy cheeks framed in shining dark hair, a good *ehleeneekoss* girl, Yorgi told everybody. Smart girl. She translated electronic systems for AT&T. The boyfriend, Hajadaki, managed a PIP printing place on East Ogden.

"Eye problem," he said. The empty socket felt like it was on fire. "Phantom pain," the nurse warned.

"What kind of eye problem?"

For hours, almost from the time he'd come back from the recovery room, he'd been thinking of what to say to Kathy, to the Malavasis, to his barber, to the mail carrier and the guy at the 76 station; to his dentist, Dr. Salerno, to the guys at Peppitone's and to any other miserable son of a bitch who asked, "Hey, Yorgi, wha' happen your eye?"

Tell 'em some fucking dinge showgirl cut him up? Yorgi Greco, chief enforcer for the Malavasi family, the guy who mashed Saul Persky's fingers? Yorgi, the *animale*, lost his right eye to a nineteen-year-old? He was *monocolo* now. They'd laugh him off Rush Street, out of Columbine's, on North. Humiliate him!

Earlier, he'd gone over a dozen different stories. Now he had a splitting headache as well as the mental torment of that hole over his right cheekbone. Phantom pain, in a pig's ass.

The nurse asked him if he wanted a shot or pain pills.

Not yet. He wanted to get his story straight. They'd all belly laugh, except dear Kathy.

Say a rock spun out of some guy's tire and went through the cab window?

Say he picked up an alley cat and got scratched in the face. Yorgi Stathos picking up a cat? Nah.

Say some guy with a knife tried to mug him in the Stardust parking lot and he whirled around, got the knife right in the head.

Fat Guido would laugh. "Any mugger take one good look at you, Yorgi, and run like hell."

Tony would say, "Yorgi, now thass a lot o' shit. Now wha' happen?"

Then he tried to think of anyone else who was *monocolo*. Finally, he remembered there was a kid on the West Side who had one eye.

42

His father had taken him fishing and was casting out. Instead of a fish, he caught the kid in the cornea. Yorgi remembered the kid with the cheap, blue glass eye. It didn't look very much like the real one.

"Accident," he said to his sister. "A casino guy took me fishing on Lake Mead an' was casting out. Hook got me smack in the eye. My right one."

"Oh, my Lord," said Kathy, voice rising in concern. "Will you be all right? Did they have to operate?"

"Yeh, I'll be all right."

He didn't want to worry Kathy. Why tell her he lost it until he faced her. He tried to grin over the phone. "I'm tough. You know that."

Yes, she did know that he was tough. She'd first seen him box when she was eight.

Then he asked how things were back there. How was the weather? Not very good. Never was in late January. How was Hajadaki, the boyfriend. Fine, she said. He was hoping she'd soon get married, like a good Greek girl. Have a lot of plump babies. Make him an uncle. Uncle Yorgi.

She said everything was fine. When would he be home?

"A few days." First he had an operation to perform.

Did he want her to come to O'Hare and pick him up. She could get off from work, she said.

"No, no, I'll get a limo."

"Take care of yourself, Yorgos. I love you. *Ahndeeo.*"

"I love you, too, Ekaterini. *Ahndeeo.*"

Then he rang for the nurse and said give him a shot. What was this crap about "phantom pain"?

He closed his eyes, thinking about Guido and Molly Bodden. Why had Guido told him all that *tizzone* stuff about the showgirl? She wasn't even a teaser! Why had Guido set him up? Guido was a tricky wop, Yorgi had always thought. Nothing like his father. Yorgi was sure that Guido had said from time to time, "Let's get rid of that ugly Greek," and Tony had probably replied, "He's a good man, Guido, a good man."

Tony had begun openly treating Yorgi like a natural son and that was the problem. Tony would die some day and who would inherit the business? The *porco* son? Or tough Yorgi Greco?

Before he faded away from the Demerol, he figured out that Molly Bodden had palmed a small knife on him. They had them now. Women's purse knives. Just like they had tiny women's guns. Whatever happened to the good women? What happened to the ladies of the world, like Kathy.

Those were his last thoughts as he slipped under.

Molly must have looked out the Thirteenth Street window a dozen times during the day, not quite willing to believe that they could keep someone like Joe Carlucci in the hospital very long. He seemed like the kind of man who would get his clothes on and just walk out. She felt trapped . . . her brown '72 Volvo wagon was across the street . . . she could see it easily. But to get to it meant to run down the stairs, down the front steps, across Thirteenth. He could be waiting just inside the apartment . . . up at the end of the block . . . *anywhere.* Her mouth stayed dry all day, no matter how much water she drank.

Yorgi awakened in late afternoon just before the eye surgeon came in to look at the chart and to ask how he was feeling.

"When can I get out of here?" Yorgi replied, ignoring the state of his health.

"Several days, maybe even tomorrow if you'll stay in that bed and behave. You've had ophthalmic surgery, Mr. Carlucci. Removal of an eye is a serious procedure." It wasn't all that serious, but most patients didn't want to hear that.

"What if I don't stay?"

Dr. Steinberg replied steadily, "You may hemorrhage, and that you'll regret." Chances of hemorrhage were slim, too, but the very word made most patients behave.

44

"I've got to get back to Chicago," Yorgi insisted. After taking care of Molly Bodden, of course.

Teddy Steinberg said, "I'll do my best to get you back there day after tomorrow. Meanwhile, stay flat on your back, use the bedpan, behave yourself. Do you have an eye doctor in Chicago?"

"I live in Naperville."

"I'll recommend one in Chicago. He can take care of the prosthetics appointment. Friend of mine. Try to relax, Mr. Carlucci. You seem highly agitated, and that doesn't help recovery. We'll take good care of you."

The young doctor in night emergency had said he guessed that Carlucci was Mafia. Probably right, just from his manner and looks. An ugly, violent hoodlum. He'd add five hundred to the surgical fee and give it to the United Jewish Fund.

At about the time that Yorgi was listening to Dr. Steinberg, Molly was talking to Howie Piaggi, stage manager for the Stardust showroom. Howie was a concerned mother to the twenty-eight girls, providing everything from fatherly advice and chitchat to bunion pads and maxi-pads. He was a hyper five-foot-four, did the tanning parlor every other day and fought gray hair with formula.

"I got a problem, Howie," Molly said, a few minutes after four.

"What is it, babycakes?"

"The usual. A guy is pestering me, hanging around outside the apartment, waiting in the parking lot, and I don't want to drive for the next few days."

"Guy from out of town? Staying here?"

"I'm not sure." Joe was, she knew.

"Consider it done, babycakes."

"Have the driver come up and knock on my door, say who he is. Okay?"

"Done, my love."

The girls, especially the unmarried ones, were always having men problems. Some jerk from Keokuk falling in love overnight, calling;

following. Security was always glad to help. Abernathy, the chief, had standing orders to take care of the girls.

After Dr. Steinberg departed, Yorgi got around to calling Guido, saying he'd be a couple of days late and that he hadn't sent the briefcase Federal Express.

Guido exploded. "I've been on their asses all day. I've tried to call you a dozen times at the Stardust. Why didn't you send it like I told you? It's a half million, you jerk."

Yorgi was surprised at the yelling, the tone of voice. Jerk? What the hell was wrong with Guido?

Yorgi said calmly, "I wanted to make sure it was safe. I'll bring it Friday or Saturday." The Malavasis had always trusted him with money. At least, Tony had always trusted him.

"Why the delay? What's wrong with you?" Guido was downright surly.

"I got an eye problem." Why tell him now.

"You get in a fight, for chrissakes?"

Yorgi said no, he hadn't gotten into any fights. "I'll tell you when I get back."

"No later than Friday, goddamit," Guido said.

"Either Friday or Saturday."

"I'll be waiting," Guido said, slamming the phone down.

What the hell was wrong with him?

Yorgi spent the rest of the time before dinner trying out his new field of vision. Everything to the left was the same, of course, his sight bending around from a little past the nose—to the right— almost to the ear on the left. Like everyone else who had two good eyes, he'd always accepted vision the way it was. Like everyone else, he'd never contemplated being one-eyed.

To the right was a blank now, and he had to turn his head to that direction to see anything. From now on, if anyone was talking to the right, he'd have to turn his whole head in that direction to see them. If a car was coming from the right, he'd have to turn his whole head to see it. No more seeing out of the corner of that eye. If he had to

46

make a hit to his right, shoot that way, his whole head would have to turn.

He held up a finger on the right side to determine how far it would have to go before he saw it. He started the finger at his shoulder. Almost to the nose, he decided.

There was now an extra hazard in his line of work, coming at him from the right side. He'd have to turn his head instantly.

So Molly Bodden, in addition to leaving him half-blind, had robbed him of something very critical to his line of work. Crippled him, in a way.

Wednesday morning Laburnum Hotchkiss called collect from St. Thomas, and Epp asked him some questions about the Bovoni Hill property. Find out if it was still available? What did they want down?

"Do I get a finder's fee?"

"You didn't find the property. You were sitting next to me when the guy told me about it. That make you a finder?"

Laburnum laughed. "Well, I should be able to get a fee for something."

"You'll get a case of Molson if you get me some information."

"That's a deal."

Epp could picture Laburnum at his desk, in coat and tie. Even in high summer heat, he always wore a bright tie with his seersucker jacket and never seemed to sweat. Ashanti black, if seen around the UN building in New York he could be mistaken for a diplomat from the Sudan. Laburnum was diplomatic most of the time but also capable of armlocks and shootouts. Always a formal man, Laburnum didn't like to be called Lab or Hotch.

"Call me this afternoon, if you can," Epp said.

"Will try," Laburnum said.

PART II

1.

WEDNESDAY NIGHT THE CAFÉ CONTINENTAL was back in business, and Epp of the Oakland Raiders was introduced to the audience: leading AFC receiver in the season just ended. Epp took his bow with a big grin and wave of hand. A writer for the Charlotte, N.C., *Observer* had nicknamed him "Fingers" because he'd led all small college receivers in '75, catching sixty-six balls for Elon. Epp had "soft hands," which made him beloved to quarterbacks like Kenny Stabler, once of Alabama, and Bear Bryant.

Not ten minutes had passed when Jimmy Rosenberger brought a girl up to Epp's table, saying, "Epp, you two have something in common. This is Molly Bodden." Jimmy's eyes twinkled. He'd done a good deed. He was white-haired and fatherly.

Whatever they had in common was just fine with Epp, who rose up and took the long-fingered hand. "I saw you on that big photograph in the lobby. You're about the prettiest thing I ever did see. Join me."

She thanked for the compliment as the Stardust press rep walked away.

"Now, what do we have in common," said Epp, smiling widely.

"We're both from the Virgins," she replied.

Epp could feel eyes on them from the surrounding tables. Old jealousy rearing its sometimes welcome head. They were yellow roses and not from Texas.

"The Virgins!" Old home week. He'd just talked to Laburnum Hotchkiss.

Her mother and little brother still lived on St. Thomas, out by Red Hook, she said. "I went to school there. Nisky Elementary and Wayne Aspinall Junior High . . ."

"I'll be. I'm trying to buy a lot down there," said Epp.

51

Come to Vegas and find something high-cotton sexy. Islands girl! "Then St. Thomas High. I graduated two years ago, first in my class."

"You're kiddin'," Epp said. "We do have something in common. I first saw light o' day on St. Croix. Let me order us some champagne. Let me do exactly that."

She looked at him as if examining jewelry. "Just for you. I don't drink before a show. But I'll have some tea. Then I've got to go backstage."

Skin a half-shade darker than his own light lemon, lips full, nose straight and narrow-bridged, East Indian, he bet. Trinidad had a passel of them. Huge brown eyes. Along with every other red-blooded male who'd passed the life-size blowup in the lobby, he'd had an erotic flash, a pull on the cord.

Saying, "We'll skip the champagne," he signaled for a waiter to order tea. "How long you been up here?"

"Ten months."

"Straight from St. Thomas?"

"No, San Juan. I worked on the Condado for five months. A man from the Stardust caught a show and here I am."

"Doin' the same thing?"

She nodded.

"I don't remember that much about St. Croix, much less St. Thomas when I was a kid. Ask me 'bout Philadelphia, though."

"I've never been there," she said.

"It's not as stuffy an' grubby as people say."

He noticed she seemed distracted; kept looking around with those huge brown eyes. Over his shoulders, off to the sides of the crowded room; even turning to look behind her.

During the first show, she could have sworn she saw Joe Carlucci sitting at a table on the second tier. A half-bald man with large dark glasses. She was at the very end of the runway and had the urge to run as fast as she could. She almost panicked again.

Before coming out to meet Epperson Watts, she'd stood beside

Jimmy Rosenberger, looking at the house with the lights up as the audience filed in. She'd swept it, side to side, while Jimmy was saying, "What's wrong with you?"

I'm scared to death, Jimmy.

"Nothing." He might tell management. They'd fire her instantly.

She studied Epp Watts, feeling instantly comfortable with him, the way he smiled, the way he talked. He had an honest, open face; he had her color, even lighter.

Epp said, "But I went back down there to bury my mama, then to Carnival a couple of times, feeling like a tourist. They had a "day" for me two years ago. Island's sure grown. We moved to Philly when I was seven. My papa is still there. That's where I'm goin' now. See him. Mama died three years ago."

"Carnival's the same but bigger each year, not as much fun," she said, still preoccupied, half turning in her seat to study the shadows again, looking for Joe Carlucci.

"Is something wrong?" Epp asked.

"No, no," she said, shaking her head.

"Is it my company?"

"Oh, no," she said. "I was just looking for someone." Her fingers lightly touched the back of his hand and he felt a tingle. "No, no, it isn't you. I'm sorry. I apologize."

"No need," said Epp.

But he thought she was like a fawn when a cougar is in the nearby trees. Skittish, ready to run to the thicket.

She smiled faintly, "So you're a football player? A professional? I don't know much about it."

Epp nodded. "Outta college and right into the pros. I figure I got eight or nine good years. That's about average. Some guys do twelve, fifteen, but you peak 'bout eight or nine, I'm told. That's when I plan to hang it up." Stopping himself, he grinned. "Less I get hurt bad earlier. That happens, too."

"You have a real plan?"

"I think so. Develop some real estate. You got one?"

She nodded, smiling a little more. Not so tense.

They were getting along famously, Epp thought.

Then the smile vanished and she stared at him, looking for something. He couldn't imagine what it was. She checked her watch. "I have to go."

He stood up. "Well, it's sure been great talkin' to you. I'm headed for Philly in the mornin'. Papa's got a heart condition an' I don't know how long he'll be around. He's still working but slowin' down. I'm gonna spend some time with him before mini-camp. But I'll be back, Miss Molly Bodden. I do plan to see *you* again. That, I do."

She stood up but lingered by the table, eyeing him. Then she said, *or he thought she said,* "Would you like to take me home tonight?" Dead serious she looked, waiting for an answer.

Epp could hardly believe what he'd just heard or *thought* he'd heard. Blinking, he stammered, "Why, yeh, ah, yeh. I'd like to do that. Yeh, you bet." She did say it.

Take her home? Take her anywhere she want to go. Take her to Colonel Sanders, McDonald's, take her to the supermart, the laundry, the car wash. He broke out in a big smile.

"All right, just stay here after the show is over. Don't mind the busboys and waiters cleaning up. Just sit right here, and I'll come and get you."

Grinning wider than ever, Epp said, "Okay, I won't move an inch." Four days after Mavis O'Connor. What a week!

He watched as she wound through the tables toward the back of the room, heads turning. She was due it.

Well, hell, he'd sit there until dawn waiting for her. Wait a week. Wait a month.

And did they have something else in common besides being from the islands? Epp was guessing that a little rich, sticky black blood was swimming along her arteries. One close look at Molly Bodden and he could tell that. Some big buck from Port o' Spain had diddled Molly's East Indian mama, leaving the seed in the right place. One look at himself in the mirror and there was no question about Epp Watts, either. His big papa had likewise diddled Thready one starry night on St. Croix.

Oh, yes, they did have something in common. Epp and Molly:

probably less than quarter-breeds. Both of them neither-nor, a hell-uva t'ing to be. *Painful t'ing to be*, sometimes.

When Epp was old enough to think about it, care about it, talk about it, Papa Watts had said, "Now, near as I can figure, you're somewhere between quadroon an' octoroon, leaning toward the latter. Maybe quintoon, though." Big, deep chest laugh. Nothin' to fret about. Epp shook his head. Those words were out of reach. But he had smoke gray eyes like Thready and her white-boned nose. Thready had been a barefoot waitress on St. Croix, serving Papa Epp's plates of conch and kallaloo stew, when they met. That's what he did when they went on to Philadelphia: seafood cook at Book-binder's; still doing it in his early sixties, on arthritic feet.

Molly said to Howie Piaggi, "Tell Security I'll be okay tonight. A friend is taking me home."

Howie said, "You sure?"

Molly nodded. Showtime was eight minutes away, and she was fitting the ostrich headpiece that wreathed her face for the opening number.

"I've never seen you worried this much about anything," Howie said. "Something happen last night?"

Molly looked around from the mirror and smiled up. "It'll go away."

"Why don't you give *it* a name and I'll tell Roy."

Roy Collins was Abernathy's plainclothes strong-arm man.

"I'll be okay," Molly insisted. She wasn't about to tell him what she'd done to a guest. Exotic dancers could be replaced in no longer than it took to make a call to L.A. or New York.

Howie shrugged. "Change your mind, let me know."

The five-minute buzzer sounded.

Epp had come along just about the time when pure anthracite black was becoming beautiful. And there he was stuck with his lemon skin, some cheek and forehead freckles, brownish-reddish octoroon or quintoon hair. *And black was now beautiful.* He took more crap from blacks in high school and college than he ever did from the whites. Now he was taking more of it from big tar-faces on the franchise lines. Every Sunday from defensive backs.

On the line of scrimmage, just before the ball was snapped, Fingers on his toes ready to go out ten yards, then cut on flying feet for the sideline, there was a lot of talk from some crouching pure black representing the Chiefs or the Browns or the Jets or the Dolphins, any of the AFC franchises: "Hey, you high-yaller sunnavabitch, you know whose white pecker got into your mammy?"

Well, he'd heard that kind of talk since Central Bucks West High School in Philly. And Papa Epp thought that was very funny, because for two centuries the lightskins down in the islands were the ones who got all the best jobs and favors, the ones who went off to Howard University or Hampton. They got the girls too, including some cute white ones. The shiny flat-nosed black-blacks, who looked like they just came over from Guinea, hand-lined for *feesh*, changed linens and scrubbed toilets in the white-run hotels; broomed the yards with dried palm fronds. And, *oh mon*, did the lightskins look down on the blackskins.

No more. Pure black was now God's splendrous handwriting. *Baby, 'es writin' in charcoal.*

Even if he got lucky, all-pro in the NFL, Epp knew he'd never have the respect in the Virgins that Griffith got when he won the world's middleweight championship. Emil was blackamoor black. Not as many people came out for "Epp Watts Day" as they did for "Emil Griffith Day."

Knowing it was eleven o'clock, showtime at the Stardust, the high-yellow coming out in long strides, arms spread, smile so wide her jaws ached, Yorgi was wide awake, almost seeing her, still wondering why Guido had set him up with Molly Bodden. Looking out the window with his one good eye at the desert night and all the

56

stars, hospital noises fading in and out down the hall, he was still trying to figure out just what Guido had in mind.

Telling him that teenage dinge was a firecracker when he knew she wasn't. Getting him all worked up. Telling him she had more tricks than The Great Thurston. Maybe she didn't put out to *any-body*. That kind. That body, all those looks, and she kept her knees together. You don't waste time and twelve hundred on those kind. Why did Guido do it?

Epp didn't take his eyes off Molly from the time she came on stage until she swept off, gliding without any seeming effort. Dancing in three production numbers, several times she came within three feet of him on the runway, acknowledging him with a quick look behind the set smile. Yet Epp felt that she was phoning her routines in, going through the motions while scanning the big room, still the fawn with the cougar in the trees.

The finale was big and loud, then the company scurried offstage, Epp staying at the table as the room emptied, clatter of silverware and dishes taking over from the brass and drums of the band. He sat wondering what it would be like to date a showgirl. Little Elon College in textile-mill country, truck-farm country, hadn't provided that kind of education. But maybe she just wanted to talk about the islands. Swap stories. Maybe she was just homesick.

Then, suddenly, there she was, in faded jeans, an old brown jacket and tennis shoes, looking little like the glamorous half-nude of thirty minutes ago. No makeup, smile faint. She said, "Let's go. Do you have a car or should we get a cab?" A huge, scarred leather shoulder bag was in her right hand, and she slung it over her back.

Did he have a car? He grinned widely. "I surely do have a car." The silver-gray Porsche was out there. Last year he'd driven papa around Philly in it. The two of them on Walnut and Chestnut and South. Out to the suburbs in Upper Darby, Drexel Hill and Marple, out where the rich white folks lived.

She led him through a back exit and as soon as they cleared the door moved closed against him, putting her arm through his, matching his every step, hurrying him.

"I bought it three days after Super Bowl. Four-speed 924, sunroof . . ."

She wasn't really listening. She was looking around the parking lot. This long tall showgirl was scared clear to her anus, he decided. He'd guessed that in the club, but now was sure of it. Okay, if she wanted a protector, he was willing. He'd beat up on the bastard. Risk his wide receiver hands.

"Where are you parked?" she asked, tight and urgent.

"Over there. We're headed right."

A hundred yards away, the figure of a man was moving on a parallel course, and Molly, quickly going around to the other side of Epp, said, "Let's run," in near panic.

"What the hell for?"

Molly said, "Please, let's run, he may have a gun—"

"Who?" said Epp, startled, beginning to run with her.

"That man."

She *was* the fawn.

As they ran, Epp tried to watch the man as well as the pavement ahead. Whoever he was, he seemed to be walking steadily along, minding his own business.

They reached the Porsche, and Epp quickly unlocked her door, then ran around to his side and unlocked; he jumped in, turned the key and the silver-gray car was gliding backward within seconds.

Hitting his lights, he turned, aiming at the man, thinking he'd run over him if he saw a gun. But then he heard Molly saying, "That's not him, thank God." The words came out with a full exhalation that seemed to leave her limp. Glancing over, he saw that her face was drained.

"What's all this about?" he asked, as they drove away from the Stardust.

Sitting in silence for a moment, she finally said, "Someone may be after me."

"Who?" asked Epp, for the second time. Who was he? Local hood? Had a gun?

Silence again as they waited for a light, then she said, "I'd rather not talk about it."

"Okay. But which way do we go?"

He was beginning to have mixed feelings about Molly Bodden, not needing any trouble this late January, twenty-five and bucking for a salary jump from Al Davis. Hadn't he just been thirty feet away from a shoot-out in Bakersfield? What the hell was happening to him?

Left turn on the Strip, then down to Bridger. Right turn on Bridger, then over to Thirteenth Street, below Maryland. The two-story building on Thirteenth looked almost new but not at all posh. Same as middle-class apartments in Philly, Oakland, Kansas City.

Inside, after she'd double-locked the door, she seemed nervous, shy. "You want coffee?"

Shaking his head, standing in the middle of the living room, looking around, he suddenly felt nervous and shy himself; tongue-tied, awkward.

"Something to eat?" she asked, still nervous.

"Nope."

She'd taken off her jacket. A pink men's shirt was tucked into her jeans. She looked like an innocent schoolgirl, younger than on-stage. Sixteen, seventeen.

He shook his head again. "If you jus' wanted someone to look out for you on the way home, then I've done my job. I'll go back to the hotel." He could swim in her eyes, he thought. Do a full gainer.

"No," she said. "I need someone tonight. Will you stay?"

"Guard you?"

"Be with me." She paused, thinking. "Yes, guard me."

He nodded. "Okay." His pleasure.

"Excuse me," she said, and went off to the bathroom.

He wondered if she meant sleep on the couch like a brother. All right, he'd do that, too, if that's what she wanted. She really *was* afraid of someone. Of that, he was convinced. She hadn't been acting in that parking lot. He could feel her fear.

In a moment, he heard the shower drumming.

Maybe she'd just want to sit up and talk. That was fine, too. Not often did he get a chance to talk to someone who was quadroon or quintoon or whatever the hell she was, he was. That kind of talk could last two days, three days, once they got into it.

But who was after her? Ex-boyfriend? Man who carried a gun around? Showgirls in Reno and Vegas went out with guys who were in the mob, he'd heard. Well, on considered second thought, that's the very last thing he needed on the way to Philly, or anywhere else. He still hadn't shaken off Bakersfield. So he'd just talk with her all night, guard her best he could, then head east in the morning.

The bathroom door opened, and she came out in a well-used blue cotton robe, nothing glamorous, saying, "I put a bath towel for you on the edge of the tub. There's a guest toothbrush on the basin."

She'd removed her lipstick and all the way across the room came the fragrance of a delicate soap. She had that fresh, steamy look of being well-scrubbed. Without saying anything else, she padded across in front of him and went on into the bedroom.

So why was he acting like a sixteen-year-old himself? He thought he knew: her up on the stage, bathed in a spotlight. Now here she was in the next room and he was still in awe. This wasn't the big-grin, fast-foot, sticky-fingered, cocky "oh, joy" Epperson Watts, Jr., that he'd usually known. And this was a younger female, not a Mavis O'Connor.

He went into the bathroom, stripping down, climbing into the shower, using the same fragrant soap she'd used. Let happen what would happen, in bed or out.

Toweling off, rubbing hard, he suddenly decided he did indeed want Molly Bodden very badly this night and awe could damn well get lost. In fact, he was already erecting. Then he went over to the basin to borrow some of her Crest and Scope.

Finishing, he wrapped the towel around his waist, collected his clothes, putting them on the couch, and was in the process of placing his shoes down on the floor when Molly's voice drifted out. "Turn the light off."

Epp shrugged. One of those. He reached over to pull the lamp chain, then felt his way into the bedroom in the sudden blackness. His knees finally touched the side of the bed, and he said, foolishly, simultaneously wanting to pull the words back in, "There *you* are, you gorgeous Miss Molly."

She didn't answer.

He dropped the towel from his waist and slid into the bed.

She said, "Just hold me awhile."

Reaching for her, pulling her up against him, he felt an incredible warmth, a body as firm as it had looked up on the stage, a body that fit his own like the pieces of that erotic puzzle in the apartment overlooking Alameda Bay.

Hard as new brick against Molly's left thigh, he didn't move a muscle for what he thought was a good ten minutes, suffering. Then he felt her head lifting and her tongue came prying into his mouth, exploring gently. Then a hand went down past his navel.

He murmured, "Oh, sweet Jesus."

Later, Molly talked and talked and talked: Port o' Spain. Spindly little girl walking along Churchill-Roosevelt Highway, hand tucked in the horny paw of big Tom Bodden, past the forests of red-orange flowering trees.

She remembered the hundreds of East Indian women walking along in their saris in the fresh early morning, shawls over their heads, rings in their noses and elaborate tattoos on bare arms. Her mother, Chaktri, was like those women except she had no ring in her nose. Nor was she tattooed.

Epp just listened in the darkness, asking something now and then, saying mostly "uh-hmh," thinking this lonely girl hadn't talked to anyone *close* for a long time. She wanted to tell a lot.

Epp finally shushed her and ran his hands down over the curve of her hips, caressing slowly.

She said, "I'm no virgin, but I've never given myself to a man like tonight."

Epp found himself believing her.

"I mean it. Part of it was fright but most is you."

They made love and then she talked again.

"I do have a dream, Epp. I want to be a fashion designer. I've had

61

that dream since I was a little girl. I know I have the talent for it. Tomorrow morning look in my closet. All the clothes there I designed and made myself."

"You'd look good in a fish sack."

"Don't tease me," she said. "I have this dream about opening a boutique on Main Street, something near Bolero or Riise's. I want all those tourists off the cruise ships to come by Molly Bodden's and see the fantastic thousand-dollar dresses in the window. I want to take my designs to Paris and Rome . . ."

"Anything you want you can get," he said, again gently stroking her back. She *was* young and he felt comfortable with her now.

". . . have shows. Be Molly Bodden, of the island of St. Thomas, down where the tropic breezes blow . . ."

"Anything you want . . ." he said, wanting to enter her again. He hoped it would never get light. He could stay in this cocoon for a month; forever.

"I'll do it, Epp. I swear I'll do it. Ideas for color combinations and different fabrics rush around in my head all the time. Even when I'm working. The lights are in my eyes and I see the blur of faces out there, and I'm thinking about oranges and reds and greens, just moving to the music. I try never to think about the audiences. One night I designed a dress during a show, every cut of it, out there on the stage—"

"Molly," he said, "oh, Molly," and closed her mouth once again with his own, his tongue slipping inside, met strongly by hers.

Yorgi awakened about three A.M., took a moment to realize where he was and what had happened to him, letting out a bellow of rage in the darkness. The bellow, just sound, no words, lasted about fifteen seconds, then decompressed.

The floor nurse came running down the corridor, her rubber soles squeaking, and plunged into Yorgi's room, asking breathlessly, "What's wrong, Mr. Carlucci?" She turned the overhead light on. "What's wrong?"

He stared at her with his good eye and said, "Nothing."
"My God, you scared me, yelling like that."

Tom Bodden was a stevedore, she said.
"He almost passed as white but all the East Indians knew he was Creole and that made me 'dogala . . .'" Hindi word for bastard.

"We couldn't live in Debal or Penal, and my mother was spit on while shopping. We lived in an *ajoupa* in the Bridge District. Mud walls, slab floor, galvanized roof."

"And I thought we were poor," said Epp.

Then in the early sixties, just after brother Nedley was born, during the time when the Afro-Creoles were chasing East Indians out of Trinidad, Tom Bodden was killed in the Seaman and Water-front Worker's Trade Union strike.

"Knifed on South Quay Street . . ."

Worst of all, Molly was raped at age six by a half dozen of the Ras boys, Bridge District hoodlums who sold cocaine, pot and "bush" rum in their slum syndicate. "I'll remember that first pimply Ras boy until I die. He was East Indian, not black."

So Chaktri took Molly and baby Nedley north, following other East Indians. "We finally landed on St. Thomas, where a few merchants from Trinidad had already settled. My mother took in sewing."

The Sinanans and C.B. Abidh and the Sookpalees plus a few Chinese who'd been chased out of Trinidad had set up shops.

She needed to talk and talk.

2.

EPP AWAKENED AFTER DAYLIGHT, finding himself alone, staying still for a few minutes, listening to soft noises from the red and yellow kitchen. Thinking about the night past he was tempted to lure her back to bed.

Go slow with her, he told himself. Go to Philly, see Papa a while, see friends, then drift back to Vegas. See her again when mini-camp started in spring in Santa Rosa. Call her every so often from Philly. Send flowers.

Getting out of bed, he found the towel on the floor and put it around his waist, going on through the living room, looking into the kitchen and seeing her there: black hair piled up on her head, yellow rose skin glowing. No trace of the showgirl with eye shadow and phony lashes.

"Good morning," she said with a half-smile. He thought she was also saying We fit well without saying it.

"Marnin'," he said, with a big smile.

"You don't often talk island," she said.

"I do, too. I go back there an' in twenty minutes I'm talkin' like a native. *Hey, mon . . .*"

"I'm the same," she said, eyes soft, nostalgic.

"Not all bad," said Epp.

"Would you like some breakfast?"

"Whatever you have."

"I'm a vegetarian, so I don't have bacon or sausage."

"Whatever you have."

"Egg omelet with mushrooms, a few chives."

"Perfect," said Epp, on his way to the bathroom.

In the shower, soaping himself around the groin, he again fought off the temptation to go out into the kitchen and say, "Molly, let's forget the omelets." But he reached over and turned the water to cold. Go slow. Kamasutra would return in all its glory.

Picking up his clothes off the couch, he went back to the bedroom to dress; turning the light on, he noticed a photo on the dresser. A woman in her fifties who once looked a lot like Molly. Chaktri, he thought. A boy who looked to be around thirteen, fourteen.

In the kitchen doorway, Molly asked, "Toast and marmalade all right. You want honey?"

"Toast is fine," said Epp. "That your family in there?"

"Yes, my mother and little brother, Nedley."

"He doesn't look so little to me."

"He's fourteen. Nice kid. Wants to be a basketball player."

The dining alcove overlooked Thirteenth, and he glanced down. No one out there. No man with a gun.

She'd squeezed oranges, and lifting his glass, he said, "Thank you," sure she'd understand it was for *now* as well as last night.

"Thank you for staying with me," she said.

Epp said, "My pleasure," and that was putting it mildly.

"*Sitäräm,*" she said, "it's another Hindi word. Gratitude."

"Says it all. You're a very special lady. I know that already, an' if I didn't have to go to Philly this mornin' I'd be here for a month." Might as well ask her: "What was that all about last night? Someone after you? Man with a gun? Who is he?"

The smile vanished and he wished he'd let it alone.

She took a deep breath, sighing. "I'd really rather not talk about him."

Epp nodded. "Okay, but if you're frightened of him, I can stay a while longer. Hang around. I can call Papa an' say I've been delayed. He'll understand."

Molly shook her head. "No, I don't want you to do that. I'll be all right. One of the security guys will drive me back and forth. They do that a lot. We're always having problems from men who come in, see us half-nude, then think we're available for all kinds of things. Most of us aren't. Some are."

* * *

A few minutes after nine, Epp was at the front door to say goodbye to Molly Bodden, not knowing exactly what to say.

Say he'd keep in touch, peck her on the cheek, hold her hand a minute. Not mention last night and a rain check. Not be a smartass. A mutual happening, he believed. They both wanted it. Good talk, making good love. So that's what he did. Pecked her cheek, held her hand. Wide smile. See you later, Miss Molly.

"I'll be in touch."

Outside, just before opening the door to the Porsche, he looked all around. Maybe the guy, whoever he was, whyever he was threatening her, had come back to the neighborhood this bright, sunshiny Nevada morning to check on who was going in or coming out of her place.

But Epp could see no one suspicious and glanced up at Molly's apartment, check whether or not she was looking out on thirteenth Street, giving him a last thought, a wave, a blown kiss.

She wasn't in the window.

He got into the Porsche, shifted gears and headed back for the Stardust to pack up, get on the road to Philadelphia.

A few minutes later, Molly called Humana Sunrise to ask if Mr. Carlucci was still in the hospital.

Yes, he was, said the operator. "Do you want me to connect to the floor nurse?"

"Please."

The floor nurse came on and Molly asked about the condition of Mr. Carlucci."

"He's doing nicely."

"How long do you think it'll be before he's released?"

"That's up to the doctor, but his chart indicates tomorrow."

Molly thanked the nurse and hung up, deciding to ask Irene if she could come over for a few days starting tomorrow.

3.

A LITTLE PAST ELEVEN, Yorgi was released with another warning from Dr. Steinberg to behave himself and have the Chicago ophthalmologist examine the socket the next week, arrange for the prosthesis man. Amazing things were being done with plastics, Dr. Steinberg said, eyes so natural that even friends had a hard time deciding which was which. Dr. Steinberg was upbeat this Thursday morning. His fee had been paid in cash. He said cheerfully, "Good luck, Mr. Carlucci."

Yorgi nodded, staring bleakly with his single orb, grunting a nasal "Yeh," and departed, wearing his socket bandage and a two-inch gauze strip over where she'd sliced his cheek and neck. Underneath, the skin itched. Yorgi knew he looked like the walking wounded, getting into the cab outside Humana Sunrise.

After standing in front of the lobby blowup of Molly Bodden, observing every curve of her, remembering all the bullshit and her woman's knife, fighting off a temptation to rip up the life-size photo, he checked out of the Stardust, retrieving the briefcase with the half million in it, no one at the desk asking silly questions about his bandages. He left a letter addressed to Molly, saying to the clerk, "See she gets this," dropping a ten on the counter.

Then he checked into the Desert Inn, diagonal across the Strip, registering as Joseph Carlucci, giving the usual address on Rush Street in Chicago, mail pickup for the Malavasis.

In the room he turned on the TV and got the last reel of a western starring Henry Fonda and Anthony Perkins, the guy who'd been that nutty Boston baseball player in another movie and played the killer in *Psycho*. Perkins looked and acted like a natural weirdo.

Sprawled on the bed, he used his cupped palm for a shutter, blanking out the film, then opening to a peephole, then half-vision,

67

then full. That's how it would be until he died, he realized. Certain body parts could be replaced, like a hip. Even a heart. But he'd never heard of a full eye transplant. Cornea, yes. Not the whole goddamn eye.

Sliding off the bed, he went over to the single piece of hard luggage he'd been checking through airports ever since leaving Chicago. Digging down, he came up with the Walther .38 wrapped in bath toweling. He fitted the silencer on, then sat down in the chair beside the bed, aiming the gun at Fonda and Perkins with his left eye. He did that until the film credits came up and the channel shifted to the news. The first story was about Jimmy Carter trying to give the Panama Canal away.

Not wanting people to stare at his bandages, he had lunch in the room—hamburger, fries and a glass of house white—then put the tray outside on his way to get a cab. "Good used-car place," he said to the cabbie.

Buy a car, don't rent one; check out of the hotel after midnight, take care of Molly Bodden, dump the car, then catch the two-fifteen A.M. red-eye to Chicago.

He got a '71 black Chrysler in pretty good shape for eight hundred, then found a hardware store on North Main and bought a linoleum knife, a roll of three-inch duct tape and a flashlight.

Parking back at the Desert Inn, he left the knife, tape and flashlight on the front seat, then went to the room to floss his teeth.

At about three, after staying in the apartment all day, deciding not to answer any door knocks, almost afraid to answer the phone, Molly called Howie Piaggi and again requested a driver from Security to pick her up about four-thirty. Even though the nurse had said Mr. Carlucci wouldn't be released for another day, Molly wasn't taking any chances.

If she drove to work, she was worried about getting to the Volvo at night in the parking lot; walk from the stage exit being several hundred feet away; worried about getting out of it when she returned home about one. That time of night there was very little auto traffic on Thirteenth Street; usually no pedestrians around.

Howie said, "After the show, when you get ready to shove off, just ask any of the guys. Abernathy has you up on the bulletin board for a ride. So just ask any of them."

"Which city, please?"

"Las Vegas. A number for Molly Bodden. B-o-d-d-e-n. She lives on Thirteenth Street."

"One moment, please."

Epp waited.

"Sorry, no listing under that name."

He wasn't surprised.

Next, he tried Jimmy Rosenberger's office at the Stardust, but publicity was closed for the day, the operator said.

He was in a Best Western, in Gallup, New Mexico, and it was now a quarter to six. Well, he'd call her from the next stop somewhere in Texas. Just to say hello. Ask how she was. Talk for a little while, just keeping in touch. Riding Interstate 40, through Kingman, Flagstaff and Winslow, listening to country most of the way, he'd thought of her almost constantly. Thought he might be falling in love with her, overnight. Didn't mind at all.

Taking the southern route across this time of year, he was trying to keep out of the snow with the Porsche. He'd already seen a lot of it on the mountain peaks. The air was as clear as ice, and just as cold, pine-scented.

In a short, stained, seersucker gown, Molly was making-up for the first show when Howie Piaggi came into the dressing room holding an envelope and saying, "Front desk sent this back."

Molly nodded and continued applying the color base, murmuring, "Thanks," but not looking down at the oblong he'd dropped.

Then she worked on her eyes: highlighter, eye shadow, eyeliner. Finally gluing on the false eyelashes.

Usual pre-show chatter was mixed with a girl's portable playing Julio Iglesias; Irene, sitting next to Molly, was talking about her babysitter selling pot to neighborhood kids.

"I get a call from this irate mother saying her twelve-year-old son got grass at my apartment. I said, 'Lady, you got the wrong address.' She said, 'Your name Turkel?' and I said, 'Yes.' Then she gave me my own address. Okay? The kid had said that's where he got it. I said, 'Your kid is wrong. I don't deal dope. I don't even smoke it.' She said, 'I'm going to the police.' I said, 'Go ahead.' So this afternoon there's a knock on my door, and two guys are standing out there. They show me badges and say they're from Las Vegas Narcotics. They ask me if I have a fifteen-year-old babysitter named Harriet. I said I did. They asked me if I knew she was selling marijuana in my front room every day except Tuesday between five and nine? Like clockwork. Fifteen years old. I said, 'Oh, Christ.' I've got a two-year-old and here the sitter is dealing . . ."

Molly was only half listening as she outlined her lips with a colored pencil, then began filling in with lipstick. "Who can you trust anymore?" she said.

"So they came back the next day," Irene continued, "and busted her in front of my eyes. She admitted it, brazen little bitch."

Guiding the tube, Molly said, "You talk to her mother?"

"She yells at me—tells me I framed her daughter."

Molly said, "Sometimes it's hard to win. Can I change the subject?"

"Sure."

"Okay if I stay with you for a few days beginning tomorrow?"

Irene glanced over, frowning. "You got a problem?"

Molly nodded. "The usual."

Irene sighed. "I think most men on earth should have their cocks cut off, including my ex-husband, the son of a bitch. Yeah, sure. Sleep on the couch."

"Thanks," said Molly.

She finished her lips and then reached down for the envelope, ripping it open. On hotel stationery was printed *Two For One*. No signature, but Molly knew. She knew.

Her hands began to shake.

"Can I make it tonight instead of tomorrow?" she asked Irene, voice squeezed with terror.

"Jesus, you do have a problem! Tonight, sure."

"I have to get a few things from home, then I'll be over. I've set it up with Security to have someone drive me."

"Okay," said Irene. "Who's chasing you."

Molly shook her head.

"You heard what I said. Snip 'em off."

Yorgi was a Johnny Carson fan and watched "Here's Johnny" every time he had the opportunity, in Naperville, or on the road. He liked how sly Johnny was, that look that Johnny gave Ed McMahon, the raised eyebrows, how he cocked his head. Yorgi thought that Johnny was a very funny guy.

While Molly was dancing over at the Stardust across the street, Yorgi was watching Johnny in his room at the Desert Inn.

This night he had a Hollywood stuntman as one of his guests, Richard—Yorgi didn't get the last name—who was a bow and arrow expert. While Johnny joked with Richard about bows and arrows, another stuntman strapped on a steel chest-plate covered with wood and let Richard hit him right where the heart is at sixty feet. The arrow drove in and quivered. The audience oh-ed and ah-ed.

Then Doc Severinson brought out a big red apple, and there was five minutes of repartee about the apple until it was finally placed on Johnny's head.

While Severinson and his band played the *William Tell Overture*, Richard split the fruit from fifteen feet, Johnny doing his "that was nothing" reaction.

Yorgi applauded. During the hour he'd laughed a lot and almost forgot he was one-eyed; almost forgot Molly Bodden.

Then at twelve-thirty, when Johnny signed off, Yorgi went into the bathroom and saw himself in the mirror, all of the rage coming back. His temples burned with it. Ripping off the bandage, he exposed the thin scar with its railroad track stitching. He'd go crazy if he didn't get her.

Five minutes later he put the Walther .38 into his overcoat pocket, put the Borsalino hat on, grabbed his packed bag off the bed and went down to check out. Another five for that and signing the briefcase out of safekeeping. In the car, he opened the case, picking out twenty hundreds for contingency, then drove across the Strip to the Stardust.

He knew which exit Molly used, having seen her come out of it Monday night along with some of the other showgirls and showboys. Parking four rows away, he slumped down in the seat to wait and watch. While waiting, he cut a strip of the duct tape for her mouth, another longer one for her wrists. He'd used duct before. Once, in Texas; another time in Louisiana, when he'd thrown a hit into Lake Ponchartrain, his mouth plastered, eyes bulging.

At one-ten A.M., Bobby Chapman said into his walkie-talkie, "This is Bobby. I'm taking Molly Bodden home. Be back in fifteen."

She was standing by the door in her usual wash-whitened jeans and brown leather jacket, hair ponytailed after the show, the big leather bag hanging from her shoulder. Schoolgirl.

A tinny voice answered, "Okay, Roberto."

Bobby, who was twenty-four, a part-time guard making ends meet so he could study business administration, held the door for her, continuing, "So they raised the rent thirty dollars just because they painted the outside. The guy told me that." Bobby had dark curly hair and a boyish face. He didn't look like he could guard cream puffs.

"Why don't you move?"

They went out into the night, Yorgi spotting them in the slat of light as the door opened and closed. He quickly got out of the Chrysler.

Bobby said, "Move where? We looked at those mobile homes off 604 below McCarran and they want five hundred. That's one-twenty more'n we're payin' now."

They were headed toward a pair of Stardust cars that belonged to Security, sitting alongside golf-type maintenance carts used for carrying everything from dirty linen and concrete mix to patrol swings.

"They raise us anymore and I'll have to quit going to college an' work here fulltime."

"Don't you get government help?" Molly asked.

As they got to the golf carts, Bobby said, "I've got a—" but the "loan" didn't come out of his mouth as a tire iron crushed the back of his skull. He pitched forward with an "aah" and Molly heard Yorgi's terse whisper, "Walk this way," and felt a gun barrel against the side of her head. Yorgi's left arm was suddenly around her shoulder, his fingers digging painfully into the collar bone, body held tightly to his.

"Your're mine, bitch," he said, mouth hard against her right ear. "Don't yell or you're dead."

She felt her legs collapsing. He held her upright in a bear hug as they went toward his car, Yorgi saying, "Walk, bitch, or you get shot in the head."

She couldn't scream. No sound would come out. Her diaphragm was locked. She wasn't aware that she was breathing. The gun felt like a poker pressing through her hair.

Reaching the Chrysler, Yorgi opened the passenger door with his left hand and shoved her in, moving behind her, keeping the Walther barrel just above her left ear.

She watched as he ripped the duct tape off the glove-compartment door and applied it over her mouth, then ordered, "Put your wrists together."

Molly began to weep, sitting there motionless, frozen, eyes closed.

Yorgi said, "Clasp your hands, goddamit," and used his open left palm to slap her, his face as empty of feelings as when he'd shot Jin Lee.

She hardly felt the blow, but her wrists came together as she clasped her hands and he quickly, expertly, wound the other piece of long tape around them, then sprang out of the car to go around to the driver's door, the professional operating smoothly.

Behind the wheel, he reached across to lock her door, then said, "Get down on the floor," again holding the Walther to her head, moving the seat back as far as it would go.

She slid down, compressed, knees near her face, heels pointed toward her buttocks. She was a tight ball.

"You play any games this time an' you're dead. Unnerstand?"

Molly nodded, eyes still closed, scoured with fear as the car went out of the Stardust lot, turning north on the Strip, accelerating.

She had not looked up at him to this point, but finally forced her eyes open and in the light of the East Fremont crossing saw the white patch over his right eye, the pencil-point scab running down over his dark cheek into his thick neck.

The tip of the razor had done all that. She'd done all that.

Oh, God, help me, she said, silently.

Illness suddenly flooded in over the terror and she thought she might vomit, wanting to suck down draughts of cold air. What started flashing through her head, like those electronic repeating strip messages on top billboards, was *Two For One.*

4.

THE CHRYSLER FOUR-DOOR took the on-ramp to State 95 at East Mesquite, then finally got on the Tonopah Highway, heading west-northwest out into the Mojave Desert, through the desolate valley floor. There were vast areas of sand and rock out there, uninhabited except for rattlesnakes and geckos. Next door was California's Death Valley.

She made throat noises to Yorgi and her eyes were pleading. Her taped hands came to her face as she choked and struggled vomiting.

Yorgi glanced down at the writhing, choking figure but made no move to help her.

"Look what you did, puking in my car."

She finally tore the mouth patch away with her fingertips.

He didn't need the mouth tape anymore. She could scream her head off out here. There was no one to hear her.

Forehead on the seat, panting, Molly spit out remnants of the food, trying to fill her lungs with air. She was still gasping. Her upper body felt as if her ribs had been ripped apart. She'd never known how it was to choke.

"Well, you don't look much like that girl in the lobby. You ain't no beauty tonight."

Molly turned to him. "I'm sorry . . . for what I did." She was still panting. "I'm sorry . . . so sorry, I'll pay all your hospital bills—"

"Sorry doesn't give me an eye." He reached down to the seat beside him and opened the hardware bag, pulling out the linoleum knife. "Know what this is?"

Odd-looking knife.

Molly shook her head.

He shined the torch on the silvery hooked blade and squat wooden handle.

"Cuts linoleum. You draw a little line, then pull the blade back toward you. Can cut half a inch."

Molly studied the knife and then quickly looked away, feeling sick again. In the yellow circle of light, the knife . . . no question what he planned to do. The message on Stardust stationery hadn't been idle.

He wasn't just trying to threaten her, scare her, wave it under her nose, place it against her throat, touch it against her breasts, toy with her until her heart would sound like an inner drum and she'd begin to babble. No, he actually planned to scrape out her eyes, holding her head in a hammerlock, of which he was so capable.

The reflection of Vegas, all the glare tossed at the clear night sky from the Strip and East Fremont, visible for miles, was dwindling as the Chrysler went deep along the Tonopah into the desert. Traffic had thinned out. No one was passing them. Most, not all, gamblers had gone to bed.

Brights on, Yorgi slowed, looking for any road that went off to the right that didn't have a ranch or residence sign by it; no mailbox, one of those county roads with a red gravel surface. A road where no car, this time of night, was liable to come pounding up, throwing the tiny rocks.

He didn't plan to go too far in, maybe two miles or so, then do what he came out here to do and dump her. See how she'd like getting back to the highway sightless. He could imagine some trucker spotting her staggering around in the distance, seeing her waving her arms, slowing down, then getting a look at her bloody face, eyeballs gone, saying, "No way, José," shifting back into second and pushing his foot down, building back to seventy. She'd be damn lucky to get a ride back to town in daylight unless a cop came along.

A cop?

Suddenly, he knew he hadn't thought it through. She knew who he was, knew where he lived, knew Guido. Once she got back to Vegas she'd tell everything. That little pink tongue would flap all over the place. Blinded showgirl.

76

Tony and Guido would say, "You do a dumb thing! You don't use your head, Yorgi!"

So take her pretty eyes, see her stagger away, follow her, let her know how it feels to be *monocolo*, then shoot her.

He saw a turnoff ahead that wasn't marked with a sign or mailbox, and slowed even more, turning into the road, hearing the pop of gravel in the wheel wells, the crunch under the tires.

Molly heard and felt the change in the roadbed, felt the car going to the right, and knew she didn't have much time. He'd soon stop and use the knife. She'd driven up the Tonopah before and knew how desolate it was back here. Roads fading off into nowhere in the desert range, dotted cactus and volcanic boulders. A body could rot and then be skeletonized in a few days by the buzzards, not found for months or years. In the winter, sub-freezing at night; on blue-sky summer days, one hundred thirty degrees.

In the dimness of the console light she could see the gun by Joe's side, on the seat, beyond the knife. She looked at his face. He was squinting, intently studying the road and land ahead, paying no attention now to the knotted form on the floor.

Her hands moved slowly above her head and back, every muscle straining in the odd position, hurting as she hyperextended, fingers searching for the door-lock tab, finding it, lifting it.

She brought her hands down and rested them a moment, looking up at his profile. She'd have to be quick. One chance at the gun. Just one. Extend her arms, grab it and point at his head. Her fingers would have to be exact, index curling around the trigger the moment she grasped the handle. Thank God he hadn't taped them as well as her wrists. Thank God she'd sliced his right eye instead of his left.

The Chrysler kept spearing on into the cold starlit night, headlights sweeping the sand to either side, gravel peppering the wheel wells, setting up a mesmerizing crescendo of harsh sounds that filled the interior of the car.

His face remained aimed dead ahead, resembling a mask.

Now, Molly told herself, coming out of the crouch, lunging for the Walther, hands in a diver's mode, grabbing it, index twining around the trigger, pointing at his jaw, hearing herself yell, "Stop the car," going to a kneeling position.

His head turned and the left eye, in the dimness, seemed to burn at her like the flame from a welder's torch. Then he looked ahead again, not slowing. "Safety's on," he said without raising his voice, almost ignoring her.

She saw his right hand drop off the steering wheel and land on his thigh, guessing the next thing that would happen would be for it to flash out in a fist. He'd turn his head and knock the gun away.

The head turned and his hand flashed out as she pulled the trigger, not expecting to hear the explosion nor his yell of pain as the bullet, at three feet, drove him to the left. She was as much surprised as he was: she, because of the safety; he, because she didn't take the bluff. The bullet had gone into the roof of the car.

Her ears rang and gunsmoke blew back into her face as the Chrysler lurched leftward, teetering along the banked shoulder on that side, gravel spinning away from it.

"Stop the car or I'll shoot again."

She'd hit him but didn't know where. Not his head or throat. Probably his shoulder.

The car slowed and stopped teetering and she saw that his right arm was hanging limp.

"Stop it," she yelled, still holding the gun on him.

Yorgi brought the car to a halt and stared at her, breathing heavily from shock, the one eye riveting her. He said, "Try to get out, bitch."

There was no way to hold the gun on him and also reach behind her for the door handle. Maybe she should take the car and drive away? Sitting there, staring back at him, trying to figure out what to do, she finally resolved it. "You get out, Joe. Use your good hand."

He didn't budge.

"I'll shoot again," she said, pushing off a feeling of faintness, at the same time disbelief at what she'd done, at what she was saying.

He made no move to open the door.

Raising the Walther to the level of his head: "Open it!"

Slowly, eye fixed on her, he reached for the handle and the door swung back.

"Now, slide out, step away from the car."

Though he was wounded, she was still terrified that somehow he'd spring at her, take the gun away and do what he'd intended to do when he turned on this road.

Good eye never leaving her, he backed up.

"More," she said.

He stayed within reach.

"More," she shouted. "I swear to God I'll shoot you again. More!"

In the quadrangle of light from the open door, she saw blood dripping from the right arm that was hanging uselessly.

Finally, he spoke. "You better kill me. I'll follow you no matter where you go."

"Back up more," she answered, and after what seemed two minutes his feet began to move slowly backward. Two feet, three, four, until he was about ten feet away.

Until she died she'd remember exactly how he looked at this moment: the white bandage over his missing eye, the long thin black scab on his cheek; blood coming down his gloved right hand in rivulets, and the searing left eye that stared out from under the gray hat brim. Over his left shoulder hung a quarter moon, backlighting him against the stars.

He repeated, quietly, "You better kill me, Molly."

She didn't answer, knowing she'd have to take the Walther off him in order to shift the automatic to *drive*. Drop the gun, use her clasped hands to pull the lever from park down to drive, then accelerate.

He knew it, too, and was waiting, she realized.

She rested her foot on the gas pedal and rehearsed mentally what she had to do: timing was everything on the dance stage, everything here. He'd lunge toward the car the moment she dropped the gun. So the thing to do was drop the gun on the seat, jerk the door in, lock it, then shift gears; pray that the old car wouldn't stall. Even so, she'd be locked inside the car; still have the gun.

The engine was still running.

Do it, she said to herself, *now.*

She opened her hands, the gun dropped, and she saw him starting to move as she grabbed the door handle and pulled in. Door slamming, she tapped the lock tab.

A second later, Yorgi reached the side of the car.

Molly pulled the lever to *drive* and pushed down on the accelerator.

The Chrysler jumped forward and she caught a glimpse of his face out of the left window, the white eye patch a blur. He was yelling something, but the engine growl and pelts of gravel drowned him out.

Building to sixty, she was free of Joe Carlucci, at least for the moment, and drove with her elbows against her stomach, fingertips keeping the steering wheel nearly straight. She burrowed on up the road for several miles, then slowed and stopped, unable to go further without resting.

Drained, she sat for a while, taking in deep breaths, hands and legs shaking. Parched from fear, she kept licking her lips, then put her head down on the steering wheel to rest, and fought off sickness.

Finally, when the trip-hammering of her heart began to subside, she raised her head and had the first close look at her wrists. He'd wrapped the silver tape four or five times. The end of it was on the backside of her wrists but if she tucked them up against her cheek, she could gnaw it free.

The quick forward motion of the car had spun him down and from his knees on the dirt and gravel Yorgi had watched the black car streak up the road. He had watched it until it stopped, way ahead. She had the car, she had the gun; sooner or later she'd find the briefcase with the half million in it. Why didn't she just turn around and head for Vegas. There was nothing he could do. Not now, anyway. A day or two but not now.

His shoulder throbbed, but he thought the bullet had exited. She'd fired from point-blank range, three feet away. Hopefully it hadn't hit bone, and the bleeding seemed to have slowed or stopped.

He continued to look at the far-off lights up the road, the only light he could see in that direction, wondering what she was doing up there; then thought—the tape. *Getting it off.* He shook his head. He should have taped her whole hands as well, then none of this would have happened.

Well, nineteen-year-old Molly Bodden had had herself quite a night, but unless she came back and finished him off he'd spend the rest of his life looking for her. That, she could count on. Now, for the second time in three days he needed a hospital. It was beyond belief what she'd done to him and all he'd wanted was a wild roll in bed, a sensational fuck. He couldn't *believe* what had happened to him.

He took a deep breath and turned to begin walking slowly south along the road, headed back out for the Tonopah, the shoulder sending darts of pain down his arm with every step he took.

In the high beams, Molly picked up the overcoated figure several hundred yards ahead and tried not to look at him as she passed at seventy, staying well to the left-hand side of the road. But she was relieved that he was still alive, walking. The last thing she wanted to do was kill him. All she wanted to do was be left alone.

A mile on up, she stopped the car, getting out and burying the gun about fifty feet off the road.

Reaching the highway, she turned east toward the crown of light over Las Vegas, deciding, as the miles lessened, that the only way out was to leave the Stardust and go back to St. Thomas, San Juan or to Atlantic City. Those casinos were to open soon.

She tried to think of what she'd told him. She remembered she had said, trying to make conversation, that she was from St. Thomas, an easy place to find *anyone.* You got on the island by plane or boat, the same way off. She couldn't remember if she'd told him her mother and brother were still there.

Had she told him about dancing on the Condado, in San Juan? She couldn't remember. If she went to the police, reporting what had happened in the apartment, then what happened in the parking lot and out on the dirt road, shooting Joe Carlucci, she'd be black-listed. No casino wanted any employee involved with that kind of thing. Television and newspapers would eat it up, she knew. Atlantic City wouldn't hire her. Not even San Juan.

Joe Carlucci wasn't about to go to the police, either, she believed. He owned the gun, he was mob.

She wondered about Bobby Chapman and if he was all right.

Just say she was homesick and quit, collect the week's pay and leave. Say she was going back to St. Thomas. There were a half-dozen girls who wanted to be the lead nude, get the extra money and were qualified. Several only a year or two older than she was. There was no problem in replacing her.

She exited 95, taking the south Las Vegas Boulevard off-ramp, going along the Strip for a few blocks then turning east on Fremont for another few blocks, away from the sawdust joints. Finally, she slid along the curb and parked the Chrysler, dropping the keys on the floor.

The car, with its bloodstained seat, was now a police problem. She'd seen enough late-late shows in San Juan and here in Vegas to know she should wipe the steering wheel and door handles of her fingertips.

A few minutes before three A.M., now Saturday, she walked toward the Strip, found a phone booth and called Irene, awakening her.

"What happened to you? I thought you'd be here long ago."

"I'm taking a cab. I'll be there in a few minutes."

Irene's wasn't far away.

First Molly wanted to wash her mouth out, then stand under a hot shower for a long, long time. After that, she'd tell Irene what had happened. She had to tell Irene, if no one else.

5.

YORGI HAD REACHED THE TONOPAH about two-forty, cold to the bone, stiff, weary, footsore, Italian shoes not made for walking on Nevada red gravel, the hole in the shoulder sending up SOS messages. He turned east and began trudging along.

Nearing three-thirty, after several cars had whined past at seventy or more, leaving a buffeting chill breeze in their wake, ignoring the man in the smart overcoat and hat with his thumb out—he was come and gone in an eyeblink—a meat-packer truck hauled up and Yorgi ran for it as fast as he could.

The burly driver frowned as he saw the eye-bandage and ugly scar on the chunky hitchhiker, but said, "Get in, buddy. Car break down?" The door banged shut.

Yorgi said, "Yeh." The cab was warm.

"Didn't see it back there," the driver said, meshing gears.

"On a side road. Thanks for picking me up."

He couldn't remember when warmth had felt so good. His hands felt frozen. His feet were numb.

"Only way to get road service this time of night is if you got a CB."

Yorgi said he didn't have one of those.

"Wha' happened your eye?" the trucker asked, looking over.

"Fish hook." Everyone would ask it.

"Jesus Christ, that so? Lose it?"

"Yeh."

"Ouch. But I heard of that on a party boat out of San Diego. Albacore boat. Coast Guard had to go lift this guy off, hook still in his eye. They'd cut the fishing line."

Yorgi put his hands over the heater vent on his side, noticing he was still wearing the gloves, dried blood on the right one. He stripped them off, sticking them in his overcoat pocket.

"Shitty way to lose one," Yorgi said, hands beginning to thaw.

"You got that right. Wha' happened to your car?"

Yorgi had to think. "Fuel pump," he finally said. His brain was mushy. He felt exhausted, and not from walking.

The trucker talked fuel pumps for the next few minutes until he took the Rancho Road off-ramp, saying he had deliveries to make at the Sahara, Flamingo, Stardust, Dunes and Tropicana. Sahara first.

"I'll get out there," said Yorgi. Take a cab if one was around. If not, get the doorman to order one. Walking along the road, he'd decided to go to one of those emergency clinics. Pay the doctor to keep his mouth shut; threaten him if he didn't.

The Sahara came into view.

Barefooted, in his shorts, Epp sat on the bed in the Amarillo Ramada, talking to the Stardust operator, asking for Jimmy Rosenberger's home phone. She said, nicely, "We're not permitted to give home numbers of the executives, but Mr. Rosenberger is in his office. I can connect you."

Seconds later, Epp heard Rosenberger say, "She's at a friend's apartment. I talked to her ten minutes ago."

"What are you doing at work this hour?" Epp asked. "Seven A.M., man."

"I been up half the night. We had a guard clobbered out in the parking lot. He may not live. Hit with a tire iron, skull crushed in. That's why I was talking to Molly. He drove her home. UNLV student. Super kid, cute little wife and two-year-old baby."

"Took her home?" Epp asked.

"That's what she told Security. So he got hit when he came back from her place on thirteenth. Somebody had it in for him, or he found someone doing breaking and entering or grand theft auto. You know some of the cars parked out there have thousand-dollar stereos."

Epp said, "Hey, wait a minute, she was scared shitless the other night when I was with her. Said some guy with a gun had threatened her."

"Guy with a gun?" Rosenberger suddenly sounded tense, as if he was sitting up straight, suddenly taking notes. "In the hotel?"

"I don't know. The morning I left her she said she'd get someone in Security to drive her back and forth the next few days. She was jumping out of her skin."

"That happened. She was picked up yesterday afternoon and then Bobby Chapman, the kid who got clobbered, drove her home last night."

Epp said, "I asked her about the guy with the gun twice and she said she didn't want to talk about him. I thought he might be mob so I shut up."

"She didn't describe him?"

"No."

"Didn't say where she met him?"

"No. Said she didn't want to talk about him, period. But I got the impression she was scared silly."

"Well, I think Security will damn well order her to talk about him. We've had police here since two-thirty. Bobby may die and even if he lives he'll likely be a vegetable. He's lost half his brain."

"Okay if I call her?" He asked for the number.

"Sure. If you find out anything, let me know."

Rosenberger gave him Irene's number.

"Epp," he said. "Are you all right?"

"No," said Molly. "I'm in a lot of trouble, Epp." She sounded worn, on edge, fighting tears. He could see her in that old blue cotton robe, barefoot, vulnerable and frightened.

"What kind of trouble?"

"I can't tell you on the phone. Where are you?"

"Amarillo, Texas. What kind of trouble?"

"It's too compli-cated." Weeping now, softly.

"Does it have anything to do with that security guard getting his skull busted?"

"Yes." Still weeping. "Ye-sss."

"Is that guy who threatened you involved?"

"Ye-sss."

"Well, I screwed it up. I told Jimmy Rosenberger about him."

"God, Epp, why did you do that?" Sudden fright in her voice, overriding the tiredness and tears.

"I didn't know, Molly. I'm no mind reader. You didn't tell me not to say anything."

"I've got to get out of here, Epp. I'm quitting the Stardust and going to Atlantic City. I've got a friend out there."

"Because of the guy?" Epp was frowning into the phone.

"Yes, because of him. Epp, I'm so scared I can't eat."

"Go to the police, Molly. Tell the Security people and they'll bring the cops in."

"You don't understand. I've got to get out of here . . . now! The hotel won't protect me. They'll fire me."

"You sure?"

"Yes, I'm sure. You do anything to someone in the mob and you're gone."

"What did you do?"

There was a pause that seemed forever and then a deep sigh. "I cut him in the eye, then shot him."

Epp got off the bed, standing up, eyes wide and unbelieving.

"I cut him accidentally but shot him on purpose. He was going to blind me."

"*Godalmighty,*" Epp said, shaking his head, looking around the room, stunned. "Shot him?" Shot a Mafia guy?

"Yes."

"Was he the one who hit the guard?"

"Yes, but I don't want to talk about it."

Same as the other night. Secretive, flaky, dangerous, lovable, beautiful. "That's what you said the other night. You didn't want to talk about it. *You've got to talk about it, Molly.*"

"I can't. No hotel in the country would hire me."

Epp didn't know what to say except, "Hire you?" She didn't make sense, worrying about a job. He reminded himself she was only nineteen. It was showing.

"I have to leave here. He's still alive and wants me dead."

"Where'd you shoot him?"

"In the arm or shoulder. I saw him walking along the road where I shot him. Out in the desert."

"Christ, Molly."

Nobody shoots the Mafia except cops and the FBI, or they shoot each other. Mostly each other.

Then Epp stood in silence, thinking. Get himself involved? He'd have to be out of his gourd. Everything to lose.

She finally said, "Are you still there?"

"Yes, I'm here," he said, with a big doubtful sigh.

"Listen, I'm coming back there. Don't go anywhere. Stay where you are and keep the door locked. It'll take me the better part of a day and night. I'll drive you to your friend in Atlantic City. It's not that far from Philly."

"I don't want you to do that."

"Never mind. You're in trouble! Say what you want to those security people and think about going to the police."

"All right." Now she sounded twelve instead of nineteen.

"I'll see you early Sunday."

He hung up and sat back down on the bed, shaking his head. Was this Elon's 3.8 liberal arts major, light-yellow "Joy boy," big-man-about-campus man? Was this the sensational Raider wide receiver? Or was it his dumb pecker saying these crazy words?

He looked at the phone a moment, reached over for his address book and then dialed St. Thomas.

Detective Sergeant Laburnum Hotchkiss came on in his best Tower of London voice, "Detective Sergeant Laburnum Hotchkiss here," so formal.

"Laburnum, what's the deal?"

"You can take it for forty-five thousand cash. They want ten thousand good-faith money."

"Okay. I'll have my agent send 'em ten. And thanks."

"It's a steal. That lot has a one-eighty-degree sea view. No one can build in front of you."

"Laburnum, need your advice on something else." He told the cop about Molly Bodden and the Mafia guy.

"Stay out of it," Laburnum said.

"She seems so helpless, scared shitless of that guy."

"Stay out of it, and remember my case of Molson."

Forty minutes later, the silver-gray Porsche was on Route 40, heading west, Epp hearing his papa say, "Nebba trouble trouble 'til trouble trouble yoh." Then hearing Laburnum say, "Stay out of it." Let well enough alone, you jerk. What he should really do, he thought, was haul his ass around and roll straight to Philly, forget Molly Bodden.

He kept going west.

After the usual once-weekly "how-are-you and how-is-Nedley" small talk, Molly said to her mama in St. Thomas, "I'm quitting the Stardust and going to Atlantic City."

Chaktri said, "Well, Molly, this is a surprise. I didn't know you were unhappy."

"I'm not all that unhappy, it's just that the opportunities are better in Atlantic City. They're opening up in three months. I'll be closer to home."

"I'll be glad about that," said Chaktri. "When will you go?"

"Tomorrow."

"Tomorrow? So soon."

"I'll be staying with Lucille Fernandez until I get my own place. I just talked to her. You remember her, don't you? I brought her home when I was dancing in San Juan. The Puerto Rican girl."

Chaktri said she did remember.

"Write down this address and phone number."

Chaktri said, "Let me get a pencil."

When she got back on the phone, she said, "You seem so wound up, Molly. Is there anything wrong?"

"No, Mama. I've got to pack."

"I don't understand why you're leaving in such a hurry."

"You know me," said Molly. "I do things in a hurry."

"Yes, I know you. You should be at home making dresses, not in any Las Vegas."

"Mama, let's don't get into that."

"All right, give me the phone and address, and let me know when you get there. Are you flying?"

"No, driving across."

"Alone?"

"No, I'm going with a man that I met."

"Someone you know?"

"He's from St. Croix."

"A black man?"

"He's not as black as I am. He's a fine man."

Chaktri sighed her feelings all the way from the Caribbean. "Get separate rooms."

"Yes, Mama. Listen, if anybody calls don't tell them where I am. Do you understand? You don't know where I am. *Anybody.* Tell Nedley."

"I don't see why—"

"Just please do it, mama."

"Where are you now?"

"In a friend's apartment."

"What's your phone number?"

"You don't need to know, mama."

"You're hiding things from me . . ."

"I have to. I'll tell you later. Good-bye, mama."

Hanging up, Molly blew out a breath.

Bobby Chapman had died mid-morning.

"He came on at eight for his four hours outside, with two breaks, then he started his four hours inside at midnight, also with two breaks," said Vince Abernathy, head of Stardust security. It was early afternoon in Las Vegas.

"Anyone see him drive off in that car?" asked Detective Lieutenant Walter Nishgo.

"Not to my knowledge. At least, no one has come forward. I got word out to all employees, asking for information."

"So no one saw them drive off," said Nishgo.

"Not to my knowledge."

"Okay, let's talk about the girl. Was she spreading her legs for Bobby Chapman?"

"I can guarantee she wasn't."

"Vince, you were a cop once. Don't go making rash statements."

"I can guarantee she wasn't," Vince repeated. A chubby soft-skinned, ruddy-cheeked man in his late fifties, with horn-rimmed glasses, Vince could have been mistaken for a credit manager or cashier, even a casino host. He didn't look like a San Francisco ex-cop, and that's what the Stardust bosses wanted.

"Whatever." Nishgo was in his forties, a six-footer and dark-skinned. Loud bow ties were usually around his neck in the winter. Summers, short-sleeved shirts and string ties.

"A guy had been pestering her this week and she wanted protection. I gave it to her. She asked Bobby to take her home last night, and he checked out on the walkie-talkie. What happened after that I haven't the faintest idea. Next thing we know he's on his belly in the parking lot, head bashed in. But I've heard she was scared to death of a 'guy with a gun.'"

"Christ, one of those," said Nishgo, with disgust. "A guy with a gun, a guy with a knife, a guy with a baseball bat. Why don't you people stop showing tits in that show? You know all the freaks who come through here. We're like a bowl of honey."

"We'll be showing tits for the next hundred years. You know that."

Nishgo nodded. "Who told you about the guy with the gun? I hate him already unless he was manufactured by the cooze. I'll say one thing, he picked the best-looking young broad in town, if he exists. I saw her last month and got a hard-on. But I don't trust any showgirl in this town to tell the truth. Who told you?"

"Jimmy Rosenberger. He got it from a pro football player named Epperson Watts."

"The Raider pass catcher?"

Abernathy nodded. "That's him."

"How the hell did he get hooked up with her?"

"Jimmy. He introduced them Wednesday before the last show, and Watts took her home or she took him home. Nice kid, I believe.

He's only twenty-five. They're both from the Virgin Islands. That's why Jimmy got them together. We were comping him."

Nishgo laughed. "Minorities, goddamn minorities." He was three-quarters Navajo himself, distant kin to some of the rich trucking Indians in Arizona. But Walter was about as American Redskin as a Tongan and didn't care for tribal activities. "Where is he now?"

"Somewhere in the heart of Texas. He's going to call me tonight."

"Tell him to call me," said Nishgo. "I'm going over to see the girl."

He left Abernathy's office, dropped five dollars in quarters in a three-play slot, then went on back to his own office, which wasn't too far from where Molly Bodden was staying.

Watching a TV movie, Yorgi was naked, stretched out on a bed in the old paint-peeled Desert Breeze Motel, on the Strip, right shoulder bandaged. The doctor in the emergency clinic around the corner, shooing his nurse away and gladly accepting five hundred in cash to treat the wound and keep his mouth shut, said to take it easy for several days. So Yorgi postponed his return to Chicago until Monday, letting Kathy know. Screw Guido. He wasn't in a mood to talk to Guido and had no idea how to explain the half million the dinge stole.

The elderly, sleepy-looking doctor said Yorgi was lucky, which had drawn a very negative look from his patient, the bullet having gone through the fleshy part of the shoulder, "beneath the clavicula, exiting through the trapezius."

Yorgi said to stop all the medical bullshit and just do what he had to do.

Under a local, the doctor prepped the area, back and front, cleaning the wound, administering an antibiotic, then recommended bed rest for forty-eight hours, dispensing a packet of Percodans for pain, one every four hours as needed.

Then he made the mistake of asking, "What happened to your eye?"

Yorgi told him to mind his own goddamn business.

The doctor had recommended the Desert Breeze and helped him

walk over there. Yorgi's legs felt as if they were made of balsa.

Throughout the morning, while trying to gain strength, get on his feet, he'd thought about the five hundred thousand—it would be his own ass if he didn't bring it back to Oak Park, no matter the story. Whoever had put out the original contract on Jin Lee would come gunning after him, thanks to Guido. He decided that his only chance was to locate Molly Bodden and do whatever he had to do to get the briefcase. Break her hands, burn her, cut her up. Whatever.

About noon, he slowly and painfully got dressed, then started toward the door and blacked out for the first time in his life.

6.

THE PORSCHE, ON ROUTE 40 WEST, had long ago put Texas behind it and was now crossing New Mexico, Epp stopping only for food and gas under a chill, dazzling blue, February sky. He'd called Papa Epp in Philly, saying he'd be delayed a few days; going to drive somebody to Atlantic City. Have some company on the way home.

Papa had sounded a little disappointed but not too much. He'd seen his son before and after Super Bowl, big celebration to be long remembered. Epp had flown him to Miami, first class, both ways. He'd had a fine time, sitting up there in the wide seats in a new sports jacket, sipping Jack Daniels and nibbling on paté-spread crackers, telling ebry-body his son was a pass-catcher for the Raiders.

Epp had paid for Laburnum's round trip from St. Thomas, plus his game ticket, putting papa and Laburnum in his suite at the Doral. They'd had a grand old time.

Papa had been in on parties and had yelled himself hoarse on the fifty-yard line, sitting between Epp and Laburnum. So he hadn't been neglected lately. But while Epp was at Elon he hadn't had much time for either his papa or Thready. He'd had them down for a weekend in his senior year, but hadn't shown them around very much. They were neither-nors. Thready was gone into St. Croix sand, but now he'd try to make it up to Papa Epp. Between circling back from Texas and adding a day to get to New Jersey, he'd only be three days late.

At a Mobil station in Tucumcari, he again called Molly, asking her if she was all right and telling her to get packed so they could leave right away.

She sounded tired and uncertain, but said, "I'll be ready. Are you sure you want to do this?"

"Yeh, I'm sure," said Epp, frowning to himself. Was he?

"You've thought about it?"

"I'm headed back your way. Isn't that enough? I'll see you in the morning. Keep your door locked."

"Okay," she said. Then quickly, "You don't know what this means to me. Having you come into my life."

Epp grinned. "Tell me tomorrow." What the hell was a few days late to Philly?

"What's Irene's address?"

He wrote it down, then ordered, "Stay there."

What was a few days late to Philly?

But after he was on the road again, rolling at seventy-five and eighty, here was a girl who'd done something pretty crazy. And now he was going to pick up her pieces.

Repeat: what was he getting into? He'd started a career in a big way—listen, there weren't all that many wide receivers picked in the first round. He was going great in Oakland, fans hanging banners over the railings: a hand and "Fingers."

Yet he knew that what had happened Wednesday night, so wonderful between the sheets, had left him open to his groin, if not his head.

There'd been what you call a funky white girl from Hickory, North Carolina, daughter of a furniture factory owner. Mary Margaret McCallum. The three M's. Mary Margaret talked real Southern *how-dee* and said she liked it that Epp was quadroon or octoroon or whatever he was, and loved what was between his legs. Mary Margaret couldn't get enough of Epp in motels in Greensboro and Winston-Salem and Raleigh.

There'd been others like Mary Margaret, going back to Central Bucks West. Lately, there'd been Mavis O'Connor and her jigsaw puzzle. She now seemed ancient history. But none of them had ever been mixed up with the mob.

Had he really fallen for Molly Bodden or again was it just his brainless pecker? He didn't really know as he bypassed Albuquerque.

* * *

Theodore Taylor

Molly awakened on the couch about two to the insistent ring of the doorbell and stiffened, debating whether or not to answer. It might be Irene coming back from the park with the baby, but she'd be calling out, "Molly, open up!"

The drilling of the bell changed to hard knocks and Molly got up unsteadily, standing back three or four feet from the door, checking to make sure the double safety chains were on. All the Vegas girls had them.

"Who is it?"

"Detective Lieutenant Nishgo, Las Vegas police."

"What do you want?"

"Talk to you."

She opened the door to the extent of the chains, and he held his ID in the crack.

"About what?"

"About Bobby Chapman."

"You'll have to wait a few minutes."

"I'll wait."

She went into the bathroom, splashed cold water on her face, combed her hair, brushed her teeth, then put on a denim jumpsuit Howie had brought over from her apartment and padded back to the door.

"I was asleep," she said.

Coming inside, he said, "You even wake up looking good."

Molly knew how she looked. Wrung out. "Thanks."

"Mind if I sit down?" He took the couch, shoving aside her blanket.

She shook her head, feeling groggy, pulling out a chair for herself, not meeting the detective's eyes.

He sat down opposite her, saying casually, "Bobby Chapman died at ten forty-two this morning."

Hand coming up to her mouth, she said, "Oh, no."

"I've got a homicide to handle."

A small tape recorder appeared out of his inner jacket. "You object to this?"

She shook her head.

95

"Bobby's dead," she said, tears brimming.

Nishgo nodded. "What do you know about it?"

She bit her lip, looking away from his steady gaze, swallowing, wiping her eyes. "Nothing. Nothing."

"You must know something."

"I don't."

"He drove you last night."

She nodded, looking out the window, thinking of poor Bobby Chapman. *Her* fault he was dead.

"How long did he stay?"

"He didn't stay, just dropped me off."

"You saw him drive away?"

She nodded.

"I wish you'd look at me when you answer," Nishgo said.

She swung her head back, eyes reddened, feeling a hundred years old.

"Bobby had a wife and a baby. I think he deserved a little more than getting killed, don't you?"

Molly nodded, guilt eating her up.

"Okay, you don't know anything about how he got his brains scrambled, so tell me about the guy with the gun, the guy that caused you to ask Vince Abernathy for an escort. You did make that request, didn't you?"

"Yes, I did." A trap was closing around her and she knew it. She began to feel heat. "Would you like something to drink?"

Nishgo said he'd take whatever she had.

She went to Irene's refrigerator and his voice followed her. "Who is the guy with the gun?"

She stood looking in at the sparse collection on the shelves. Some soft drinks, some fruit. Banana bread. Margarine. Some salsa. A bottle of artichoke hearts. A small bag of wheat flour. An unopened can of Graber's olives. She said, "Graber. Frank Graber."

She took out two Cokes and went back to the table.

"How do you spell that? G-r-a-y-b-e-r?"

"I'm not sure."

"Friend of yours?"

"I had a date with him."

"When?"

"Tuesday night." The trap was closing so slowly that the jaws didn't even look like they'd moved, but she knew they had.

"Where'd you go?"

"The Hilton, for roulette."

"He local?"

"No."

"Where's he from?"

"New York."

"Where was he staying?"

"He didn't say."

"And you didn't ask?"

She shook her head.

"When's the last time you saw him?"

"Early Wednesday morning."

"That when he threatened you?"

She nodded. Half of it was true.

"With a gun?"

"Just with his hands, just the way he acted."

"Where does the gun come in? You see him with it?"

Molly took a deep breath. "I just thought he had one."

"And you told that football player?"

"Yes."

"Why did you think he had a gun?"

"He was that type of person."

"You mean criminal?"

She nodded. "I think so."

"Why would you date a criminal?"

"It was a blind date, a friend made it."

"Who was the friend?"

Molly could feel the sweat along her hairline and over her upper lip. "I don't want to involve him."

"We've got a homicide here, Miss Bodden. You ought to be thinking about Bobby Chapman while we're talking. I need to know everything there is to know. Is your friend local?"

97

"No."

Nishgo smiled. "You can tell me later. But first I want to know if you're still frightened of this Frank Grayber."

Molly nodded.

"Why didn't you come to us the morning after he threatened you. We could have at least run him down and talked to him. You know we always cooperate with the casinos. We don't need rough play here. We sure as hell don't need homicides."

Molly said, "I should have, but I thought he'd just leave town."

"And go back to New York? Not bother you again?"

Molly nodded.

Nishgo pushed the recorder to off and sat back. "Well, I'll probably be talking to you again. I don't know what we have here. After Bobby got back to the parking lot he could have walked up on a couple of guys hot-wiring a sixty-thousand-dollar Mercedes. Or he could have had some guy who was pissed off at him. We already checked him for dealing drugs. No known record. Here was a nice young guy with a nice wife and a ten-month-old, and sometime this evening he'll be on a porcelain table and they'll examine his organs, one by one. An autopsy is mandatory. Think about him getting sliced open, Miss Bodden, and give me a call if you think of anything else. And if Frank Grayber happens to call you try to find out where he is, then you call us. If he's really threatening you, I can get him behind bars, real quick."

He stood up, smiled, thanked her for his drink, and she saw him to the door.

Out in the hall, he said, "Student with a baby. Makes me sick, Miss Bodden."

She nodded.

Then she relatched the chains before calling Howie Piaggi to tell him she was quitting the Stardust and wasn't up to working the shows tonight. Please send her last check in care of Lucille Fernandez back in Atlantic City. *And don't tell anyone where I've gone.*

Then she went back to the couch, image of curly-haired Bobby tucking in beside her. She'd slept on and off for most of twenty-four hours.

Irene came back with the baby about three.

An hour later, Walter Nishgo called Vince Abernathy and said he thought Molly Bodden was lying. "I'm not sure why, but I think she knows a lot more than she's saying. Just the way she acted."

How she acted was the best telltale of all, Vince well knew. But he said, defending, "She's just a kid."

"She's been around," said Nishgo.

"Yeh, but she's still a kid, only nineteen."

"She did give me the name of the guy who threatened her. But she said he didn't do it with a gun. Frank Grayber. G-r-a-y-b-e-r. Will you check the desk and see if he's been registered with you? I've got my guys checking around."

Abernathy said he'd have registration make the check.

Long after Universal's *Dinosaurus*, starring Ward Ramsey and Kristina Hanson, said "The End," Yorgi yelled his way out of the dream, damp sheet sticking to the whirlpools of hair on his back, sweat beading in the hollow of this throat, head damp with it.

He'd been standing in front of Molly Bodden's full-length mirror but could see only his eye, big as a basketball, with the nerves connecting to it like pieces of rhubarb, and tiny blood vessels wandering all over.

There were three or four parts to it: colored gray and blue and brown, balls and chambers, the eyelid, drawn-back, being pink inside.

The thing was pulsating, and there was no body attached to it, as if it were separate from Yorgi Greco, something floating out there, looking back from the mirror, staring at him, out of body.

Yorgi heard himself yelling as he departed the dream, gasping for breath, heart pounding. In the past, he seldom dreamed, despite his line of work. Now he lay there panting, thinking about the detail of the huge eye he'd just seen.

He got up, went to the bathroom, took a pee, looked at his face, gingerly touched the shoulder wound then went back to bed, angrily tossing around until almost five o'clock when he took another Percodan.

He was hungry, but didn't feel steady enough to go out, afraid he'd black out again.

PART III

1.

ABOUT THE TIME CHURCH BELLS were ringing in Vegas, that other sane Vegas, the same time casinos were coming to life again, slots sputtering metallically, blackjack and craps tables beginning to get a few more customers, Epp slid the Porsche up to the curb on St. Louis Street and got out, looking around.

She could have missed the guy she said she shot. He could have found out where she was living.

Epp again wondered momentarily what "Fingers" Watts was doing here on this bright Sunday morning, a long way from Philly, maybe in line to take a bullet himself, but he crossed the street anyway, going up the few steps into the brick building, climbing a flight of inside steps, ringing Irene's bell.

Molly's voice, wary, came through the wood and he answered, cheery as the Domino's Pizza deliveryman, "Epp—Molly, it's me."

Chains rattled and the door swung back. There she was, in a jumpsuit, hair piled up, face not showing much luster, not the Molly he'd left Wednesday morning, saying, "Hold me."

That's what she'd said the first night.

Hold me.

So he held her, bleary-eyed himself, saying, "You're gonna be jus' fine."

An attractive blonde, in a housecoat and curlers, child in her arms, stood across the room.

"This is Irene," Molly said.

"Hi," Epp said.

Irene smiled and nodded.

Still holding Molly, he repeated, "You'll be fine."

He felt her head nod against his chest. Her bags were packed and in the middle of the floor.

Then he held her off. "What now?"

The whites of her eyes needed a squirt of Murine.

"I'm ready to go." Her head nodded backward toward the bags. "Reggie's going to see that all my stuff goes into storage until I call for it."

The mannequin, sewing machine, dress bags, paintings, books, bric-a-brac, Epp supposed.

"He's going to sell the car," she added.

"That friend of yours in Atlantic City know you're coming?"

Molly said she did.

"Any more trouble from that guy?"

"No. I've been here. I haven't slept much."

Epp had stayed up all night himself driving. "We'll check into a motel down the road."

That was okay with her.

"Let's go," said Epp, taking her two bags.

He said good-bye to Irene while Molly hugged her, saying her thanks; she'd call when they got to Atlantic City.

In less than ten minutes they were headed up 93 for Kingman, Arizona. Epp planned on staying there for what was left of Sunday afternoon and Sunday night, getting on 40 early Monday and going back the same way into Texas.

A half-dozen miles out of Vegas city limits, Molly quiet, thoughtful, Epp said, "For my sake, so I know what I'm getting into, I want you to tell me exactly what happened. Don't leave anything out."

He was looking straight ahead when he said it, but looked over at her when he finished. He got the back of her head. She was looking out at the harsh, hostile brown-red sand and twisted arms of cactus and didn't answer.

He waited awhile, then said, "You hear me, Molly?"

She nodded and finally answered, face mostly in profile, looking at some point where desert met sky, two or three points on the bow.

She told him everything from her date with Guido Malavasi and

104

then Guido calling her to date his friend, Joe Carlucci. She'd kept thinking she could make it big with roulette, somebody like Guido or Joe staking her, then she'd pay back the stake and keep the rest. A guy had won big, fifty thousand, in one night at the Hilton in December. Enough to open that shop in St. Thomas. That's why she was dating Guido and Joe, and other guys. The only reason. Foolish, she now knew. Stupid; reckless. Asking for trouble.

Epp was just letting her talk.

She told him exactly how Joe Carlucci looked, one of those men covered with human fur; how evil he looked, how he acted that night. How she panicked and cut him in the eye, down the cheek. She blamed it on her fear of rape, that time when she was six and the Ras boys climbed on her one after the other. She lived in monumental fear of it happening again.

She told him how Joe Carlucci looked on the road off the Tonopah Highway after she'd shot him . . . standing there with his right eye bandaged and blood dripping down his right arm.

"He told me I'd better kill him or he'd come after me wherever I went. He meant it, Epp."

"Well, you know what you have to do. You have to call the police."

She was still looking out at the brown-red sand, the cholla cactus, the long reaches into the treeless brown mountains. "Because of Bobby Chapman?"

"That's right. Because of Bobby Chapman. You've got to call that detective tomorrow and admit you lied to him. You've got to tell him about Carlucci hitting Bobby with that tire iron."

"What happens to me then? If all that comes out in the papers, I won't work in Atlantic City or anywhere else. I've heard what these casino people can do. Any girl gets into trouble, they walk away. Everywhere. I told you that."

"Molly, you got to take the chance."

"Then Carlucci comes after me." Her head turned toward Epp.

"Carlucci goes to jail," Epp insisted.

Molly was silent a long time. "That's how it's supposed to happen. Suppose it doesn't?"

105

"You have to tell Nishgo what you're afraid of. He'll keep your name out of the papers until he has to use you. He knows the casino people."

She looked over again. "You sure of that? So I'm working in Atlantic City and out comes the news that they've arrested Joe Carlucci for killing Bobby Chapman. How long do you think it'll last before his friends get to me. How long do you think it'll be before someone tries to kill me so I can't testify? How long do you think that will be?"

Epp sighed. "Who's in Atlantic City?"

"A friend of mine from Puerto Rico, a dancer. Lucille Fernandez."

"I didn't know the casinos were open."

"One is. Caesars'll open in May. She said I could get a job."

"Same ones as in Vegas?"

"Caesar's, Sands, Tropicana. Some planned that aren't in Vegas."

Not much else was said the rest of the way to Kingman and Molly, exhausted, finally dozed, coiled up.

They found a motel just off 40 in Kingman and went to sleep in twin beds when the sun was two o'clock high. They were practically wordless.

Still feeling sickish, shoulder hurting worse than it did yesterday, Yorgi went out to breakfast about eleven o'clock, buying a copy of the Vegas Sunday paper. On the front page was a story about Bobby Chapman, the Stardust guard who was assaulted in the casino's parking lot early Saturday morning. The story said he'd died of severe head injuries and that the police were investigating. Detective Lieutenant Walter Nishgo was quoted as saying there were no suspects but that they "were developing some leads." The only "lead" that Yorgi knew of was Molly Bodden. She, alone, could make the identification, so far as he knew.

He placed a call from the Desert Breeze to the Stardust, asking for the show reservation desk, saying he wanted to attend that night and make sure that beautiful Molly Bodden, the girl in that big photo in the lobby, was going to dance.

"I'm sorry, sir, she's no longer with the show."

"What happened to her?"

"I don't know, sir."

"Did she go to another hotel?"

"I've heard she left Las Vegas." Word had gotten around the Stardust. Molly had quit and was going home, Howie said.

"Where'd she go?"

"I have no idea, sir." Jimmy Rosenberger had said to make that answer to anyone who called.

"Well, I don't want to make a reservation unless she's there."

"Thank you for calling the Stardust, sir."

Figures, Yorgi thought. She took the half million and split. Where to? Back to St. Thomas, likely, with all that money. Enough to set up a dozen dress shops.

He threw the paper across the room and went out to catch a cab, remembering she lived on Thirteenth Street. Once they got on Thirteenth, he had the cabbie drive slowly until he spotted the pink stucco. Getting out, he told the cabbie to wait and mounted the short steps.

Her name was still on the first-floor mail slot and then he saw that the building had a resident manager, E. M. Fernley.

Yorgi rang the bell, and a graying, fiftyish woman opened the door. Yorgi asked, "You got any apartments for rent?" A poodle yapped at him.

"As a matter of fact, I do," said Mrs. Fernley. "One is about to be vacated."

"I'm interested," Yorgi said.

"Let me get the key."

In a moment they were climbing the stairs, the resident manager saying, "She still has some of her things in there, but they'll be moved tomorrow. She's a showgirl. You know how they are. Here today, gone tomorrow."

The door to Molly's apartment was opened seconds later, and Yorgi looked in with his good eye. Her personal possessions were mounded in the middle of the living room.

"Left in a hurry?" he said. "Know where she went?"

"Nope. Called me yesterday afternoon to say she was leaving. Her rent was paid up. It's a nice apartment, partially furnished, Mr.—?"

"Katsanis," said Yorgi.

Back at the Desert Breeze, Yorgi called United to make a reservation out tomorrow. Go home, regroup, then find the bitch *and* the money, in St. Thomas or wherever.

At seven-thirty P.M., Yorgi called the Stardust again, telling the operator that he had to get a message to Molly Bodden.

"She's no longer with the show," said the operator.

"I know that," Yorgi said, "but I need to get a message to her. It's important. She must have a good friend who'd know how to reach her."

"I'll connect you to the stage manager, Howie Piaggi."

A moment later Yorgi heard, "Piaggi."

Yorgi said, "I need to get a message to Molly Bodden. Can you do that for me."

"What's your name?"

"Joe."

"Joe who?"

"Never mind. Just tell her that she should have killed me out in the desert and that she better get the money to me or she'll be dead."

Yorgi hung up.

Howie stood by the phone backstage for a moment, frowning, then said, "Jesus Christ" and called Abernathy at home.

Off and on all day, going through those Indian-sounding places— Picacho Butte and Rimmy Jims and Navajo—with the high-desert Arizona sky crisscrossed by jet trails, car windows feeling icy cold, air so clear outside the fleeing Porsche that peaks fifty miles away seemed touchable, they talked about calling Walter Nishgo. Molly argued, always ending with a sigh that seemed to let everything out of her chest. Now they were back in New Mexico, moving past Manuelito to Gallup, and Epp was saying, "Maybe you wouldn't have to go back for the trial. Maybe they'd just take a deposition . . ."

"How does that work?"

"You swear under oath, and someone asks you a lot of questions while a court stenographer takes it down. It's good in court."

"I just don't ever want to face him again."

"Nishgo would understand that. Look, the guy was going to rape you, then he kidnaps you, puts tape over your mouth, on your wrists. You shot him in self-defense. A prosecutor is going to understand that. You were scared to death for God's sake. The law isn't going to connect you with that."

"Scared to death is the understatement of the century," Molly said, looking over.

"And it'll be better this way than if Nishgo puts the pieces together by himself. This way you're up-front about it. Just tell him you lied to him Saturday afternoon only because you were frightened of what might happen to you. What the mob might do."

"And you don't think they'd make me come back to Vegas, get involved with reporters? I just give a deposition?"

Epp blew out a breath. It had been like this all day. Maybe she was acting this way because she was so young. "Just tell them you don't want to talk to reporters."

"Will that work if it gets into the press?"

"It'll work if you stay away from them. You see all these people on TV saying 'No comment.' You'd be like that."

"Would I need a lawyer for the deposition?"

"I don't see what for."

"Someone to sit there beside me if I have to go back."

"Look, you got friends. Jimmy Rosenberger, that Howie Piaggi, Irene, some of the older girls." He paused. "Well, hell, I'll come back with you if they need you."

Silence for a while, Molly staring out the window; Epp staring straight ahead.

109

"Okay, I'm working in Atlantic City and the Mafia sends somebody after me."

"You don't even know he is Mafia. All you got are two Italian names, guys living in the Chicago area."

"He sure looked like Mafia."

"The way you describe him he looks like a bear."

"That doesn't tell me what to do if the Mafia sends someone after me."

Epp's voice was winding down. "You go to the Atlantic City police."

"And I'm fired the next day."

The job again, for chrissakes.

"Not necessarily. But I guess you have to take that chance."

"Epp, don't push me. Please don't push me."

"I'm only pushing because the guy may still be in Las Vegas and they can pick him up. Once he leaves, they may never get him. He's a goddamn murderer . . ."

Silence again. The winter sky was orange behind them, mountains purple up ahead.

"Maybe I should talk to a lawyer first?"

"You haven't been charged with anything."

"I did shoot him."

"They'll give you a gold star." But on the other hand . . . from yesterday on, Epp had thought this was the kind of story the media would vacuum-clean and make last for days: gorgeous showgirl dancer does a job on an ugly mob guy from the Chicago suburbs . . . Maybe she should just keep her mouth shut. "Nebba trouble trouble 'til trouble trouble yoh."

Epp checked into the Holiday Motel on the bypass road off 40, and after they got the bags out of the car Molly said, "You don't smoke, do you?"

Jumpier than ever, she was into the bathroom and out of it, looking at her face in the mirror, turning away. Running her hand through her hair. Looking at the pamphlet on the dresser: Zuni Pueblo, 38 miles; Ice caves, 48 miles. She was about to come apart.

"I never did," she said.

"Neither did I."

"You want a pack of cigarettes? I'll go get 'em."

"Don't," she said.

"You want a drink?"

"Yes."

"What?"

"Vodka, I guess. I don't drink much, Epp. I don't know what to drink."

"Mix?"

"I'll drink it straight."

"You *are* uptight, lady."

"Yes, for God's sake, I *am* uptight."

"I'll go get the vodka. There's a place right down the road, walking distance."

He left her sitting on the bed, holding her head.

She was still in the same spot when he returned with the fifth. She didn't look up as he went out again to the ice machine.

Pouring half a water tumbler of vodka over the cubes, handing it to her, he sat down beside her on the bed. She took a gulp, shivered, and for a moment he thought it might come back up. She closed her eyes, waited, then took another drink and finally said, "Let's call Nishgo."

"What's the area code?"

"702."

He dialed the numbers for information, redialed for the Vegas police, got a 911, and wound up talking to the desk. Epp said the call had to do with the murder of Bobby Chapman and that he wanted to speak to Walter Nishgo.

"He's not here now, but I'll get him for you. He'll call you," said the four-to-twelve sergeant. "Give me your number."

2.

AT FRIGID DUSK, looking, from a distance, like a 3M executive just returned from a selling trip to St. Louis, Yorgi got out of the limo from O'Hare at the brick-and-wood two-story house on Glenwood Drive, not far from Knoch Park and Glenwood Elementary School, a quiet family neighborhood. There were crusts of stained snow on the lawn, patches of ice on the front walk. With temperatures in the mid-twenties, northeast Illinois was still hostage to winter.

People on the block had no idea what Yorgi did for a living and most thought that the attractive dark-haired girl they saw coming and going was his wife, not his sister. Blowing snow from the driveway and walk in the winter, cutting his own lawn in the summer, Yorgi made no attempt to have them think otherwise. Mr. and Mrs. Stathos, smiling and nodding, keeping to themselves. Shy neighbors, they bothered no one.

He went up the pebbled walkway, avoiding ice slicks, wearing big dark glasses to cover the eye bandage, carrying his only piece of luggage with his left hand. The right shoulder ached more today than it had the first two days.

Home only minutes before from AT&T in Lisle, sorting groceries on the table in the kitchen, Kathy heard the front door open and went out into the hall just in time to see her brother arrive and put his bag down at the foot of the stairs.

She went to him, twenty feet away, seeing the tiny railroad-tie stitches and the reddened arc that carved through whisker stubs. "Oh, my Lord, your face," she said.

"How's my Ekaterini," he said, smiling, holding out his arms.

"Yorgos, this is terrible. Worse than I thought. You'll have a scar. And your eye?"

Taking off the dark glasses, exposing the bandage over the socket, he hugged her against his chest with his left arm. "I'll grow a beard. You'll never know. I've always wanted a beard. Didn't I tell you?"

She stood back to look. "Just terrible. It's all the way to your neck."

"Not so terrible. It could have ripped my jugular vein, the doctor said. I wouldn't be here now." Make her feel better to hear that. "I was lucky."

"A fish hook did all that?"

Yorgi always hated to lie to Kathy but had to do it now and then. "The guy on the other end of the line was very strong."

She touched fingertips to the good side of his face. "How's the eye?"

Why not tell her now? Get it over with. "I don't have it anymore, little sister."

Kathy began to weep softly.

Pulling her to him with his good left arm, putting his mouth against her hair, he murmured, "Iss okay . . . iss okay . . ."

"I'm so sorry," she said, "so sorry."

"They'll make a plastic eye that looks exactly like the left one. None of those ugly glass eyes like they had when we were kids. The doctor in Vegas said the only thing it'll lack is real movement. People won't even know 'less they look close."

Finally, she took her wet face from his shoulder. "Why did it have to happen to you?"

"Accident. Could happen to anybody," Yorgi said, wiping her cheeks with the back of his left hand.

To tell you the actual truth, Guido got me a date. Guido played a little game and look what happened. But he wasn't about to tell her that.

She sniffed and said, "Go on up and change. I'll fix a good dinner for you."

Kathy always fixed something special for him when he came home from trips. He smiled at her again, gave her a hug and went on upstairs, Molly Bodden on his mind. She'd flown with him to O'Hare, ridden with him in the limo. Had she gone on to St. Thomas?

113

* * *

Not wanting to miss Nishgo's call, Epp had gone out to Kentucky Fried, and they were now having dinner in the motel room.

Molly barely nibbled at her piece of extra-crispy, finally putting it down. "Am I doing the right thing, Epp? For me? The right thing for me?"

"We've been over it all day. It's the only thing you can do."

"But it just seems that I'll get in deeper, involving police, the courts." Molly looked over at the phone. "Ring, dammit," she yelled at it, "before I get cold feet."

Me, too, he thought.

Beyond the loss of an eye, something else had happened on this trip, Kathy sensed. She wasn't quite ready to believe the fishing story. Yorgos hadn't gone fishing for years. He was withholding something from her, she believed, something to do with the Malavasis. Maybe Guido. She knew Tony was down in Florida, at the Fontainebleu.

Kathy had been around Tony and his wife, around Guido and others of the "family," ever since Yorgos quit boxing. She knew they were mafioso but didn't know exactly what her brother did for them. He said they had various businesses and he was like a collection man when customers didn't pay their debts; like the IRS when people didn't pay their taxes. She could imagine Yorgos going around, doing the collections. Just his looks made some people uneasy. She knew that.

The Malavasis themselves sometimes joked about Yorgos, especially Guido, calling him *animale*, but they didn't know how kind he was underneath. They just saw what was on the surface of Yorgos Stathos, she thought. He was a good brother to her, always loving, always looking out for her best interests. The house was in her name, paid off, as well as the two cars, Yorgos saying suppose he was killed in a plane crash on one of his trips or something like that. So far as she knew, Yorgos owned nothing except the fine clothing on his back.

The Kentucky Fried Chicken boxes had long gone into the waste-basket when Molly said, "If he doesn't call tonight, it's all off."

"He's going to call," Epp said.

"Well, dammit, why hasn't he done it? It's eight o'clock. I can't stand this."

"He's probably out on a case somewhere. Or home. He's got more than Bobby Chapman on his hands."

Molly repeated, "If he doesn't call tonight, it's all off. I'm losing my nerve."

"Okay, I'll try him again," Epp said, moving over to the phone.

The "family" was always good to her, that Kathy couldn't deny. Tony Ox and Josephina always came by on Christmas Eve with expensive presents. When anyone in the family got married, Kathy was always invited along with Yorgos. Tony Ox always hugged her and said nice things to her when they met, saying how pretty she was.

The few questions that Kathy had ever asked her brother were always answered with, "Jus' business, Ekaterini. Nothin' for you to worry about."

Yet she'd always worried, thinking that sometime she'd get a call from Tony Ox, saying that Yorgos was dead. Or she'd read a story in the *Tribune* about her brother being arrested for one reason or another. She had no idea he was a hitman. He was just a collector, she thought.

Yorgi was toying with the lamb and potato stew, the *yahni*, that he usually liked. He'd had four *grappas*, unaged brandy he imported from Italy, instead of his usual two, and he still had a legitimate pain in his shoulder, not the phantom pain the nurse had told him about.

Kathy was talking about the boyfriend, Hajadaki. "I said, 'Nikos,

115

why do we have to have enough for a down payment on a house? Why can't we just rent?' "

Yorgi thought the son of a bitch was dodging marriage. He was almost as old as Yorgi and had been going with Kathy for four years. Yorgi had said, last spring, "How about me talkin' to him? Ask him what he plans?"

Kathy had said, "Oh, no! Please don't." Kathy had an idea how that talk might go, Nikos getting punched.

If another summer went by, Yorgi decided he'd pay a visit to the PIP printing shop, anyway. Encourage him a little, slap him around a little. But Yorgi was finding it hard to concentrate on anything she said about Hajadaki, because of the dinge. Until Molly Bodden came along, the only one he'd ever hated, despite all the killing, was Nino Bonaventura, the guy who'd broken his jaw in three places, ruining his career. Nino was now fourteen years in the past, lately serving time in Statesville, he'd heard, for armed robbery. So that overhand right didn't get Nino too far, at that.

Kathy was talking about the tulips and lilacs she'd planted in the fall, and how she hoped even half of the Holland bulbs would come up.

Yorgi was thinking about Molly. He yawned and said he was pooped. Jet lag. He had to go to bed. He bent down and kissed his sister, saying he was glad to be home, thanks for the dinner.

Climbing the stairs, he hoped he wouldn't dream again about that pulsating eye as big as a basketball, suspended in air. Christ, the next thing would be eyeballs on bird's wings, diving on him, chasing him.

He thought he could feel the plastic sphere implanted in the socket.

Nishgo didn't call until a quarter to twelve and Epp, reaching across Molly's warm body to pick up the phone, said, "Don't you sleep at night?"

There was a half-laugh on the other end. "Is it still night? You have something about Bobby Chapman?"

Epp cupped the phone. "It's that detective. You want him to call back in the morning?"

Molly turned over and then sat up. "No, I'll talk to him now. Then maybe I can sleep."

Epp turned on the lamp beside the bed and Molly pulled the sheet up sedately over her breasts, talking and answering questions for the next forty-five minutes.

"First, you're sure his name is Joe."

"That's what he told me."

"Joe."

"Yes."

Nishgo had decided not to tell her, for the moment, about this call "Joe" had made to Howie Piaggi. The money, the death threat. But he did ask, "You owe Joe any money?"

"Why do you ask that."

"Lot o' times people get upset over money matters."

"Well, he staked me to twelve hundred at the Hilton."

"You lost it?"

"Yes, I lost it."

"Molly, some people, quite a few, in fact, will kill for twelve hundred. I'm not saying Joe Carlucci will but it's possible. In the apartment or out in the desert, did he ask for the twelve hundred."

"No, he didn't."

"All right, let's go on to Bobby Chapman."

They went over the parking and Bobby Chapman three times, Nishgo saying, "You sure, you sure . . . ?"

"I'm sure."

"Okay, let's talk about this Guido a moment. He said his name was Malavasi?"

"Yes."

"Do think I've heard the name—Malavasi, Malavasi."

Molly said that was right. Guido had said he lived near Chicago.

"I'll feed it into the system and see what pops up. The bureau has something, I'm sure. He goes in with Joe Carlucci, but we'll also look for Mr. Carlucci locally."

After Nishgo had his fill, Molly asked, "What happens now?"

117

"Paperwork, a lot of it, including you filing a complaint for kidnapping, assault with a deadly weapon; then we get him on suspicion of murder for Bobby Chapman—issue an abstract warrant. Teletype it around the country, including Naperville. If he's gone back there and they can apprehend him, then we'll go to the state, get a signature for extradition and try to bring Mr. Carlucci back here to stand trial. Meanwhile, we'll get a grand jury indictment on him for all three charges. All this may take weeks, months. But we'll start it tonight by trying for him here."

"Can I go on to Atlantic City?"

"Sure you can, just keep in touch with me, and thanks for telling me the truth. Sleep well."

Molly said goodnight, passing the phone back to Epp, sinking down in the bed, sighing deeply. "Now, I *won't* sleep—not at all."

Epp pulled her close to him. "I'm damn proud of you."

"I'm still scared shitless."

"I have a little something for that."

"What?"

"We go take a warm shower together and then come right back here."

"And get in this bed?"

"In this bed."

3.

EARLY TUESDAY, even before Kathy was awake, still dark outside, Yorgi went to the garage and slid the fifty-gallon steel drum of powder-form concrete cleaner, strong, green soap-smelling stuff that eradicated oils, away from the top of his safe. He'd personally sunk it into the six-inch floor ten years ago. Kathy didn't know it existed. Yorgi's salary was five hundred a week from West Michigan Loan Associates, and like a good citizen he willingly paid state and federal taxes on every single dime of it. But neither Illinois or the IRS was aware of the existence of Yorgi's roomy safe or what was in it, collected over the years from freelance jobs such as Jin Lee. That money was his stake whenever he retired.

Walking over behind Kathy's car to make sure the garage door was securely locked from the inside—Kathy or anyone else just walking in—Yorgi returned to the safe, ran the combination and visited the cash on hand, which was around four hundred eighty thousand in banded big bills. Shaking his head in a fury over the sorry deed he had to do, he extracted all but twenty thousand, laying the money into a cardboard fancy-fruit box. Then, breathing heavily, he closed the safe, spinning the combination, and slid the heavy drum back over the spot beneath the tool bench.

Kathy was still asleep when he returned upstairs, the transfer having taken less than thirty minutes, and he recounted the money while waiting for her to wake up. This was one time he didn't want to cheat himself.

Kathy went off to Lisle a little after eight, and Yorgi soon had to come face-to-face with the mirror. There wasn't much more to like today than there was yesterday. The scar seemed a little less red as he guided the electric razor as if it were on the edge of Grand Canyon. The scab on the shoulder wound was purplish black set in a circle of pink, and he turned around to look over his shoulder at the backside. The same. Three inches higher and the bitch would have nicked bone. As if he needed it, the mirror was another reminder of Vegas.

At eleven o'clock he was on the Burlington Express, the gourmet fruit carton by his side, looking out the window, deep in thought, scarcely noticing as Lisle, Hinsdale and LaGrange passed by. Even if Tony was back from Miami, there was no way to explain the loss of the money. Even Tony wouldn't accept such a story, let alone the people who owned the four hundred fifty. So he was out-of-pocket for that amount and had to swallow it. Ten years of savings blown, thanks to *her.*

Yorgi met Guido for lunch at Peppitone's, on North, and said, "Here it is," handing Guido the box.

Pissed-off in general, pouty, showing it, the *sottocapo* said, "I still don't understand why you didn't send it Federal Express. Tell me why." He sat there like a pasty Buddha.

Yorgi tried to shrug it off. "Thought it was safer with me." One helluva mistake, he now admitted to himself. A terrible mistake.

"I told Tony—you counted right?"

Yorgi raised his hands, stick-'em-up fashion.

"The other party was gettin' anxious, you know."

"So they had to wait a few more days," said Yorgi. "Tell them I got the job done, didn't I? What more do they want? You got the money. Ten in there for you and Tony."

Yorgi didn't feel like getting bounced around this noontime by anybody. He'd rather be strangling Molly Bodden.

There'd been shouts in Peppitone's when Yorgi came in: "Hey, Yorgi, wha' happen your eye?" "Hey, Yorgi, who cutcha?"

He'd expected them.

"You're a mess, Yorgi," said Guido, picking at flakes of crab in his salad.

Yorgi was wearing a black patch over his eye like the Hathaway man of old. He had to go to three pharmacies in Naperville to find one.

"You mean that hook snagged your eyeball, then went down into your neck?"

How many times would he have to tell it? How many?

"Ended up stuck in my neck. They had one of those Medevac helicopters come out to the lake." Yorgi remembered what that truck driver had said on the Tonopah. "That's how I went to the hospital, hook in my neck, holdin' a rag to my eye."

Guido shook his head, triple chins shaking with it. "You shudda stayed in the casino. I never fished in my life, but didn't know it was dangerous."

"Freak accident," said Yorgi, forking up a slice of tomato, anchovy draped over it, watching the *sottocapo* closely. He had a big head but small, puffy turtle eyes. Could the SOB have paid that girl to cut him, shoot him? Had it been a plot? No, even for Guido that didn't make sense.

Guido cocked his head one way, then the other, as if judging a beauty contest, finally saying, "Makes you look meaner to see that scar, all those stitches." Then, chuckling to himself, he added, "As if you could look any meaner."

Yorgi didn't say anything. He felt like backhanding the *sottocapo*, then working him over, punching him out.

"An' you're gonna get a glass eye?"

"Plastic. Just like my left one. It'll move. I got my first appointment on Friday, on LaSalle."

"Gotta get a new nickname for you, Yorgi. 'Greco' doesn't fit anymore." He looked around thoughtfully. It was busy, noisy, smoky, at one-fifteen in Peppitone's.

Striking on a name, Guido grinned. "Cyclops, the one-eyed Greek. Yorgi *Ciclope*?" Then he took it back. "Naw, that doesn't fit. Yorgi *Scarface*? Naw, that one's been used, mostly in Cicero." Hah, hah. "I'll think of something."

Do that, you fat son of a bitch.

Still watching the *sottocapo* closely, Yorgi said, "Guido, about that girl . . ."

"Yeh, I was gonna ask you about her. She all I said, eh? Fantastic, *mortaretto*?"

Yorgi nodded, his good eye holding the *sottocapo* like a gray fist. "Yeh, Guido, that penthouse off the Strip . . . Jeez-us, those thick rugs . . . she take you up there? Yeh, of course she did."

121

Guido was suddenly frowning.

"Started takin' her clothes off soon as I got the door shut, had 'em all off 'fore she got to the bed, yellin' at me, come on, Joe, come on, Joe . . ."

Guido's frown widened.

"That has to be one of the greatest female tongues on earth . . . she was lappin' all over me in that sunken tub—"

Guido let out an uncertain laugh.

"We did it every way except on the window ledge six stories up. Fantastic, Guido. *Mortaretto*, like you said, an' I do thank you."

Yorgi had rehearsed every word of it, coming in on the train.

Guido partially recovered to say, "Like I told you."

Just from the look on Guido's face, Yorgi knew something hadn't worked. The girl had been bait for something else. The last few days he'd been making guesses about what it was: Guido had let out for business two contracts—one for a thief named Jin Lee, one for an employee named Yorgi Greco. Despite the mashed nose and banged-on ears, Yorgi was never as dumb as he looked. He'd been told that. "Hey, Yorgi, you're not as *stupido* as you look." That was true. That man, a Kansas City resident, was no longer on earth, proof of the statement. Guido, in time, would learn.

Walter Nishgo sat at his desk, looking at the teletype printout, tapping his pen on the bottom of it. There was a good eight inches, single-spaced, on Antonio "Tony Ox" Malavasi and about three on his son, Guido. Nothing on Joseph Carlucci.

The eight inches on Tony went back to when he was first busted for assault with a deadly weapon, aged seventeen. He'd wriggled out of two homicides before he was thirty. Guido's record was mainly loan sharking and extortion. He hadn't served any time. Neither was in the league of their late Oak Park neighbor, Sam Giancana.

Nishgo drew a short black line on the bottom of the printout, then printed AKA by Joseph Carlucci—deciding that wasn't his real name. Turning to Harry Jeffcoate, who was sitting in a wooden chair next to the desk, long legs stretched, he said "Okay, let's go over what we've got to date."

Harry, face like a wedge, with a Pancho Villa mustache and pop eyes, four years a detective-sergeant on the force, had been doing the fieldwork on Bobby Chapman. Harry said, "We got Carlucci at the Stardust Sunday through Thursday, but the maid said his room wasn't slept in after Monday."

Walter was writing on a pad.

"We pick him up at Humana Sunrise early Wednesday morning, eye and face cut open. Has surgery, checks out of Humana, checks out of the Stardust an hour later, pays cash all the way, and goes across the street to the Desert Inn. We gotta guess he recoups the rest of Thursday, room service for lunch and dinner. Buys the old Chrysler from Jack's Merit Used Cars about two o'clock Friday, clobbers Bobby Chapman and grabs the girl about one-fifteen A.M. Saturday. Takes her off the Tonopah to ream her eyes out. Instead, the fucker gets himself shot. I gotta laugh . . ."

"He's one tough son of a bitch, isn't he. Eye gone, he gets a bullet and still operates," said Walter.

Harry went on reading from his own pad: ". . . gets himself shot, the girl takes the car and drives it back here, dumps it at Longene Court and Fremont, then catches a cab to Irene's place. The asshole with a bullet in him catches a ride, we guess, back here. Where Joe Carlucci, or whoever the hell he is, then went to get his shoulder repaired, we don't know, and the girl is just guessing that she shot him in the shoulder. That's the last of Joseph Carlucci in this town. If he flew back to Chicago he didn't fly under that name, and you can bet your balls he paid cash . . ."

Walter said, "I'm not betting my good balls on anything to do with Mr. Carlucci."

"I talked to that Dr. Steinberg yesterday and he said he gave Mr. Carlucci the name of an ophthalmologist in Chicago. Guy by the name of Manning. I called Dr. Manning, and his girl said no one by the name of Carlucci had contacted them . . ."

"You told her to call us if Carlucci checked in?"

"Jesus Christ," said Harry. "You have to ask me a question like that?"

Walter sighed. "I guess it doesn't make much difference we don't know where he got the shoulder fixed—if she got him in the shoulder. I say again he must be one tough son of a bitch. Most people I know take a bullet, they head for the hospital. You haven't turned up anything at the emergency clinics?"

Harry shook his head.

"Well, I guess I better start talking to the gendarmes in Chicago, see if they can do anything with the Malavasi tribe. Maybe they know Tony has an ape on a long leash. That girl swears he's as hairy as an orangutan."

"He also ain't got but one eye now," said Harry. "I.D.?"

"You are a good man, Jeffcoate," said Walter, smiling at the string-bean wearing a loud summer cotton plaid jacket this overcast winter morning. Rain was threatening Las Vegas, something that didn't happen very often.

They'd crossed Oklahoma and were between Clarksville and Lamar, near the Arkansas River.

"Listen, I'm *dogala,* pure, unadulterated bastard in the eyes of the Brahmin, poor child of an East Indian and a black man," said Molly. "That's a no-no, forever. Most East Indians don't like blacks, Epp. They're afraid of them. They look down on them."

"I'm *dogala* in another way, and screw the Brahmins. They're all in Trinidad. Has nothing to do with the U.S.A. Anyway, we've got a lot in common. Why the hell do you keep telling me all these negative things?"

"So you'll know."

"I think I already know. I'm finally falling in love, like I said last night."

"Careful."

"Why don't we try living together? I'll come over and stay in Atlantic City until summer camp. See papa once a week."

Molly considered the proposal, then shook her head. "Out of the question."

"Why?"

She laughed. "Your skin is lighter than mine."

"You'll wind up marrying some snooty East Indian Vaish who won't give a damn about you being *dogala*. All he'll want is your hot body six times a day."

Molly laughed and shook her head again. "I won't marry at all."

"Dat's a turrible t'ing to say!" He gave her a grinning sidelong glance.

"I have a bad temper and would make no man a good wife. I have my career in design coming up, and I have to take care of my mother, my brother!"

"You're only nineteen and don't need to take care of anybody except you. And your brother is soon going to be old enough to be kicked out!"

"That leaves my mother."

"I can handle your mother, sight unseen, and I can't believe you've got a bad temper. I thought all you Hindu lovers of sacred cows were always laid back and meditating."

"Some are, some aren't. *I aren't.*"

"Beneath all that beauty lies a kind and gentle disposition."

Molly laughed softly. "You'd soon find out."

"Give me the chance."

"The picture of all East Indians as Ghandis and gurus is not at all true. Some of us are quite violent and I do have a bad temper."

Epp grinned. "I think I could handle your temper, even your violence."

"Maybe," Molly said as they went by Lamar at thirty-five mph, Epp having no desire to tangle with Arkansas patrol cars.

"Let me tell you what's going to happen," said the ocularist, Roger Wethersby. He appeared to be in his mid-fifties, gray-brown hair combed to the left side to cover a bald spot. He looked like a softie, with his silver-framed glasses, sitting there in his white coat on a movable stool that allowed him to scoot across the floor. There was a faint chemical smell in his laboratory.

Yorgi was sitting in a comfortable steel-framed black leather chair opposite Wethersby. They were almost playing kneesie.

"First of all, your surgeon did a fine job on the socket. Everything is healing nicely, and that's good to know. The back-wall implant is perfect. You should have a fair amount of movement." He'd examined it, opening the lid wide, looking in with a tiny light.

"You a doctor?" Yorgi asked, good eye scanning. An optician friend of Dr. Salerno's had recommended Roger Wethersby.

"No, I'm a technician," the ocularist replied. "But I've been doing this twenty-six years, and I've made hundreds of prosthetic eyes."

"So what happens?"

"Next week I'm going to make a soft wax impression of the right socket, and from that I'll make the eye of methacrylate. That's a white acrylic, a resin."

"You don't say."

"All of the work is critical but for the cosmetic effect, the hand-painting of the prosthesis."

"You mean my eye?"

"Yes, your new eye. That step is the most critical. I'll do it with you in this same chair, looking straight at me with your left eye. I'll get even the tiniest red veins. Like posing for a portrait."

"And my right eye will look exactly like my left one?" The latter was lancing skeptically into the ocularist.

"Most people will never know the difference, Mr. Katsanis."

"How many times will I have to come here?"

"Normally, five or six."

"When's the first one?"

"How about a week from today, same time?"

Yorgi nodded, rising.

As Yorgi was going out the lab door into the waiting room, Wethersby said, "You're going to love your new eye, Mr. Katsanis."

Yorgi turned back to shout, "Are you crazy?" then went on to the receptionist's window to pay for his consultation in cash.

On second thought, he just might go the rest of his life with the eyepatch. He was getting used to it. Made him look distinctive, he thought, like a storybook pirate. He still hadn't decided to go with the beard, afraid of itching.

Aaron Cobfield, the court-appointed attorney, had just come from the Las Vegas Assistant D.A.'s office and was telling Floyd Cramer, being held in city jail, that the search was legal. The cops had the Mustang towed on the traffic violations without touching the inside—they swore—and then got a search warrant for it.

Floyd was frowning. "I could say the gun belonged to someone else, just like the car belonged to someone else—that dumb broad."

"We plead guilty to that one, huh? Concealed weapon, guilty, okay?" Cobfield was young, with a head of permed blond hair, lots of curls.

Floyd nodded. "But what about that Malavasi guy, the one back in Illinois? The only reason I had it with me was because of him. He's the one who hired me to hit Joe Carlucci."

"You got any proof of that? A letter? Anyone overhear you two talking? Xeroxed check?"

Floyd shook his head. "No proof. Just what I can say about it."

"Which is—tell me again," said Cobfield.

"That he hired me to take out Joe Carlucci. Offered me ten thousand. I was supposed to pick it up last Wednesday in Oklahoma City. Son of a bitch hasn't even sent me the twenty-five hundred he promised. He hung me out to dry."

"Forget him," advised Cobfield. "You see, Floyd, all that has nothing to do with you shooting Earl Maxwell in Winnemucca. It just makes it look worse for you. Conspiracy to commit murder one. Forget Malavasi, whoever he is. Forget Joe Carlucci. You had the gun for self-protection. The mistake you made was having it under the seat. Right?"

"And Malavasi has no part of this?" The man from Cordell was finding it hard to deal with forgetting Guido.

Cobfield said, "None at all. You accepted the job. It didn't work out, thank God. Okay?"

Floyd shook his head slowly, thinking there had to be a way to involve Guido Malavasi.

"Now, let's talk about Earl Maxwell. That one we can claim self-defense and try to make a case of it . . ."

Kathy's car pulled up in the driveway, then she walked in the kitchen door, bag of groceries in her arm, saying, "Hi, how'd it go?"

Yorgi got up, crossed over, kissed her forehead and relieved her of the grocery bag. "He'll start next week."

Maybe she'd gone to Reno to work? They had girlie shows over there, he guessed. Who'd know where she went?

"And do what?"

"Make a mold of the eye."

She had to tell some of the other dancers at the Stardust. Leave an address with someone, for chrissakes.

That's fascinating," said Kathy, taking off her gloves and coat. "They stick wax in the socket?"

"Something like that," Yorgi said absently. His mind wasn't anywhere near what the ocularist was going to do. *She might have gone to St. Thomas and her mother's house.*

Kathy asked, "What's it going to be made of?"

"Some kind of plastic. He told me, but I can't pronounce it. Methasomething."

The mother, Yorgi thought. The mother.

Yorgi sat back down, took a sip of his *grappa,* reached under the bar for the phonebook and flipped through the pages until he found the area code and number for St. Thomas.

"How do they color the eyeball?" asked Kathy, putting fruit away into the refrigerator.

"Hand-paint it," said Yorgi, dialing 809 and then the information digits, asking for Mrs. Bodden's home number.

"That how they do it?" said Kathy.

"That's how."

What would happen to the world if there were no information

128

operators? Call Athens and get the Finikas, call Mykonos for the Zenia. St. Thomas for Molly Bodden's mother.

Yorgi took it down, excused himself and went upstairs to use his own phone, unlisted.

A young male voice answered.

Yorgi said, "I'd like to speak to Molly Bodden," making ready to bet that she'd have them say she wasn't there.

"She isn't here."

He was right. But she *was* there. Now, how to find out.

"Well, could I speak to Molly's mother?"

"She isn't here, either. She plays Bingo every Tuesday night."

"Who are you?"

"I'm Nedley, Molly's brother."

"Well, you sound like a bright young man. How old are you?"

"Fourteen."

"That's a good age. Nedley, I need to get in touch with Molly. My name is Wethersby, and I asked your sister to design and make a dress for my wife."

"She does that, though she's a dancer right now."

"Yeh, I know. I met her in Las Vegas. Tell you what, I promised I'd send her half the payment, six hundred dollars, but I haven't gotten around to writing the check. Now, I understand she's left Las Vegas."

"Yes, she has."

"Well, where is she?"

"We don't know."

"She hasn't been in touch with you?"

"No."

"What time will your mother be home?"

"Ten or ten-thirty, I'd guess."

"Okay, I'll call back."

"What did you say your name was?"

"Wethersby," said Yorgi.

He hung up and sat by the bed a moment longer.

Returning to the kitchen, Yorgi peeled potatoes—they were having liver and onions and mashed russets—listening, or trying to listen, to Kathy tell about her day with AT&T in Lisle. But he was thinking more about Atlantic City than what went on in the telephone business. After dinner he helped her with the dishes, then said he was going up to his workroom.

Kathy smiled at him, saying, "Yes, why don't you do that." Here he was, after losing an eye, carrying bravely on.

In the den were two of his models, the SS *Constitution* and the seven-master schooner *Thomas W. Lawson*. He knew the history of all his ships. He'd been building them since he was a kid. The *Lawson*, for instance, took ten minutes to tack. When light, she'd often miss her stays and in shallow water had to be brought out "club-headed" with an anchor; in deep water, she had to be wore around. She wrecked in 1907. He knew the history of all his ships.

In his workroom, located beside his bedroom, were a dozen other models such as the *Golden Hind,* the *Cutty Sark,* the HMS *Bounty* and the SS *Kearsarge,* which destroyed the Confederate's *Alabama.* Underway this winter was the *Sea Witch,* a clipper of 1846 vintage.

On his workbench were chests of X-acto knives, gouges, routers, pointed tweezers and blunt tweezers, Dremel Moto tools. On his supply shelves were three-thirty-seconds single and double plane blocks, three-sixteenth jackstay eyebolts and spools of rigging cotton, zero-fifteenth diameter and up.

Yorgi used a special pair of miniature surgical telescopes over his reading glasses when doing intricate work such as threading rigging line through the blocks and deadeyes, sometimes a jeweler's loup. Flying home from Vegas, he'd worried about how his diminished field of vision might affect the crabby tweezering.

He sat down, fitted on his magnifiers, and got a strand of rigging cord and tried to reeve it through a block, stabbing five times before the end went in. It was different with one eye.

A little later, Kathy came by and looked in on Yorgos, thinking what a determined man he was. She paused in the doorway, saying, "That eyepatch makes a difference in your face."

He turned. "Does it?"

She nodded. "I think there was an old-time movie actor with an eyepatch. Or maybe I'm thinking of that aviator that flew around the world. I remember seeing pictures of him in a history book."

"Is that right?" Yorgi said.

She nodded again and walked away, then returned. "Then there was John Wayne when he played Rooster Cogburn."

"Yeh, he had one," said Yorgi gloomily, turning back to the bench.

Goddamn Molly Bodden for the thousandth time. It was getting so that she was all he could think about.

Spending a nearly sleepless night, rolling back and forth on the bed, Yorgi thought of, and discarded, a dozen ways to find her. Calling her mother was probably useless. He'd even thought of calling the Vegas police and the Stardust again. Someone might slip up.

It was when the first gray light began to unfold over Illinois that he remembered that stack of her things in the middle of the apartment room on Thirteenth Street. They had to be shipped somewhere. He sat up in bed.

What was the name of that resident manager? He could remember her face, the way she talked. Graying, fiftyish. Her name was on the slot. What was it?

Mrs. Field? There were initials, he remembered. He'd thought *she* would be a man.

Mrs. Foley? E. W. Foley? No.

Going over to the window, closing it, looking out into the cold, he fed a half dozen similar names into the hopper, then said aloud, "Fern. E. W. Fern." That's who she was . . .

He dialed Las Vegas information and asked for Mrs. E. W. Fern, on Thirteenth Street. The operator took a moment, then said, "There's no Mrs. Fern listed on Thirteenth. There is an E. M. Fernley . . ."

Yorgi said, jubilantly, "That's her."

He scribbled the number and then waited an anxious two hours before making the call, so it would be seven A.M. in Nevada.

"Mrs. Fernley, this is Bekin's Van and Storage in Chicago. I'm sorry to call you so early."

"I was up. Just getting ready to walk my dog."

"Mrs. Fernley, we have a problem here with a shipment of household goods that belongs to one of your former tenants."

"Who's that?"

"A lady by the name of Molly Bodden."

"What's the problem?"

"Well, we're transferring the shipment to another van this morning, but we seem to have lost the bill of lading with the destination address on it. Did you sign off on the shipment?"

"Yes, I did."

"Do you happen to have a copy of it?"

"I think so. Just a moment."

Yorgi's fingers were tapping the bed stand.

"Here we go," said Mrs. Fernley. "It was shipped to Atlantic City in care of a Lucille Fernandez, Shalimar Manor . . ." She read off the street number and zip code.

"Thank you very much, Mrs. Fernley," said Yorgi, and hung up.

It wasn't until minutes after the connection was broken that Mrs. Fernley recalled that Allied Van had picked up Molly Bodden's things. To hell with it. She shrugged and went out the door with the poodle.

PART IV
Atlantic City

1.

ATLANTIC CITY, FEBRUARY 1979.

Almost midnight, ocean breeze raw and cold from Absecon Inlet all the way to Great Egg Harbor, big whitecaps out there and even little ones on the Inland Waterway. Quiet on the Million-Dollar Pier, Boardwalk nearly deserted, just a few bundled-up late-night health walkers moving along it. But the construction crew lights at Caesar's Boardwalk Regency, Arkansas and the Boardwalk, were burning brightly, work going on around the clock, getting ready for the suckers of May. Resorts International, first casino to open, at North Carolina and Boardwalk, was already a mass of lightbulbs and gamblers. Bally's Park Place was scheduled for December.

"I feel responsible," said Lucille Fernandez. "I shouldn't have tipped that blade for you. I remember telling you how the Babalu girls did it, then showing you. But it never occurred to me that you'd use it. I was just showing you what some of the girls did, breaking a triangle off. I'm sorry, baby."

"Don't feel that way," said Molly. "He would have had me. I know he would have. I swear it. I didn't use my head, but I know if I hadn't done *something* and gotten back into the bathroom he would have had me."

"I should have told you to buy mace. God, anything but using a piece of razor. You don't know how, anyway." Lucille hit her forehead with the palm of her hand.

"Stop it, Lucille."

"You could have missed him, you know. Then he would have broken your arm and gone on to do what he wanted to do."

"Come on, Lucille."

"I don't know that I would have had the presence of mind to do what you did."

135

They were in Lucille's apartment on Fairmount, wine glasses almost empty, Molly unwinding from the trip across with Epp. Not as pretty as Molly, shorter, Lucille was from Arecibo on the north side of Puerto Rico. What she lacked in face she made up in body. She had chorus-line calves and buttocks; did a fiery flamenco as good as anything in Barcelona or Madrid. She was much darker than Molly and a better dancer. They had met on the Condado, doing two shows a night.

Lucille was twenty-six, laid off from Resorts until the Easter show, meanwhile selling cosmetics six days a week at Roundtree's, one of those perfectly made-up girls at the Revlon counter.

"I never knew what fear was until last week," said Molly. "I had no idea what fear was."

"I've had it a few times, but don't think I really know," Lucille said.

"It was all a terrible mistake. Dating him, letting him stake me, taking him back to the apartment, not warning Bobby Chapman that a guy was out to blind me . . . kill me—"

"You have to quit thinking about it . . ."

Just talking about it, she had worked the fright up again. "He won't give up—he said that, Lucille! He'll come after me wherever I go. I just want him in jail for a long time."

"You're safe here," Lucille insisted.

"For now. Maybe. I won't sleep all night again until I know the cops have him. I get panicky every time the phone rings, someone knocks on the door . . ."

"I tell you, you're safe here."

"It's mental and physical all at the same time. Your whole body feels squeezed with it, paralyzed, but then something takes over and you fight back. That piece of blade and grabbing his gun in the car were things I didn't really think about. They just seemed to happen."

"Animal instinct."

"The first time it was fear of being raped, the second time fear of him taking my eyes. I was more afraid of that than of him killing me.

136

I wasn't even thinking about death. I just saw that awful-looking knife he had and knew I had to do something. The gun was there!"

"He got exactly what he deserved," said Lucille. "I just wish, for your sake, you'd finished him."

"It's bad enough as it is, that security guard dead. Only two years older than I am . . ."

"All the more reason why you should have kept pulling the trigger."

"That would have been murder."

Lucille got up to go into the kitchen and filled their glasses with chenin blanc. Then she stood in the door, looking worriedly at Molly.

"I got a call from Howie Piaggi Sunday night. He said he'd gotten a call from 'Joe.' He didn't know any of what you've told me. He said that Joe wanted his money back."

Molly shook her head. "I got him to stake me at the Hilton for twelve hundred. If he wants it back, I'll send it to his friend Guido."

Lucille nodded. "Maybe you should do that, Molly." She'd decided not to relay the death threat. Molly had had enough. "I'd do that tomorrow if I were you."

"I have to transfer my account from Vegas. What's a good bank here?"

"First Jersey."

"I'll call Vegas in the morning."

Lucille nodded.

"Okay, let me tell you about Resorts. The room has fourteen hundred seats, and they opened with Steve and Eydie, then Bill Cosby, Don Rickles. It's been that way ever since. Top people. Thirty dancers, more or less, all AGVA. You feel like you're in a giant green womb, no different than feeling you're in a giant red womb at the Stardust."

"Isn't it an old place?"

"Used to be called Chalfonte-Haddon or something like that, resort hotel. But they've spent a lot of money, a hundred million. Look, it's the same business everywhere. You go to work for Resorts,

137

it's not much different than working for the Stardust. They tried to play cute just before we opened and wouldn't meet the AGVA scale for rehearsal, three-fifty minimum, but we picketed on ribbon-cutting day and the shitheels opened their wallets. Same as Nevada, same faces. But go over there tomorrow afternoon, looking young and beautiful, and ask for Cecil Statler—he's the producer—show a little flesh, blink your eyes. Tell him I sent you."

Yorgi got some money out of the garage safe, then told Kathy, just before she left for AT&T, that he'd be gone for a night or two.

"Another trip so soon?" she said, dismayed.

"Only a night or two."

Then he called Guido to tell him the same thing.

Guido asked suspiciously, "Where you going?"

"St. Louis. Get another opinion on my eye."

"What for? You said you had a glass-eye maker on LaSalle."

"The guy in St. Louis is supposed to be better."

"Call me when you get back," said Guido.

"Don't I always?" said Yorgi, hanging up. He couldn't wait for Tony to return from Miami, end of February. When the *capo* was home, he hardly had any dealings with Guido.

He was booked as N. Katsanis on a United eleven-forty A.M. flight from O'Hare to Philadelphia, then Allegheny to Atlantic City, just about enough time to read the *Tribune* sports pages. There wasn't near as much fight coverage as there had been when he was boxing. Yorgi pulled a 9mm Parabellum Beretta out of the lower dresser drawer, which once also secreted a favorite Walther .38, wrapping it in toweling, taping it heavily, then putting it into the hard-pak suitcase for hold luggage, not to be inspected. The Beretta was good for fifteen rounds, more than plenty for what he had in mind. Aside from his shaving gear and a change of underwear, the rest of the suitcase was soon taken up with balls of newspaper. He locked it securely.

He had a hunch she'd brought the money to Atlantic City, maybe in the same briefcase. He couldn't see her stashing it somewhere in

Vegas. Well, she was one nineteen-year-old who'd played the wheel once too often. What counted now was the briefcase and her health as a witness. There wasn't much choice, nineteen or not, was there? *Ahndeeo!*

The Airporter stretch-limo pulled up on Glenwood Drive promptly at ten A.M. and Yorgi climbed aboard, favoring the shoulder a bit, as natty as any 3M salesman on his way to Kansas City. Dark blue Kuppenheimer today with a maroon, blue-dotted Grethel tie. His cheek looked a little better, all but three stitches having disintegrated.

Because he always had a lot of waiting to do, everywhere, Yorgi often remembered how it was with fights: sitting on a bench in the dressing room, Polack from the Y taping his hands, always saying something like, "This boy'll jab your brains out you let him. Gotta good left hand. Get him in the gut. In the ribs. Make 'im drop his hands." Yorgi nodding, chewing his mouthpiece. The waiting time before the ring was always hell. Butterfly time. You hoped there'd be a knockout in the match going on so you could go in. Yells and shouts of the Golden Gloves crowd out there. Then about thirty feet away was the black guy you were going to fight, getting taped up. The only way to get rid of the butterflies was to stare at him, even if you were only fourteen at the time.

Like kids out of school they came from under the lighted canopy of the Shalimar Manor, a beach-looking place that glittered in the sun from gold stucco specks but looked ordinary and boxy at night; three of them laughing and talking.

Yorgi was across the street, diagonal, quarter of a block down, parked in a rental Ford compact like a narc-squad stakeout, slouched there, radio playing softly.

Earlier, just about dusk, he'd seen the guy in the red sweater get out of a Porsche with California plates and go in, having no idea he was about to visit Lucille Fernandez and Molly Bodden. He might complicate things, whoever he was. Fernandez's boyfriend?

They passed by on the opposite side—dark-skinned girl, Latino-type, likely Lucille, the six-foot-or-so young guy in the sweater, lean as a hurdler, and Molly. Yorgi blew out a frustrated, angry breath. There she was, laughing. He shook his head at ever getting involved with such a crazy kid—he'd stick strictly to hookers from now on—waiting a moment before getting out and following them.

They finally went east along Arkansas, having a fine old time, Yorgi saw, the guy breaking out in front to do a little dance step for the girls; then north along the Boardwalk, crossing over to disappear inside the construction jumble of Caesar's.

Yorgi took up station across the Boardwalk, waiting for them to come out, wondering why they went in. He wanted to get a better look at the sweater guy, figure out who he belonged to, whether or not he might stay the night. Screw things up.

They weren't a hundred feet inside the maze of scaffolding and power cords, piles of plasterer's sand, paint-spattered plastic sheeting, when the security watchman got up from his stool, yelling, "Hey, you can't come in here."

Lucille quickly crossed to him, smiling widely, calling him "Officer," soaping him up. She said, "Sir, we're dancers. We really are, and we're going to be in the show in less than three months. Can't we just walk around? Please. We won't touch anything."

Molly came up beside her, smiling. "Please?"

"Oh, what the hell," the guard said. Two good-looking girls. "But watch your step. You get hurt an' I'll swear you sneaked in."

Lucille grinned at him, pecking his cheek. "That's a deal."

Smelling half-cured cement and wood shavings, walking in thick dust on the concrete slab flooring, they wound around sawhorses and stacks of lumber, wheelbarrows and table saws. The night crew seemed to be mostly electricians working in the steel girders overhead. But welding sparks were cascading too.

Lucille had come in here before. "You can't tell much, but here's the showroom and the stage is down there," she said. "It'll seat five hundred. Not too big, but they've already got plans for a Circus Maximus, I hear."

"Half as big as a football field already," said Epp, looking around, impressed. "Quarter as big."

Molly ran forward and jumped to the stage, doing a pirouette, then throwing up her arms in a finale.

Epp clapped.

"This used to be a Howard Johnsons" Lucille said, "but they put the tower up, adding a bunch more rooms. The whole exterior is new—Art Deco inside and out. I hear they're also spending a hundred million."

There was a steady pop-pop in the cavernous room, sheets of four-by-eight plasterboard being tied to the studs forming the inner wall, two men holding and one using a compressed-air gun to fire inch-and-a-half drywall nails.

A workman in a hard hat passed, and Epp remarked, "Lot easier than using a hammer."

"You betcha, buddy."

They walked on out, waving thanks to the watchman.

On the Boardwalk they went north, up toward the piers, and Yorgi fell in behind them, at about a hundred yards, until they turned once more, this time crossing over to an ice cream parlor. Wouldn't you know? Wouldn't you know? Molly and her ice cream. He remembered the big nut-sprinkled sundae she'd had in the Hilton coffee shop while he was making plans to lay her.

They took a window table and he stayed over on the Boardwalk, now and then pounding his gloved hands against the night cold, like one of the bums. He still couldn't figure out which one the guy in the sweater belonged to. His face seemed sort of familiar, but Yorgi couldn't place him. Finally, he saw a waitress bring out a dish with a candle on it and they all seemed to be singing. Oh, ho, little birthday party for Molly Bodden. Her last, if he had anything to do with it. She puffed out the candle.

Deciding he'd seen enough here, he walked on back to the Shalimar Manor, checked the mailboxes to make sure Lucille Fernandez lived in No. 35, then went up to the third floor to see where her apartment was located. "L. Fernandez" was on the door. Okay.

He went down to the compact, started the motor to get some heat, and turned on the radio again, ready for some more waiting, having come from a long line of patient, simple people from the Pindus. What he needed to do was separate Molly from the other two, somehow get her alone, get her outside the apartment if he was lucky, then get the money back.

About nine-thirty the birthday trio came loping home, still jabbering, Red Sweater's arms around *both* of them as they went into the apartment house.

An hour later, Red Sweater came out, got into his Porsche, and off he went.

Yorgi sat for a few minutes, thinking that going up and knocking on their door, probably having to kick it in, would only get him screams, two squad cars and drawn firing pieces. Tomorrow would be, should be, better, safer.

Taking the Ford back to his motel on Brigantine, he got dinner nearby—catch o' the day, Nova Scotia salmon—and went to bed about midnight after watching *Fantasy Island* and *Kojak*. Johnny Carson had a replacement from Vegas, Don Rickles and his insults. Rickles wasn't all that funny, in Yorgi's opinion. He watched a few minutes, then turned off the TV, hoping he wouldn't dream about that basketball in midair, with its cornea and sclera.

2.

YORGI PARKED NEAR THE SHALIMAR MANOR not long after full daylight, about seven-fifteen, letting the engine idle for heat, hood
pointed toward the apartment house. Snow was threatening, the
sky a frigid gray. Drinking from a double styrofoam cup of coffee, he
was half reading the *New York Daily News* laid across the steering
wheel, but concentrating mostly on departures from the Shalimar.

Lucille Fernandez came out about eight-thirty, crossed to his side
of the street, unlocking a green VW. Gussied up, stockings and high
heels, fur-collared coat, she was off to earn a day's pay.

By eight forty-five, butt and legs beginning to numb up, Yorgi was
about to get out, stretch a little, take a little walk, when the girl of
his dreams came down the steps in jacket, jeans and boots, blue
bandanna on her head, not dressed to go too far. She was carrying a
plastic bag. Yorgi guessed she was off to the dry cleaners.

Sliding down in the seat six inches, raising the *News*, hiding
behind it, in case she looked his way, he counted a few seconds, then
lowered the tabloid, seeing she was on her way to the corner of
Fairmount and Arkansas, galloping along. Swinging feet over, he
quickly disembarked, running up behind her, holding the Beretta
in his right pocket so it wouldn't bounce out. He came up on her left
side, saying, almost in her ear, "Don't scream or try to run."

Head coming around, eyes widening, seeing Joe Carlucci again,
in person, his scar, the black patch, she said, "Oh, my God," almost
stumbling, almost falling down.

"Do an about-face, an' go right on back to the apartment," he
said, holding the gun against her, shoving it into her ribs. "I want
my money."

"Please don't do this," she managed to say. "Please don't—"

Aside from a girl with a baby carriage way up Fairmount, there was no one on the street this gloomy icy morning.

Yorgi said, turning her, "I've come after it . . ."

"The twelve hundred?"

"No, the half million."

The gun was prodding her along, digging into flesh.

"I don't know what you're talking about," Molly said, beginning to shake all over, feeling the terror she'd felt in the desert. "I don't know what you're talking about—"

"The four hundred ninety-five thousand in the briefcase . . ."

"What briefcase?" The voice edged on hysteria.

They were almost back to the apartment steps; she was hoping someone would be coming down. Anyone.

Anticipating, he said, "Keep your mouth shut."

They went up the six steps together.

A boy of about ten, books and a brown bag in his hands, was coming down the first flight, and Molly tried to motion with her eyes. The boy, taking steps two at a time, didn't even look at her.

They took the second flight. No one coming down, no one in the halls. Her legs felt boneless.

Then they were in front of No. 35 and he said, "Open the door," looking both ways.

"Don't do this to me again—"

"Open the goddamn door."

Reaching into her jacket pocket, she drew out Lucille's second set of keys, fumbling with them, then crying out in pain as he rammed the gun deeper, snapping, "Come on, open it, *open* it . . ."

The door swung back, Molly staying in the threshold a moment, saying, "I don't know anything about any briefcase—"

"Get in there, goddamit," he ordered, shoving her, closing the door behind her.

The Beretta was now out of his pocket.

"I *swear* I don't."

"It was in the back seat."

Theodore Taylor

Molly said weakly, "I didn't even look back there. I swear I didn't."

"Don't lie to me." The gun was an inch from her nose, so close she could smell it. A flat metallic odor.

"Honest to God."

"Listen, nigger bitch, all I want is the money an' we'll call the score even."

"I never saw it. I don't have it, Joe. Believe me. If I had it I'd give it to you. You think I'm crazy? Taking four hundred ninety-five thousand from you? Taking anything from you?"

"Let's look around," he said. "Where's your stuff?"

She hadn't seen him in daylight before, and the boxer's beat-up whiskery face, cauliflower ears, the new thin scar that stretched from his black socket patch down into his neck, drenched her with more fear.

"In there." She nodded toward the bedroom.

"Go ahead of me," he said, taking the Beretta down.

She led the way. Both suitcases were opened on the floor, near the bed. "I haven't even unpacked. See?"

Kneeling down, holding the gun with his right hand, he tossed panties, bras with his left. Slips, belts, hosiery, blouses came flying out.

Standing up, he ordered, "Open the closets."

"That's all Lucille's."

"Jus' open the goddamn closets."

She slid the doors back, and Yorgi, still pointing the gun at her, used his left hand to feel around the dresses and shoes.

"Pull the mattress back."

"Joe, I swear I don't have it."

"Jus' pull the fuckin' mattress off . . ."

Once, long ago, in a terrible dark mood, she'd told Chaktri that she'd never live to be twenty-one, that she wanted to be buried in a flowing white dress, have a lot of people at her funeral, everyone singing *Que Sera, Sera* . . . But now, right now, in this apartment, she'd never wanted to live as much, and unless she was as

145

crazy as he was—*she didn't know about any money*. She didn't know.

Tugging the double bed apart, she fell backward with the mattress.

"Turn the springs over."

Beginning to weep, Molly was saying, "It's not . . . here-uh . . ."

"Well, where the hell is it?"

"I don't know . . . don't *know*."

The silencer cracked against her lips; she felt blood trickling down.

"In the kitchen," he said, giving her a shove out of the bedroom.

She fell, got up, half walked, half staggered into the kitchen, holding a hand to her bleeding mouth.

"Open everythin' up."

She moved around, pulling the knobs on the broom closet, the doors beneath the sink, the cabinet doors. "Joe, believe me, I don't have it."

He looked and felt into each space, finally standing in the middle of the kitchen. "I don't think you fully unnerstan', bitch. I'm gonna blow your fuckin' brains out 'less you give back that money. You leave it in Vegas?"

"No, I didn't leave it in Las Vegas. I've never had it."

"Go on in there an' sit down." He waved her out of the kitchen with the gun, following her, then stood in front of her. "Open your mouth, Molly."

She opened it.

He stuck the end of the silencer in. "Let me tell you somethin' 'bout this gun. Don't look big, but it'll plaster the back of your head against the wall. Now, you cut me, caused me to be half-blind, shot me, stole my money." His voice rose to a yell. "Think you'd get by with all that, nigger bitch? Is that what you thought?"

Steel against her teeth, tasting oil and smelling the gun, Molly knew she wasn't going to leave the apartment on her feet.

"You ever been burnt? Ever had someone hold a match up against your nipples? Stick a hot knife up your *treepah*?"

Molly shook her head, wanting to pass out.

"An' it won't stop here. You got a mother an' kid brother down in St. Thomas. I'd as soon whack them as not you don't give back that money. Are you listenin' to me?"

Molly nodded, suppressor still in her mouth. His good eye had a crazed look in it, so intense it might jump out of the socket. The false eye stared, cocked up a little.

She talked into the gun. "I'll tell you . . ."

"What'd you say?"

"I'll tell you."

"That's better. Where is it?"

Taking a deep breath, she said, "In a bank. I threw the briefcase away." At least this might get them out of the apartment.

Say anything, do anything.

"Where's the bank?"

"Just off the Boardwalk."

There was no bank just off the Boardwalk. But say anything, tell him anything.

"Where's the deposit slip?"

She thought desperately. "Safety deposit box. I have a key."

She'd noticed a small numbered key on the ring when Lucille had given her the second set.

"Show me."

She got up, crossing to the table where she'd dropped them. "This one," she said, showing him a thin key with 215 stamped on it.

"You lie to me, Molly, an' you won't see another birthday."

"I'm not lying to you, Joe."

"You did a few minutes ago. You been pullin' shit on me since the first night I metcha."

"I didn't know who it belonged to."

"It was in the back of my car, for chrissakes."

Molly shook her head. Poor girl got confused, didn't mean to steal

147

the man's money, didn't mean to cut the man, shoot the man. Just a dumb high-yellow girl from the islands.

"Okay, we're gonna go get it. I'll be an inch from you, unnerstan'? You pull anythin' an' you're dead. Then your mother is dead, your brother is dead . . . Unnerstan'?"

Molly nodded. The main thing was to get out of the apartment, out on to the street. Even if she got shot running, the odds were better than being in the apartment with him. "I understand."

There was a shout from the hall, "Grocery boy. *Open de doah.*"

Molly groaned.

Yorgi's head swiveled around. He whispered harshly, "Who the hell is that?"

"A friend."

A foot banged against the door. "Molly, you in there? Open up. I got two heavy bags o' groceries here. Molly?"

Yorgi put the Beretta against her temple. "Open it. No games."

She did as told and Epp came in, both arms filled with big brown bags, saying, "Hey, what the—," seeing her there, gun at her temple, dried blood streaked down from her lips, seeing the mob guy with the eyepatch.

"Kick the door shut, grocery boy," said Yorgi. "There's fifteen rounds here. Eight for you an' seven for her if that's the way you want it. Now, put those bags down an' stand with your back to me, hands flat on the table. I'll blow her brains out you make any wrong moves."

What John Madden used to shout to the big defensive linemen went through Epp's head: "Get 'em mad, piss 'em off, get 'em rattled, make 'em make mistakes."

But this guy had a gun, like the Afro in Bakersfield, not an open palm, not a fist, he wasn't hunkered down on the line, and this wasn't overtime in the Astrodome. No game this morning. Calling him a wop shit-heel didn't make much sense. Turning to tackle him, throw a punch at him, grab him, wrestle him, didn't make much sense, either. He could kill both of them, so easy.

Theodore Taylor

Bent from his shoulders, hands flat on the table, the police spread, looking out the window at the falling snow, Epp said, "Why don't you put that gun on me, not her."

No answer.

Well he had to say something. "I get outta this alive, your ass is a goner. I promise you that." Hollow words, even to his ears.

Still no answer.

"You hear me, shit-heel."

Nothing. All he could hear was Molly's breathing.

"Has he still got that gun on you, Molly?"

Her voice was squeezed. She said yes.

Over against the front wall Yorgi saw what he needed.

"Stay steady, boy," he said to Epp, moving Molly with the gun toward the wall. "Remember what I got against her head." Under a clay pot of mimosa were three bricks. Yorgi said to Molly, "Reach down and hand one to me, slow and easy. Play games an' I pull the trigger. Keep thinkin' 'bout that."

She did as told.

Shifting the gun to his left hand but still holding it against her, he palmed the brick in his right hand, stepping up behind Epp to connect five pounds of baked clay with skull bone, a high crashing blow with most of one-eighty pounds driving it.

Epp went forward soundlessly, then tottered backward, landing on his shoulder blades.

He looked dead to Molly. "Oh, my God . . ."

Yorgi stood looking down at the body thoughtfully, then aimed the Beretta at Epp's right kneecap and fired, the explosion no more than a loud pop. He glanced at Molly, saying, "That's just in case your friend wakes up. I don't think he'll walk so good."

Epp's body jerked in spasms of pain.

"Why did you do that, you bastard?" Molly sobbed and covered her eyes.

As if he hadn't heard her, Yorgi said, "Banks open at ten, let's go."

They left the apartment. Epp hadn't moved.

* * *

149

There wasn't more than twenty or thirty feet of murky visibility as they went up Texas toward the Boardwalk, snow falling almost vertically and sticking, headlights small yellow moons in the whiteness of the morning, cars creeping along, what few there were, chains clanking dully, all sounds muffled.

Teeth chattering from cold and fear, Molly was again moving unsteadily on puppet legs, on Yorgi's right side, boots slipping and sliding, the gun in Yorgi's pocket digging into her hip. His left arm was draped over her shoulder. Except for the snow, this was the Stardust lot all over again, the moments after he'd slugged Bobby Chapman.

If only it were a bright sunny day people would see there was something wrong with this hunched pair, the girl's face contorted. They were walking strangely, even for a snowstorm. In clear weather someone might guess the man had a gun and she was his hostage.

Joe hadn't said anything the first block but now he was talking. "You play games at the bank an' a lot o' people'll get hurt, not only you."

Molly kept silent, flakes pelting her face.

"You jus' ask for the key. We get the money an' walk out. You hear?"

She nodded.

One of Lucille's shopping bags was tucked under his left arm.

"You made a big mistake—stealin' from me top o' what else you did . . ."

"I told you I was sorry."

"Like you told me you were sorry for usin' that knife."

So what would happen at any bank when she handed over the key to get a matching one? The girl would say, "I'm sorry, this isn't ours." He'd march her outside, take her off somewhere, yelling at her she'd lied again, torture her no matter how many times she told him she didn't have the money.

Jerk loose from him, pull out from the grasp of his arm and run. Take the chance.

She'd always been a good runner, ever since childhood, and she had ten years on him, she thought.

He might not get a good shot at her with all the snow.

Then again, she might slip and fall.

But she had to take the chance like she'd taken it off the Tonopah. They plodded past the Atlantic and Pacific intersections, two figures in the murk, Boardwalk a block away.

There was a buzz in Epp's ears, angry wasps circling, as he slowly came to. He opened his eyes, out of focus; closed them, opened them again, looking at the wavering ceiling, wondering where he was. There was excruciating pain in his right leg, and the back of his head was throbbing. He lifted his arm, then dropped it involuntarily, yelling out as it hit the carpet.

After a moment, he raised it again and reached back, fingers coming away sticky with blood. He reached down to his knee and there was more blood down there. He'd never felt such pain.

Then he remembered: Lucille's apartment . . . he'd come in with two bags of groceries . . . guy standing there holding a gun on Molly . . . remembered being bent over the table, looking at the snow falling, talking to the guy.

Epp sat up, buzz still in his ears, dizziness making the room swim; some queasiness and that pain. There were the groceries, the table; snow still coming down.

He sat there upright for a good half minute trying to make the dizziness go away, trying to collect his thoughts. Then he looked all around, realizing that Molly and the man she called Carlucci were gone.

A brick was on the carpet near his knee. No wonder his head hurt. But what had happened to his knee? Had Carlucci smashed it? Shot it?

Putting a hand down for support, he tried to get to his feet, but fell back and decided to drag himself over to the phone, on his back. Room still out of focus, it was as if he took a hit in midair, coming down on the artificial turf, helmet slamming; distorted faces looking down on him, asking him what day it was, how many fingers the trainer was holding up.

Epp had trouble reading the dial but finally found *zero* and pulled it around, saying "Police" when the operator answered.

"Sir?" she said, making sure.

"Police," he repeated, and she said, "I'll connect."

The desk sergeant said, "Okay Mr. Watts, I got it all down an' I'll send a car an' a medic wagon soon as I can. You jus' stay right there . . ."

"Goddamit, find the girl and the guy that's got her. I can't move. I told you I was shot in the leg."

"Mister, we're in the middle of a blizzard, in case you don't know. I can't even see across the street. How the hell do we find her if we can't see her. Just stay right where you are an' put a cold compress on that leg."

The day-watch sergeant hung up, saying to a cop who was standing outside the cage, "Man says someone shot him in the leg an' kidnapped his girlfriend. Said the guy is mafia. I got this same kind of call last week when it wasn't snowing. Shit, turns out the guy was an off-duty dick from Newark and caught his wife shacked up in the Bluebell over on Brigantine."

No one was silly enough to be taking a February snowbird constitutional on the Boardwalk, at Columbia Place, but dimly ahead was Caesar's, rising ghostlike with it's herringbone art deco in the white flakes. The exterior worklights punched holes around the entrance, and Molly was praying that the wide chain-link construction gate was open, as it had been last night.

Moving steadily closer, Joe's hard hand still clutching her shoulder, she saw that the gate was swung back, thank God. From there to the entrance of the building was about twenty-five feet.

He hadn't said much since they reached the Boardwalk, only

muttering, "Money better be there," almost to himself, his needle stuck in that particular groove.

The last hundred yards or so she'd leaned more against him, her hands clasped up around her jacket collar. He hadn't given her time for gloves and her fingers were numb.

As they reached a position opposite Caesar's entrance, she balled her right fist as best she could and rammed her elbow into his stomach, hearing his "ahhhhh," wrenching away from his shoulder grasp.

Then, as she ran for the entrance, feet going up and down faster than they'd ever gone, like she was in a fifty-yard dash, she knew he was hammering along behind her. She heard a "whadda you doin'" shout, as she went through the entranceway and raced on inside, hearing him now, footsteps on the concrete, harsh breathing. She didn't look back.

Then they were both inside, veering around the stacks of construction material, the plaster mixers, and she yelled at the first hard hat she saw, a man carrying a red hose: "He's got a gun!"

The hard hat's mouth dropped open and he froze.

Running the only way she knew in this cluttered building, mind skimming over the mental map from last night, she dashed on into the showroom, looking frantically for an exit on the opposite side.

Yorgi had closed within fifty feet of her as she crossed the middle of the big room, headed for the stage, shouting up to green hardhats on the platform that was just ahead, warning them that the chaser had a gun.

She saw several bodies up there, men in hooded sweat parkas. They seemed to be staring at her as if to say, What the hell is goin' on? It was as if she were watching them in fast forward.

She didn't see one of the hard hats as he aimed at Yorgi ten feet away, nor hear the hollow pops of released compressed air as five drywall nails found the chest of Joe Carlucci.

He went backward, mouth open in surprise, Beretta skidding and twirling in the floor dust, three hard hats leaping down off the platform to pin him.

* * *

Walter Nishgo was telling his number-two man, Jeffcoate, about it. "A Puerto Rican with a nail gun got him five times with drywall nails. You imagine that? That's so wild, every cop in the country'll break up. Little spic nailing a Mafia hit man, knocking him flat on his ass."

"In Puerto Rico?" Harry Jeffcoate asked.

"No, Atlantic City. He was chasing that same chickie again, that nude dancer that cut him and shot him, right through Caesar's."

"They aren't open."

"That's right. That's why the workmen were in there."

"So, he's dead. We close it?"

"Hell, no. They plucked the nails out of him this afternoon. There's an A.C. cop inside his room. Fucker'll live, no doubt."

"But we got a whole new weapons system to think about. Mount nail guns on squad cars from now on, hit those sonsabitches with roofing nails, finish nails, ten pennies . . . you imagine bringing that hard-nosed son of a bitch down with a pneumatic gun. God, look at the money we could save."

"What was he chasing her for this time?"

"Vendetta, by now, I think. He thought she swiped some of his money. That was in addition to the other stuff. So he shows up in her friend's apartment. To get him out of there the crazy kid gives him a cockamamie story about having the money in a bank. That's where they were going, in a snowstorm, when she broke away from him."

Jeffcoate said, "You'd think he'd know enough by now to let her alone. Christ, I wouldn't get anywhere near her."

"Guy went totally off his rocker, I think, after all that had happened. Followed her right into that building into a nest of hard hats. By the time the cops got there they had him tied up with electric wire, nails sticking out of his chest."

Nishgo was shaking his head, then he sobered. "But the son of a bitch bopped that football player over the head, then kneecapped him. The Raiders guy. He may never play again."

"That's too bad," said Jeffcoate, frowning. "He was just starting."

"When Watts woke up he told the A.C. cops that Molly had been kidnapped by the mob guy. Things fit together about twenty minutes later at Caesar's and they called me a half hour ago to say they had my one-eyed wandering boy, a little construction material under his chin. Sometimes I love this job. We'll start extradition in the morning."

3.

ATLANTIC CITY MEDICAL CENTER: Back of his head shaved, dressing covering the split skin and inflammation, Epp was on his back, cheek resting on the pillow, right leg held steady between two cloth splints. He looked at Molly when she came in and asked, "You okay?" She'd just come from police headquarters.

She nodded. "But you're not."

"You see him shoot me?"

She nodded again. "There wasn't anything I could do."

"I know that. The cops told me what happened."

"I wish so many things," said Molly. "I wish I'd gone straight home. I wish we hadn't met. I've brought so much trouble to you!"

"C'mon," said Epp. "Don't blame yourself for what's happened to me."

"How can I not blame myself." She sat down beside him and took his hand. "What do they say about the knee?"

Instead, he told her about his head. "The doc said I have an open fracture of the occipital bone—hairline, an' it's no worry as long as no infection sets in. That son of a bitch really clobbered me."

"I thought he'd killed you."

"Why did he shoot me, Molly?"

"He said so you wouldn't walk so good."

"He was right. He owes me if he ever gets out of jail."

"Tell me about the knee."

Epp let out a long breath. "It's shattered. The cap is shattered. They took X-rays. But their orthopedic man said wonders were being worked today. There's a sports specialist out in Los Angeles."

"What does he mean by wonders?"

"Oh, I guess he means I'll walk one way or another. Plastic kneecap."

156

He saw sudden tears in Molly's eyes.

She said, "You know he's on the floor below."

"From what I heard I guessed he would be. I'll tell you what I'd like to do. I'd like to go down and kill him. Get a gun of my own, a wheelchair . . ."

Molly shook her head. "I know. If I'd only done it in the des-
. ert . . ."

"Well, you didn't but it looks like he'll go to jail, finally. Call that detective out in Las Vegas tomorrow. Tell him you'll do whatever he wants. That's a bad guy below us. It's time he got put away."

"I promise. He threatened Mama and Nedley again today. Said he had friends who'd do something if he couldn't."

"Tell that to Nishgo. I think he's an okay guy. I think you can trust him."

"I met him, you remember."

"I'm a little fuzzy," Epp said.

"You know what's down in the lobby?"

"I can guess."

"Reporters. Maybe twenty. TV cameras. I managed to sneak by them. They were all up around the desk. They didn't know what I looked like."

"Duck 'em. Talk to the head nurse. They can let you out a back or side way. Call Lucille to meet you somewhere or walk home. Has the snow let up? I can't see out."

Molly nodded, looking out the window into the gray late after-noon sky.

"Maybe I'll go back home for a while," she said.

"That's a good idea."

She looked back at him. "You know how small that island is. You get off it in a plane, or a boat or by swimming. Tell me the places to hide if they decide to come after me."

"I can't," Epp said. "It's your island. You grew up there. I can tell you where to hide in Philadelphia."

Molly put her hand over and touched Epp's cheek. "Near Second and Walnut?"

"You better catch me when I'm down. I had some pretty good-

157

lookin' girls on the string at West Bucks. Likely some are still around. I'm in my own territory now."

"I'm tempted," said Molly. She got up and leaned over to kiss him. "See you tomorrow. You need some rest."

"Tell the head nurse to have someone take you out the back way."

Molly nodded and touched her fingers to her lips.

After she was gone a moment, Epp's jaw quivered and tears began to slide down his cheeks. He knew he'd never play football again.

Paying no attention to the patient in the bed, the young cop in the corner chair was reading a paperback that said *Vixen 03* in big red letters on its cover and it occurred to Yorgi that he might be able to jump him, get his gun away. But what then? Here he was again in one of those short hospital gowns, no idea where his clothes had been taken; his car keys, wallet. Besides, he was still a little woozy although he'd been out of the recovery room for almost two hours. He knew he was on pain-killers for the chest wounds. Probably best to wait until tomorrow and call the Malavasi lawyer, Strelich.

But the pain in his chest wasn't as great as the pain in his head. He felt humiliated. Construction workers had brought him down. If somebody had to pop him, he wouldn't have minded so much if it had been the FBI, cops or sheriffs deputies but to have a hard hat do it with a tool? They'd laugh him out of Peppitone's.

He couldn't believe what was happening to him, *what had happened to him,* within the last two weeks, because of the girl. Every single move he'd made was wrong. Looking at the young cop with his head buried in *Vixen 03,* Yorgi went back over everything since he went to Molly's apartment. He finally decided she was a goddamn witch. He'd never believed in witches. Now he did.

Later, Yorgi said to the cop, "How about turning the TV on."

The cop looked up. "You got the remote control on the table right beside you."

After the national news came the local: Ignacio Ocampo, of Atlantic City, still wearing his hardhat, hiding bushy black hair, was saying into the remote camera of WCAU, the CBS affiliate in Philadelphia, "Here come thees girl yellin' 'ees gotta gun, 'ees gotta gun, an' I see thees man runnin' behin' her, an' sure enough hee's gotta gun, so I take mine an' aim it at heem . . ."

"The nail gun you're holding," the WCAU reporter said, trying to contain a laugh, feeding into the Walter Cronkite CBS Evening News.

"Si, thees gun." He held it up, still attached to the compressed air hose in Caesar's jumbled showroom.

"You didn't know why he was chasing her, didn't know he was allegedly Mafia?"

The cop put *Vixen 03* down and was staring at the TV.

"No, sir." Ignacio shook his head gravely. "I jus' saw a man chasin' a pretty young girl with a pistol. An' when he come near my platform I shoot 'im. Ee din't look like no cop to me."

"Mr. Ocampo, have you ever heard of a nail gun being used for something like this?"

"No, sir. But thees are dangerous things. I have a fran' who shot himself in the foot three year ago. He still limp."

The camera went to a full-head single of the reporter, who was struggling to hold back a smile. "The man that Mr. Ocampo shot with five drywall nails has been tentatively identified as Yorgos Stathos, of Naperville, Illinois. Atlantic City police said that FBI sources claim he has ties to a Chicago-area Mafia family and is being held for Nevada authorities for questioning in connection with a recent homicide in Las Vegas. The girl he was chasing has been identified as Molly Bodden (big head close-up of smiling Molly), a twenty-year-old Las Vegas showgirl. In the same incident, Stathos allegedly shot Epperson Watts, Jr., a wide receiver for the Oakland Raiders. They are both patients in Atlantic City Medical Center."

Even Cronkite had an amused look on his face when he said, "For other news, we go to Atlanta . . ."

The cop looked over at Yorgi. He said, "Hey, you're famous."

With a look to kill, Yorgi switched off the TV.

In Apartment 35 at Shalimar Manor, Molly, shaking her head over

159

what she had just seen, said to Lucille Fernandez, "I'm finished. No one's going to hire me."

Lucille said, "Stop it."

"I didn't listen to you, didn't listen to myself," Epp was saying to Laburnum Hotchkiss.

"Don't blame yourself. Everybody gets involved in things they shouldn't even think about. I see it everyday. What's the status on that knee?"

"He blew the cap into a hundred pieces. He was so close he powder-burnt me."

"Ouch," said Laburnum.

"Little worse than that."

"I know," said the cop. "I've only seen a kneecap once. That's enough."

"How's the weather down there?"

"Same as ever for February. Sunny, warm. When are you going to come down and build on that lot?"

"Sooner than I ever thought about. First, I need to undergo some repairs."

"I imagine," said the detective.

"Molly—Walt Nishgo, I tried to get you three times last night."

"We took the phone off the hook."

"Don't blame you. Gotta tell you, you ever get tired dancin', we've got a place for you here. You can be the first Vegas female cop."

"No, thanks."

"What you did was sensational, and I probably don't even know the full story. But getting him to chase you into Caesar's was genius. You've got more guts than three-quarters of what we have on the whole damn police force here."

Molly said, "I was looking out for myself."

Walt said, "Well, anyway, thanks and congratulations. We're going to take him off your hands in about a week and you'll be getting a call from the D.A.'s office."

"Why?"

"The clock will start ticking on us once we take custody. We'll have sixty days to bring him to trial. And it's my guess they'll want you here two or three days ahead to work with the prosecuting attorney."

"Mr. Nishgo, I don't want to come out there. I've heard about depositions."

"I doubt they'll use you that way in a murder trial. You want to see him convicted, I hope. Depositions are used in a lot of ways but not for this kind of trial."

"What'll happen if I refuse?"

"They issue a subpoena, force you to come. It's better you do it voluntarily. State'll pay your airfare, hotel, meals, incidentals. They're not generous, but they're adequate."

"Have you seen the morning papers?"

"I've got three on my desk now, including the local paper."

"Who gave them that photo of me?"

"You can bet the Stardust didn't—Molly, that shot of you was in the lobby for six months. It was on brochures, probably sent out to five hundred newspapers months ago. Jimmy Rosenberger likely wishes he had it back. They don't need this kind of publicity."

"Neither do I," said Molly.

"You kidding? People see this photo an' you'll get all kinds of offers. Hollywood big shots'll likely be on the phone today. You're famous today, Molly."

"I'm also scared."

"The man's coming out of the hospital tomorrow to take up temporary residence behind a lot of steel in Atlantic City. As soon as he can travel, I get him. You've got nothing to be worried about!"

"He said he had friends."

"Listen, no one is going to rough you up. He's no *capo*. He's way down the line, is my guess."

In his suite at the Fontainebleau, Tony Ox was reading about Yorgi Greco in the Miami *Herald* with concern. He'd put down his oatmeal spoon and said to Josephina, "Yorgi's in trouble."

He finished the story, passed the paper over to his wife and picked up the phone to call Guido, asking him if he'd seen the papers, then telling him to have Gunther Strelich fly to Atlantic City right away.

A little while after Lucille came home, Molly said, "I saw Cecil Statler today. He said no without saying no."

"How'd he say no without saying no?"

Lucille was walking around, taking off her clothes, piece by piece.

"He said a lot of girls had applied and he wasn't sure how many they needed and why didn't I call him when the new show was set and he had a rehearsal date."

From the bedroom, Lucille said, "Well?"

Molly was on the couch, legs tucked under. "Lucille, the minute I came in the door he said, 'Read a lot about you. Saw you on TV.' Great!"

Lucille came back into the living room, barefooted, in bra and panties, holding a pair of jeans. "So?"

"It was the way he said it, like it was *me* who'd done something wrong to Joe Carlucci or whatever his Greek name is . . ."

Slipping into the jeans on one foot, balancing, Lucille said, "These people are the same. That's no secret. You know that, Vegas or here. They deal in flesh, by the inch and pound. They look at ankles, calves, boobs, asses, zits. That's all they care about. They run scared of anything else. That's Cecil Statler."

"Howie wasn't that way."

"You got a jewel then. It's different out here. The shows aren't going to be the same as Vegas. Everything's going to be a little nervous for a while."

She went back into the bedroom to get a sweatshirt. From there she said, "I'll get you a job at Roundtree's until something breaks—"

"And get the same answer?"

Out again in the living room, slipping the sweatshirt on, Lucille said, "Well, aren't we loaded with optimism? Try a club in Philly. Someone might say, 'Hey, you're the one that got kidnapped by that mob guy. Got a spot for you.' Look, you've got assets that most of us don't have—you're young enough to be eaten alive, you're beautiful, great body, and you can dance pretty good. No time to cry in your beer."

"I'm just facing facts."

"The fact is," Lucille said, "Cecil is right. There's a line forming and the competition will be coming in from as far away as Bangkok and Stockholm. We don't have any monopoly on the T&A business, baby. Forget all your unwanted publicity, just compete."

"I'll try."

"That's a good girl."

"I've been thinking that if I can't get something lined up here I'll go home for a while, then try the Condado again."

"Condado? Hmmm," said Lucille, headed for the kitchen. "Why not? You want some chablis?"

"Okay," said Molly, sighing.

"Go anywhere you want to go," Lucille said, from out there, "Paris, London, Tokyo. Sell the assets while you're young. Three years I'll be thirty and looking for a rest home."

Molly laughed softly. "Well, aren't we loaded with optimism?"

"I face facts, dollink."

Molly said, speaking of facts, "I went to see Epp again this afternoon. They're sending him to a specialist tomorrow at Philadelphia General. First of three or four operations. He's down pretty low. A man named Al Davis called him from Oakland this morning, asking if it was true what they read in the papers. That AP story said he'd probably never play again."

"Why the hell does the press always have to bring the bad news? How would they know?"

163

"They talked to a doctor here last night. He said he'd seen the X-rays."

"So that's one doctor's opinion," said Lucille.

"I think it's Epp's opinion, too. His whole world has come apart in just two weeks. And all I have to do is look into the mirror and I know why."

"Stop punishing yourself," said Lucille angrily.

"Who else is to blame?"

"What do I do with you?" Lucille asked.

Nishgo said, "How'ya doin', buddy? I was sure sorry to hear about your knee. Where are you?"

"Hospital bed in Atlantic City. I'm about to take an ambulance ride to Philadelphia."

"Hang in. Jeffcoate said you'd called me."

"Yeah, I did. Do you think that Stathos will make bail?"

"Not in New Jersey. We got word on that this morning. No bail, in view of our pending extradition request."

"What about Nevada?"

"He'll have a worse time here, I guarantee."

"But if he does make bail, would you let me know?"

There was a silence for a moment, then Nishgo asked, "What did you have in mind?"

"I'd just like to know."

"If you're thinking what I think you're thinking, I don't blame you. But at the same time, you'd be holding a lit fuse. We know a lot more about Mr. Stathos than we knew yesterday, thanks to the FBI. They've known for a long time that the Malavasis controlled a freelance hit man. They figure he's done up to a dozen of his own kind. They've never even tried to move on him because he's been like a roach killer. Good riddance to a bunch of scumbums. But don't let that crazy maneuver in the casino fool you. He's dangerous and he'd kill you. He could just as easily have put that nine-millimeter into your mouth instead of your knee."

Epp said quietly, "Please just let me know if he makes bail."

"Not me," said Nishgo. "What I honestly recommend is that you get well, get out of the hospital."

"And play football?"

There was another silence from the Vegas detective. "I know. I don't blame you. I'd want to kill the son of a bitch myself."

4.

"PLEASE TRY NOT TO BLINK YOUR EYE, Mr. Stathos," said Roger Wethersby. He'd flown out two weeks earlier to make the wax casting. Now he was back again, painting the methacrylate prosthesis, the miniature spot lighting Yorgi's face making his five o'clock shadow storm-blue. Except when cutting the lawn in summer, he was seldom exposed to the sun. His skin was usually as white as flour paste.

They were in an examination room of the Clark County jail infirmary, an armed deputy standing by; looking on as if great art were being created.

"The tiny blood vessels are the test of a good ocularist," said Roger. The resin eyeball in the small vise seemed to be taking on a life of its own.

Yorgi had not opened his mouth since Wethersby began working and remained silent now. In fact, he'd spoken very little since arriving at McCarran, linked to the wrist of Walter Nishgo.

The Malavasi family attorney, silver-haired Gunther Strelich, had insisted that the eye be replaced. Though a Vegas attorney was hired to represent Yorgi in court, since Strelich was not licensed in Nevada, the Chicago lawyer was in charge. He did not want his client to appear before a jury with a black eyepatch. He was sinister enough.

Wethersby was confused when Strelich called him to say that Mr. Stathos, the same man as Mr. Katsanis, couldn't make his appointment on LaSalle since he was now in Las Vegas. In jail. Would Mr. Wethersby kindly go to Vegas to continue the work? Roger said that he wasn't licensed in Nevada and that he didn't do work in jails. Thank you but no thanks, firmly.

The next call Roger got was from a man named Antonio Malavasi.

166

He had a hoarse voice and said, "Be a good fella an' take care of my employee out in Vegas." Roger started telling Tony Ox everything he'd told Strelich, but the hoarse voice kept saying, "Be a good fella," and Roger finally got the message. He was talking to the Mafia.

So Roger flew west with his materials and equipment and was finding work in the Clark County jail to be different, if not exciting.

"The eyes change from day to day, sometimes hour to hour," said Roger. "There are dry-weather eyes and cold-weather eyes, hangover eyes," he said with a laugh.

The young deputy offered, "You know, I've never thought about it like that, eyes changing all the time."

Yorgi finally spoke. "Why don't you two assholes *shut up*."

They did.

The new eye had not been inserted by the following week when Gunther Strelich and Tony Ox flew out to visit Yorgi.

Tony Ox went in first, saying, "Yorgi, Yorgi, how come you got in such trouble?" The *capo* was genuinely distressed, Yorgi was relieved to see—a father's concern for a wayward son, an almost-adopted son. "You look like you got into a cat fight, one of those big lions or tigers."

All of the redness had gone out of the cheek slash, but the scar was there, a thin white furrow in a landscape of whiskers.

"Don't see many of them patches nowadays," said Tony Ox. "It'd make you look distinguished outta those jail clothes. Gunther's still tryin' to get you out on bail but tells me these Nevada people are tougher'n we got 'em at home."

Yorgi said he appreciated all that Gunther was trying to do.

"Now, tell me wha' happened. Guido tol' me, but I wanna hear it from you."

If anybody deserved the truth Tony Ox did, so Yorgi dropped the Lake Mead fishing story and confessed that the nineteen-year-old dinge from the islands had done all the damage, including a gunshot Guido didn't know about, including lifting the briefcase.

167

"But Guido said you brought the money back."

"My money," Yorgi admitted ruefully. "I replaced what I got from Jin Lee. Every dime of it, Tony Ox." The honorable thing to do, but that didn't need to be said.

As much shock as ever passed Tony's face just passed it. His forehead hinted at a frown.

"Gunther told me I could get life here."

"Tol' me that, too."

"He also said that without that girl they got no case. I'll walk."

Tony nodded. "You know how to get to her in Atlantic City?"

He'd anticipated Tony's question and handed over Lucille's address. "I think she'll either be there or down with her mother in St. Thomas."

"Girl like that ought to be taught a lesson," said Tony Ox, taking out his glasses to read the slip.

"I tried," Yorgi said.

"Some people have too much luck."

"You can't tell what the hell she'll do next. I fought guys like that. Southpaws. I swear I haven't had a good night's sleep since she cut me. I get nightmares, Tony. She's a witch, believe me. A *strega*."

The eyes of the *capo* were searching Yorgi's face. "Why'd Guido ever mix you up with her?"

"You have to ask Guido."

Tony Ox said he would

His visitation time was up.

"Gunther needs to talk to you about the trial. Do whatever he says."

Yorgi nodded.

Rising, Tony Ox said, "You take it easy, Yorgi. I been through this, you know. Twice in Statesville, so I know how it is. You just take it easy here. Go with it. We'll look after things. I'm gonna fly Kathy out to see you next week."

Yorgi said he appreciated everything.

Pointing a chubby finger at Yorgi, Tony Ox said, "We'll get that money back for you, don't worry. An' she ain't gonna testify at any trial. I promise."

*   *   *

Tony Ox and his son were having lunch at Bolla's, on North Harlem, in Elmwood Park, Tony having roast leg of spring lamb, Guido having a filet mignon plus lobster tail along with a bottle of *Corvo Bianco Vino Fiore* from the vineyards of Duca di Salaparuta in Sicily.

Tony would have Italiano food at home tonight, perhaps a pasta *epizelli* and then veal or chicken, cooked in his own kitchen by Josephina. Tony Ox worshipped her in the kitchen and, once upon a time, in bed.

Bolla's was a house of mirrors. Mirrors everywhere. You could watch yourself eating veal Dorothea baked in de jonghe butter, or watch Carmelo Albini breaking bread with Franco Maggadino. Talking extortion, Tony knew. Everybody could watch everybody else.

He was saying to Guido, "I don't unnerstan' why you fixed Yorgi up with that girl. I saw her pitcher in the Miami paper. She's too young for Yorgi." He stopped a fork of lamb in midair to wave to Pasquale Nuzzi and Niccola Parenti, who were passing by, then continued, "Younger they are, more the trouble, Guido. You should know that. Yorgi don' know why you fixed him up, now he's thought about it."

Guido shrugged. "He always goes with hookers, Papa. So when I met this girl in Vegas . . . I went out there in December, you remember . . . I thought of Yorgi. Do him a favor. No hooker this time. Like a treat."

"You tell him all about her?"

Tony said hello to Judge Scolastico across the room; waved, smiled.

"Yeh, Papa, I told him. How beautiful she was, what a body she had. A *mortaretto*. All he had to do was stake her to roulette. You shudda heard what she did to him."

Tony Ox looked at his son bleakly. "I heard what she did." They weren't talking about the same things, Tony knew.

"He told you." Guido was surprised.

Tony Ox nodded. "He's in a lot o' trouble."

"That's what I hear," said Guido, loading his mouth.

"He could get life," said Tony Ox, watching his only son gobble, disliking what he saw today and yesterday and many days before. Guido was more a *porco* every day he lived. "Gunther said he could get life."

Guido mumbled that he'd heard that too, words battling past the potatoes.

Tony Ox said, "I'm very fond of Yorgi. I wouldn't want someone to set him up, Guido."

Guido swallowed, clearing his mouth. "Why would anyone do that?"

"That's what I have to find out, Guido," said Tony Ox. "He's in a lot o' trouble an' I don' know I can help. I have to leave it up to Gunther, more or less. But I'll do what I can."

In late afternoon, with Josephina in the kitchen, Tony Ox called from Oak Park to Ralph Esposito in Brooklyn to say, "I want you to go put a lil' pressure on this girl." He gave Ralph Lucille's name and address in Atlantic City. "You gotta car?" Not everyone in Brooklyn owned a car.

Ralph said he did.

"Okay, I want you to be a good fella an' drive down there. You know what to do but don' make no noise, nothin' the neighbors can hear."

Ralph said okay. He did know.

"She owes us some money."

Ralph was well acquainted with that situation. A lot of people owed Tony Ox money from time to time.

Tony said, "You call me when it's done, Ralph, an' I'll send a cashier's check. I add fifty for your car. Gas and oil."

Ralph said that was fine.

Next, Tony Ox called a man whose name was Hermanos. He lived in a second-story apartment just beyond the Miami River bascule bridge on northwest Twelfth Avenue. Tony told Hermanos he wanted him to fly down to St. Thomas and visit Mrs. Tom Bodden,

170

tell her what kind of trouble her daughter was in; that she owed a half million to a man now in jail in Las Vegas and that it wouldn't be healthy to testify against him. Just tell her exactly that and say hello to her young son. Be very polite. Then fly back to Florida. Okay? Five hundred plus the airfare and overnight hotel just to pass that message. Okay, said Hermanos.

5.

MOLLY LET HERSELF IN with her key and saw Lucille sitting on the couch, still in her coat, staring off as if she were a statue. She looked over with a tearstained face. There was a caustic acid smell in the air, like rotten eggs.

Drapes ripped, couch ripped; big white stains on the rug. TV set smashed in. Lithographs slashed, glass broken.

"Look in the bedroom," said Lucille.

Molly walked to the door. Dresses had been pulled out of the wide closet and were now rags on the floor. Coats, hats, everything hacked.

The bed covers had been pulled back, and in the middle was a butcher knife jabbed into the mattress, sticking up as if buried in a human chest, red all around it.

Molly, speechless, went closer. The knife had been plunged down through the right-side padding of a brassiere, just above where the heart would be. The red was thick and gooey, Heinz 57 from the kitchen, but the message was there, like the horse's head in *The Godfather.* Pay up, Molly, don't testify, Molly.

She said, "Oh, God, will it never stop?"

Molly called Walter Nishgo the next day at about ten A.M. Vegas time.

Walter said, "I'm not too surprised. For what it's worth, I'll ask the A.C. police for a copy of their report. They lift any prints?"

"This afternoon, I think. They told me they had better things to do than try to find out who trashed this place."

"I agree," Walter said.

"I don't," said Molly.

Walter said, "How ya' doin'?"

"Not so good."

"I can imagine. Listen, the D.A.'s office tells me we're still six weeks from trial, an' what I suggest you do is go home. Today. Get out of Atlantic City. Tell no one where you're going."

"But they know where I live. The Greek knows where I live. He called down there."

Walter took his time before saying anything else. Then: "You're still better off down there, Molly. They may decide the warning they gave you last night is enough. Just keep a low profile, lock your doors, and I'll talk to the St. Thomas police. I'll tell them we have a murder witness on their doorstep. Send a squad car around two or three times a day."

Molly said worriedly, "I've been thinking about going home the past few days."

"Go," said Walter.

"I just don't want *them* harmed."

"Go," said Walter. "Give me your phone down there."

Not fifteen minutes after Walter Nishgo hung up, Molly's mother called. Chaktri sounded disturbed. "What kind of trouble are you in, Molly?" she asked suspiciously.

Molly hung back, not wanting to say Mafia. "Am I supposed to be in trouble?"

"A man came here last night to say you owed a half million to someone who's in jail in Las Vegas. Is that true?"

"No, Mama. I don't owe *anyone* any money."

"Well, he stood right here on the front porch and said that. Why would he say that if you didn't owe it?"

Molly looked at Lucille, cupping her hand over the speaker. "They sent someone down there last night."

"St. Thomas?"

Molly nodded, then said to her mother, "How did he look?"

"Small, dark-skinned. Latino."

"What else did he say?"

"He said to say hello to Nedley, and said it wouldn't be healthy for you to testify."

"God," Molly said.

"You have to tell me what this is all about, Molly."

Molly said, "I'm a witness in a murder case in Las Vegas involving a mob guy, and I'm being threatened by them."

"Oh, Molly," said her mother. "I'm so scared."

"So am I. I was going to come home tomorrow but now maybe not. Is Nedley at school?"

"Yes."

"When he comes home, *keep* him home. I have to make a call."

"How did this all happen?" said Chaktri, her fear coming through, voice shrill. She might fall apart, Molly thought.

"I'll tell you later. Just don't go anywhere, don't answer the door. Mama, these are very dangerous people. If somebody tries to break in, call the police."

Chaktri said she would, sounding panicky.

As Molly put the phone down, Lucille used a finger to push Nishgo's number toward her. Molly said, "He threatened them."

Lucille said, "Call Nishgo."

She dialed Vegas.

Nishgo's line was busy and she left a call-back message.

Molly took a deep breath. She just wanted to make it all go away. She'd never look at another roulette wheel as long as she lived.

The phone rang and she heard, "Walt Nishgo—you called me . . ."

"They sent someone to St. Thomas."

"Hell they did . . ."

"Last night a man knocked on our door and told Mama I was in deep trouble, that I owed a lot of money to a man in your jail and I shouldn't testify. Then he threatened my kid brother. Mama said he looked Latino."

"Okay, I'll have to talk to the D.A., but we've got kind of a safe place about twenty miles from here. It's like a dude ranch. We've used it before for witnesses who've been threatened. Meanwhile, I'll tell the D.A. to talk to Stathos, tell him we don't stand witness intimidation in this state. He can add years on his sentence if he doesn't call off the Malavasi dogs."

"What about my mother and brother?"

174

"Well, let's keep them on hold for a few days. I doubt we can pay their expenses. I've already talked to the St. Thomas police and they're going to keep a check."

Molly said, "I don't want them hurt because of some terrible mistake I made. I'll pay their expenses. I've got some money saved up."

Walt said, "Lemme get back to you on them, but let's count on you coming out here. Read some books, ride some horses, take some long walks . . . then be a good witness. Put this son of a bitch away, an' everybody goes about their business. I'll call you by day's end."

At Red Hook, Detective Sergeant Laburnum Hotchkiss was showing his badge to Chaktri Bodden on the front porch of the tin-roofed house. Looking at it with suspicion through the screen door, she asked him to repeat his name and why wasn't he in uniform. Besides, he was Ashanti black. The car out front wasn't marked.

"I'm a detective, Mrs. Bodden. I haven't worn a uniform in six years. The Las Vegas police advised us you were threatened night before last. You should have called us then, right after the threat was made. We might have been able to apprehend him."

He sounded British.

"I was too frightened," said Chaktri. "It's my daughter they're after."

Laburnum nodded. "I know. I understand she's a witness in a murder case in Nevada."

"Yes," said Chaktri. "She got mixed up with the wrong people."

"That happens," said Laburnum.

Chaktri said, "He looked like he was Puerto Rican."

"Did he give you a name?"

"No." Then she repeated what the "Puerto Rican" had said.

Laburnum took his notes through the screen door, Chaktri not offering to open it.

"If he, or anyone else, comes back, don't let them in. Call 911. If

175

I'm not there, tell the desk you're being threatened . . . don't hesitate."

The young prosecutor, Agostino, had led Molly through her testimony about what happened in the Stardust parking lot that early Saturday morning and was now asking her to identify the accused.

She pointed toward Yorgi. "That man," she said, so softly that even the judge, eight feet away, barely heard her.

He said, "Please speak up, Miss Bodden.'

Louder. "That man."

He'd been staring at her all morning. Now she had to meet his eyes. Up to now she'd avoided looking at him.

"You knew him as Joseph Carlucci?" said Agostino.

She knew the right one was an imitation eye but it seemed to be as alive as the left one, drilling into her, hate and rage and revenge pooled in it, and she wanted to jump out of the witness box and flee the courtroom.

"Yes."

Last night she'd told Agostino she wasn't sure she could go through with it, just seeing him could make her tongue-tied. "You don't know what fear is," she'd said to Agostino.

"Maybe not, but there's no way he can hurt you in that courtroom. Security will be heavy."

Yet she'd been trembling from the moment she crossed the floor from the prosecution table.

"Your Honor, would the court please request the defendant to rise for positive identification."

He was wearing an expensive pin-striped suit, she saw, one of his expensive ties and matching pocket handkerchiefs. Dapper. She'd last seen him on his back in his overcoat, snow melting on it, nails sticking out of his chest, bound up in wire. Except for that time, the battered face always remained the same—the deadpan cruelty of a shark.

The judge said, "Please rise, Mr. Stathos."

Now that she *had* to look at him, Molly could feel the perspiration on her forehead, in the hollow of her throat.

Yorgi stood up.

"You're positive, Miss Bodden?" Agostino asked. "This is the man you knew as Joseph Carlucci?"

"Yes."

"This is the man who hit Bobby Chapman in the head with a tire iron on the first Saturday in February, then kidnapped you at gunpoint?"

"Yes."

Agostino had attempted to introduce the activities of Stathos in New Jersey as further indication of the violent nature of the accused but was denied, the judge ruling, "Let the State of New Jersey properly pursue that case."

She was being stabbed by the brown eyes and looked away from them.

"Thank you, Miss Bodden," Agostino said, and she sagged in relief.

Then the judge declared a recess, saying that proceedings would continue after lunch.

Carlucci—she hadn't gotten used to Stathos—continued to stare at her as she got down out of the witness stand. He stared as if his *mantra* could kill her; stared until he was led away. She felt drained.

"Do I have to be here this afternoon?" Molly asked Agostino. They were near the bench.

"I'm afraid so. You have to stick around until we give the case to the jury. There'll be cross-examination, as I told you."

"He keeps staring at me."

"That's not unusual for a defendant. But that's all he can do. You did a damn good job this morning."

"Could you see my knees knocking?"

Agostino grinned. "I knew they were. Most people have knocking knees in here. Me too, sometimes. I've got to go back to the office. I'll brown-bag there." He went over to get his briefcase. "Be back a little before two."

Molly nodded and went toward Walter Nishgo, who was standing in the aisle opposite row four. She'd seen him come in shortly after she took the stand. He was smiling.

"You did fine," he said.

"That's what Agostino just said. I was dying up there."

"C'mon, I'll take you to my favorite hamburger joint. You got a choice. McDonald's, Burger King, Wendy's or Mack, The Knife."

Molly laughed for the first time all day. "I'll take Mack, The Knife."

As they were leaving the courthouse, Walt asked, "Where's the boyfriend? I thought he was going to be here."

"He's still in the hospital."

"Poor guy."

"That's what I think, too."

Mack, The Knife was on South Main, near Bonneville, two blocks over, four down; Molly matched the detective's long strides.

"Are they going to give him the death sentence?" she asked, as they walked. "Agostino said he didn't think so."

"Neither do I," said Walt. "When's the last time you ever heard of a mob asshole getting the chair or the chamber?"

"I don't keep up with things like that."

"I do."

"Well, will they put him away forever?"

"Forever's a long time," said Walt, taking a curb.

"Not long enough for him," Molly said. "I never want to see him free."

"Tell you the truth, you may not get your wish."

"Well, what do you think he'll get? Agostino said he won't even guess, but he's got a hunch, I think."

"You think right. Don't tell him I said so, but my guess is life."

"That means 'til he dies."

"That means ten years, or less, if he behaves himself, if he doesn't shiv anybody."

"Oh, no, I thought life meant life."

"Not unless the judge or jury tacks on without possibility of parole. The jury just recommends."

They turned into Mack's, ordered a pair of burgers with everything, got their numbers and sat down on the high stools at the waist-high side counter.

"Why won't they recommend that this time, without possibility of parole?"

"Give you a five-minute dissertation on how Lady Justice really works. No premeditation here, for one thing. To tell you the truth, Stathos probably just meant to knock him out. You were the target, not Bobby Chapman, because you plucked half his eyesight. Then shot him . . . stole his money, he thinks—"

Walt stopped. "Shit, ain't that grand? You deserve to be queen of the Policeman's Ball . . ."

He took a sip of his Coke. "Where was I? Okay. Not a nice thing for you to do to the Mafia. But I'll tell you something Agostino knows and I know by now—Stathos, the man who staked you to roulette to get into your pants, is a hit man of long standing but none of us mind when he shoots up the scum. Mob buddies. So he's helped us more than he's hurt us, except with a kid like Bobby. You think cops really give a damn when someone like Sam Giancana gets whacked in Oak Park or Johnny Roselli is discovered in the fetal position in an oil barrel in Dumfoundling Bay? We love it."

"But he should be put away until he dies."

"Maybe that'll happen to him. But I'll lay you a bet he gets life and walks in less than ten years. It's better I level with you."

"So I've got to think about him and what he's threatened until I die?"

"Not necessarily. Someone may give him some steel between *his* ribs. There are some over in Carson City pen just as tough and mean as he is. We can at least hope for that."

The hamburger numbers were shouted, and Walt went over to get them. Sitting down again, reaching for mustard, he said, "Stathos sat between Harry Jeffcoate and myself all the way here and the only words he said was he had to pee. From the time we picked him up until we stuffed him in jail here, that's all he said. Now, the night before they turned him over to us, Harry and I went out slumming. From Vegas, we need to hit the big hotels and that one halfass A.C. casino that was open? No way. So we found a little club with a comedian named Cozy Morley. Guy tells nothing but ethnic jokes. Like for a Puerto Rican funeral they put the body in a stolen car in a towaway zone, or this Jewish bad boy is sent to a Catholic School and his parents ask him why he's suddenly behaving. He tells 'em, 'They have a guy nailed to the wall in every room.' So we toss these jokes back and forth, watching him like hawks. Even a Greek joke. Does he laugh, even smile? He looks straight ahead for almost four hours. He's got Frigidaire coolant in his veins."

Molly was already thinking about Yorgos Stathos walking out of prison someday. "You know that money he's accused me of taking, and I told you, and I told Agostino, I told the Atlantic City police, I didn't do it. I didn't . . ."

"I don't think anyone doubts you. I've got my own version—*he did have it*. Where he got it from, Christ only knows, but he had it in a briefcase and he had the briefcase on the back seat. You grab the car and bring it to Longene Court, walk away without locking it, some guy sees the briefcase, takes it, figures it's dope money. Adios, five hundred thousand or whatever it was. Hell's fire, I might be tempted. In fact, I probably would have grabbed it and now have myself a residence down where you live . . ."

Molly looked at the rugged, honest face of the Vegas detective and asked, "You know these kind of people, what should I do when the trial is over?"

"Get the hell out of here. Go somewhere a long ways off. Don't tell anybody where. Maybe change your name . . . dye your hair . . ."

"You think they might hurt my mother, my little brother?"

"I doubt it. Asshole like him doesn't have many friends to send around, as I said before."

"So you think I'm the only target?"

"I think this has all narrowed down to a personal thing between you and Stathos. You did a lot of damage to him, Molly, physical and mental. You foxed him three times. You rubbed his nose in shit. Hurt him, took his money, he thinks. That little dance in Caesar's that gave all of us a laugh was what really did it. That was like cutting his balls off. I read where they had to use restrainers on him in the medic wagon. Face it, you pissed all over a proud and dangerous man."

They walked slowly back to the courthouse at Bridger and Third.

On Monday morning Agostino called Molly at the dude ranch to say the case of *Nevada* v. *Yorgos Stathos*, of Naperville, Illinois, had gone to the jury. Cross your fingers.

Molly was all packed and left within the hour for McCarran International and a first-leg jet to New York; then on to San Juan for overnight, hopping to St. Thomas Tuesday. Home, at last.

Then Molly called Agostino in the afternoon from JFK and he was higher than the TWA she'd just exited. "We got the sucker, Molly," he said, grinning widely over the phone. "And it didn't take long, less than two hours. Guilty of murder in the second, guilty of assault with a deadly weapon, guilty of kidnapping. What about that? *You* did it all—your testimony did it. Not me."

"I feel like I don't have any bones. I never want to do that again."

"I hope you don't have to," said Agostino.

"What happens now?"

"Judge'll sentence him in two weeks, then he'll go over to Carson City to start serving his time. His lawyer'll likely appeal, but in my opinion that's not going anywhere. So Mr. Stathos is going to do some years."

"How many?"

"Molly, we've talked about that before. I don't know. I really don't. I told you he could get two life terms, served separately—or two served together."

"What about that without possibility of parole?"

"Up to the judge. Have a good flight home and call me in a couple of weeks. I have to get the D.A.'s permission for any calls outside the U.S., so it's easier for you to call me . . ."

Molly said she would. Two weeks from Monday. "I want him in there fifty years, a hundred years . . ."

"Don't get greedy."

"I just want to get safe, that's all."

"You're safe—"

"For now," Molly said, thinking of the other times when she thought she was safe.

She went outside to catch the shuttle to the Eastern Terminal.

The visitation period was almost over, and Kathy would head back for Chicago within two hours.

Her right hand was holding Yorgi's, and with his left he passed a note beneath the plexiglass space. He said, "You take care of yourself. Things will work out, believe me."

Taking the note, she swallowed and bit her lip. "I hope so."

They said good-bye and she left the Clark County jail.

In the cab to McCarran Field, she read the note:

> There's a safe beneath that big drum in the garage, the one with the green cleaning powder in it. If you need money, take it out of there. There's not much left, but if anything happens to me, I wanted you to know. R-36, R-42, L-11, L-23, R-19.
>
> Love,
> Yorgi

6.

HOW SHE LOVED THE LITTLE ISLAND and always had, the soft wind, the rain while the sun shined, the colors in the bougainvillaea and frangipani and hibiscus and tiny wild orchids, colors she wanted to use someday down on Main Street.

Tuesday evening at sundown and Molly just wanted to relax in the old tin-roofed house in Red Hook, down at the far end of the island, about as far away from town as you could get, on the Mannassah bus line. Go around in bare feet for a few weeks, smell the tropics, feel the warm, moist air after the dryness of Vegas, sit on the porch and watch the high-piled white clouds tumble off toward St. John, forget everything that had happened since the last Tuesday in January.

The phone rang, and Chaktri stuck her head out of the front door to say, "Someone named Epp Watts."

Molly got out of the ancient rocker in which she'd spent hours as a child, rocking, rocking, daydreaming. She went on into the sparsely furnished living room, unchanged, except for a TV set, in the fourteen years since they'd come up from Trinidad. She crossed the broom-polished wooden floor, swept at least three times a day by Chaktri, who was still taking in sewing.

"Jus' wanted to tell you I'm home, out of the hospital," said Epp.

"Everything go okay?"

"Ummmm. I know everything there is to know about my patella."

"What's a patella?"

"My kneecap. I've also learned about osteoblasts, osteocytes, osteoclasts."

"Please don't tell me."

"How you doin'?"

"Getting restless. Too much of a good thing. I'm getting lazy—I

183

haven't done a blessed thing since I got here. I've been sitting in my childhood rocker all day."

"I should come down an' join you. I'm up an' walking around."

"You're *walking*, Epp? Oh, I'm so glad."

"With a cane."

"But that's still wonderful."

"Sure."

"I guess it's not wonderful but it's progress, isn't it."

"That it is," said Epp. "I'm serious about coming down. I've got another operation next month, then it's up, up and away. And by the way, I'm officially retired from the NFL. I had three vested years."

"I've been meaning to ask you about that but didn't know how to do it. Are you all right? Financially, I mean."

"I'm fine. Aside from the car I haven't spent too much. I had a guy invest money for me. I'm in pretty good shape that way. Stocks, CDs, money market. I've got something stashed away. I own that lot on Bovoni Hill. The pension doesn't amount to doodly-squat. About five hundred a month. I'll collect when I'm sixty-five."

"That's not enough to buy groceries."

"Not the way I eat. Hey, Nishgo told me that the Greek got it good. Guilty on all counts."

Molly didn't want to think about the Greek down here. She wanted to think about *monkey-don'-climb* and *cock-a-lockas*. "I just hope he never gets out."

"Well, in one way, I'd like to see him out. Get him on my turf. He's been on my mind a lot."

"He's someone we both have to forget, Epp."

"Well, I'll never forget the son of a bitch."

"You know what I mean," she said.

They talked on for another ten minutes and then Epp said he'd call again soon. "I love you, Molly," he said, and she said, "I love you, too," but they both knew it wouldn't work . . . for the time being.

Chaktri asked, "Who is Epp Watts?"

Molly looked at her mother. "The man who drove me from Vegas to Atlantic City, the one from St. Croix."

"He's black, isn't he?"

"He's whiter than I am."

"He the one who talked you into going to the police?"

Molly sighed. "It was my decision."

"Hah," said Chaktri, and picked up her broom.

Molly got back into the rocking chair, the thunderheads south of St. John seeming to have piled higher while she was talking to Epp. She craned her head around toward the sound of straw on wood. "When's Nedley coming home?" she asked. Evening coolness was setting in.

"Soon. He gets off at seven."

Nedley was a part-time bag boy at the Grand Union.

"Your brother's a good man, a good man, an' we're gonna appeal," said Tony Ox to Kathy Stathos. "Gunther's gonna start the paperwork tomorrow an' we'll get Yorgi outta there. We always take care of our own, Kathy, you know that. We jus' din't expect that girl to testify."

"I don't understand how he got involved with her," said Kathy.

"Neither do I," said Tony Ox. "But you need anythin', you jus' call me. You got Gunther's number?"

Kathy said she had it.

"Don't worry, we'll take good care o' you, an' Yorgi," said Tony Ox.

Yorgi had been told in Clark County jail that the state pen in Carson City was an old one. That was no lie. As the van came down the cottonwood-lined street it was looming ahead, looking like it was a hundred years old, a place for cowboy bandits. He'd been told that sloth fossils could be found in the hand-quarried walls of the 1880s buildings. He wasn't sure what a sloth was. There were some new buildings up on the hill that he could see, homes for more recent sloths. He'd been told to watch his rear end when black guys in knit caps were around. He'd heard slammer stories from sur-

185

vivors long ago in Illinois, and he wasn't worried about surviving in Carson City with horse thieves.

Yorgi was escorted to his cell in late afternoon, after check-in and a physical exam, during which he was found to be in perfect health—the doctor naturally asking him what had happened to his right eye, Yorgi replying a fish hook got it, falling back on that. He'd had his first physical up in Indian Springs, the shrink there asking the same thing.

The doctor said, "Hmmm."

Yorgi's first exercise period was two days later, and he noticed a skinny guy staring at him, giving him an extra long look. He stared back as the tall con came slowly across the yard toward him. What the fuck did he want? Trouble already, ten minutes out into the sunshine.

The guy stopped about three feet away, saying, "Don't I know you?" He looked like a cowboy with a big adam's apple.

"What's more, you won't." Tony Ox had said to take no shit from moment one.

"My name's Floyd Cramer and I'll be go to hell."

"You go anywhere you want to go. Just don't get in my way," said Yorgi.

"I *will* be go to hell. You're the guy I was suppose to pop in January. You're why I'm here."

Yorgi frowned. He didn't exactly appreciate Floyd Cramer's burst of hollow laughter. "Whatta you mean, I'm the one you were suppose to pop?"

"In January, in Vegas."

"What kind o' bullshit is this?" said Yorgi. Already beginning to suspect.

"Joe Carlucci? Know that name?"

"Yeh," said Yorgi warily.

"I was suppose to get ten thousand to take you out in Vegas. Man, you were set up," said Floyd Cramer.

"Ten thousand from who?" Yorgi demanded, now very much interested in this stick of cowboy.

"You ever heard of a Malavasi? Oak Park, Illinois? He ring a bell with you?"

"Yeh, he rings a bell. You damn right, he rings a bell."

Hadn't he known all along? Guido!

"You had a good lookin' showgirl, an' I sat out in front of the Hilton for three hours, freezin' my balls off waitin' for you. I was goin' to follow you to her place, then pop you when you came out."

Do him a favor, after Jin Lee, a bonus; get him a date, *then get him shot.* "Why didn't you do it?" Yorgi asked.

"Shit, I got picked up. Comin' behind you, I ran a red light. What got me was traffic tickets for the car I used, an' an outstanding warrant for a shooting over in Winnemucca. Self-defense, honest to God, an' now I'm here. Murder One. Public defender screwed it for me. Blew it. I got life, too."

"First name of that guy in Illinois Guido?"

"Yeah, Guido. He owes me. Lawyer friend of mine in Oklahoma City got us together."

"You talked to him in Illinois?" Yorgi didn't think for a minute that Tony Ox had done it. Guido, Guido!

"That's right. I get out o' here I got to pay him a visit."

"We got a lot to talk about, you and I," said Yorgi. "What'd you say your name was?"

"Floyd Cramer, same as the piano player. I'm from Cordell, Oklahoma."

"Nice to meet you, Floyd," said Yorgi.

JFK at five-forty P.M. on a Thursday and Epp was sitting with Molly, holding her hand, near the entrance to foreign departures. He'd driven up from Philly, knowing he'd only see her for a few minutes. She'd come in on Eastern from San Juan and was going out on Air France.

She said, "It was sweet of you, Epp, but you didn't need to. I just wanted to let you know."

"I certainly did need to come," he said. "You goin' away for God knows how long?"

Her hair swept back in a ponytail, red ribbon in it, wearing jeans and a shirt and that old leather jacket he'd seen her in so many times, she looked younger than twenty. Again, people, especially males, were taking a second glance at her.

"I may not like Paris. They may not like me."

"Well, don't leave if you think that way."

"I need the job."

"Come on, you can get work without goin' to France."

"I can't."

Stubborn female. "Okay, how'd it happen?"

"I went over to San Juan and got nothing but a bunch of baloney. They said they had all the girls they needed right now, but in the fall when they changed the show, maybe . . . I got a lot of maybes. So I went back home, called Howie Piaggi, and he said, 'You willing to go overseas?' 'Where?' I asked. 'Paris,' he said. *Paris*! God. I'd thought about Paris. Imagine. 'They'll adore your skin tone, your long legs, babycakes.' Same old Howie. So he said he'd call back. Two days later he did, telling me to send photos to the Lido, a man named Marly. In case you don't know, the Lido, the Folies Bergère and the Moulin Rouge are the top dinner shows in town. The Stardust brought a Lido show to Vegas years ago. Anyway, next thing I know I get a call from this Marly and have trouble understanding him. *Exoteek*, he says, talking about the photos, I think. They sent a ticket. I'm so excited."

Epp acknowledged sadly, "You're already flying."

"I was uptight, real uptight. I didn't know how uptight I was. First night I was home, Nedley was supposed to be home around seven-thirty. He didn't come in until after ten and I climbed all over him, was sure he'd been kidnapped. I thought the mob had him. He'd been bowling. Just bowling."

"You had reason to be uptight."

"I tried to relax and enjoy myself. I love St. Thomas. But I jumped

188

every time the phone rang. I stayed awake at night, listening for the Greek. If I went into town I'd look over my shoulder before I crossed the street. I didn't know how spooked I was."

"You needed me there," said Epp.

"Maybe."

"Here I thought we'd be spending some of the summer together, you'd be working at Resorts . . ."

"No one believes me, but I'm not hirable in Atlantic City or even San Juan. And I'm not about to work those topless bars in Miami."

Epp again ignored her job problems to say, "You know I'm in love with you."

Molly shook her head. "I think you're in love with that girl in the ostrich feathers."

"Her, too."

Molly laughed. "She's the phony one."

"I'll take her," said Epp.

"Watch what you say," said Molly.

He reached over for her other hand. "How 'bout canceling the flight, sendin' that Lido guy a wire tellin' him you've changed your mind, then comin' back to Philly with me? We'll get married, an' I'll set you up in a dress shop anywhere you want."

"That's the best offer I've ever had. But, Epp, I'm not ready. I just turned twenty. I really want to do the boutique on my own. Please understand."

He sighed. "I'll try."

"Come over and see me," she said.

"I'll try that too."

Air France called its seven P.M. flight to Paris and they embraced for a moment, Molly saying, "I love you, too, in my own way."

Epp kissed her, then hobbled along with her to the departure gate, using his cane, hugging her again just before she went through security.

SECOND SUNDAY IN NOVEMBER, 1979:

Ten-thirty P.M. in Paris and Molly was getting ready for the first

189

show at the Lido. Molly loved Paris. She was beginning to speak the language, just a little, and Paris loved her, with her "exotique" lemon-colored skin and long legs and perfect breasts and sable-sleek hair. When she wasn't dancing at 116 avenue des Champs-Elysées twice nightly six nights a week she was exploring the haute couture of Guy Laroche and Nina Ricci on avenue Montaigne or Courrèges in the rue François, Sonia Rykiel on the rue de Grenelle and Dorothee Bis on the rue de Sèvres. She'd gone to all of them, Balmain and Christian Dior to Anastasia and Gudule, looking but not buying. She looked and then made her own. She'd taken a windowbox apartment in Saint-Germain-des-Prés.

STATE PENITENTIARY AT CARSON CITY:
The first snow of the new winter was falling over western Nevada from Smoke Creek Desert, up north, down south to Esmeralda and thirteen-thousand-foot Boundary Peak, east into the Stillwater and Shoshone ranges. By now, Yorgi knew a little about where he was, and it wasn't anywhere near Lake Michigan. The snow covered up some of the bleakness of the mountains and was a good change of scenery. For once, he appreciated snow.

He'd spent the time since lunch this cold Sunday afternoon lying on his bunk, thinking about his favorite subjects: Guido Malavasi and Molly Bodden. He hoped they would stay healthy until he got out of prison.

A little after two, a guard named Espinosa came to escort Yorgi to the hobby shop. Kathy had bundled up all his precision tools and had sent them out. He was now working on a thirty-inch model of the U.S. schooner of war *Hannah*, 1775, first man-of-war commissioned by George Washington. In this institution where he was forced to live, it was not practical to build larger models.

By two-twenty, his surgical telescopes were in place over his reading glasses, making him look like a diamond cutter as he went to work on the *Hannah*.

BOOK TWO

1.

FEBRUARY 1987.
When Ronnie and Nancy were still in the White House and the Giants were Super Bowl XXI champs, the prison psychiatrist at Carson City, prior to the March parole-board meeting, asked Mr. Stathos, "Do you hold any animosity toward anyone in this institution or outside of it? Any feeling of getting even for your incarceration? A police officer? A judge? Anyone like that?"

Staring at the crewcut shrink with his good eye, which seemed to glow like a dark brown gemstone, gray-bearded Yorgi said emphatically, "No. No grudges. None at all. No grudges. None at all."

He was smiling widely, showing his near-perfect teeth. He'd taken good care of them, even in medium-security, flossing three times a day and using a proxy brush. The glistening teeth were still about the only pretty things Yorgi possessed. Otherwise, he now looked like an aging oracle lost from *Planet of The Apes*.

"None?" repeated the shrink.

There was no reason, was there, to mention Guido Malavasi or Molly Bodden? Besides, they weren't cops, judges or fink guards. Guido was in Chicago, Molly down in St. Thomas.

"None," Yorgi repeated. "None at all."

"What do you think you'll do *when and if* you leave here?"

"Go back to Illinois and build my ship models," said Yorgi, good eye still gleaming.

And do a few other things, he was saying to himself. Like whack Guido and Molly. Shoot one, burn the other.

"I know you're very good at that, building those ship models. I hear you're now getting fifteen hundred each. I know I certainly can't afford one," said the shrink, hinting slightly.

193

Yorgi kept smiling and shrugged apologetically at the high price, not offering to lower it.

"Old life gone forever, eh, Mr. Stathos? Just a memory. No more syndicate?"

"Gone forever," said Yorgi, losing his smile.

No more the mob. Tony Ox was dead. No more the freelance hitman. No more "Yorgi Greco." It was now Yorgos Stathos once again, peaceful model maker from Abe Lincoln's state, the old life gone forever except the two personal jobs, Guido and Molly.

But if he'd had any knowledge whatsoever about where the guy was, he would have added the fucking Puerto Rican, Ocampo, to the list. The P.R. was responsible for those five dime-sized scars arranged in a vertical crescent above Yorgos's left nipple, beneath the matting of hair. They were also a constant reminder of Guido and Molly. He'd touched them often, rubbing them unconsciously, over the past eight years. Although Guido and Molly had set him up, it was the little P.R. hard hat who'd put him in here. But he had no idea where to find the shit-heel.

After more questions, the shrink said, "Well, I'm recommending you for parole in April."

Yorgi murmured a humble thank-you, renewing the wide, glittering smile, cracking his knuckles.

Espinosa, the regular day guard in Stathos's block, said, "I've known him eight years, he goes in and out like an accordion. One day he makes sense, the next he's flying around cuckooland. I hear him in there talking to himself and suddenly there's somebody answering him in a falsetto. I think he hallucinates every third day. You want me to tell the parole board? I'll even tape that ugly Greek."

"No, I don't want you to tell the parole board anything. The shrink has already told them. The guy may be a little weird but he's not crazy, is what the shrink said. We need the space. He's done his time."

"He's in-and-out batty, I tell you," said pot-gutted Espinosa, one of the better guards at Carson City.

"I talk to myself now and then," said the young assistant warden. "I don't think I'm batty."

Espinosa tried once more. "He's a hummer."

"He's a what?"

"A hummer. He came out of Old Max *humming*. He hums to himself. You should hear him. You go by the hobby shop and there he is, building his goddamn models, humming away. He's driven three or four roomies batty. They call him 'Graybeard, The Hummer' around here."

"Sounds harmless to me," said the assistant warden.

"Okay," said Espinosa, giving up.

Okay, okay, college-boy Assistant Warden, let the loony son of a bitch go out and kill someone else.

In April, Yorgi was getting ready to depart Medium Security after eight years, two months and nine plus days, doing his first four in musty Old Max mainly because of his Illinois reputation. But he'd been a good boy ever since musty Max.

Never was he a candidate for the newer Super Max over in Unit Seven. Those single cells were for the really bad ones. But that, too, was kind of an ironic joke in Yorgi's case. In his time with the Malavasis, he'd whacked more people than any single bad one over in Super Max.

Calling Kathy, in Naperville, he said, "They're letting me out Tuesday."

"Oh, Yorgos," she said, "I can't wait. You want me to come out there, come back with you?"

If ever there was a wonderful, devoted, loving sister she was it, Yorgi thought. "No, I'll get a bus over to Reno. Fly out of there. I'll call you when I know the flight."

"I can't wait," she said, so excited.

Not liking two seconds of it in those oblong chambers with case-hardened door bars and fortress windows and lidless toilets, Yorgi had jailed pretty well. Only once did he have to protect his ass. A beefy Chicano, making baskets in the hobby shop, winked and said,

195

"*Te quiero,*" and Yorgos lifted his X-acto, fastening his good eye on the spik, answering, "Beans, you better watch your *bicho.*"

Now, he was departing Nevada thanks to the shrink.

Floyd Cramer, nearest to a close friend Yorgi had acquired during residence in Carson City, had departed the hard way three years earlier, succumbing to inoperable stomach cancer. The day Floyd told him the clock was ticking behind his navel, Yorgi said, "I'll get Guido Malavasi for us. *Both of us.* I'll get that fat fucker, I promise."

Then it would be Molly Bodden.

What little hair was left on his head, soot-black when he entered, was now cinder-block color. Espinosa saw him nude and said, "You look like you got flocked. Steel wool glued on you." He had to trim his beard every two weeks. It sprouted like lawn.

On leaving the sandstone establishment at the foot of Fifth a few days before his forty-fourth birthday, Yorgi knew he appeared fifty-four instead of forty-four because of all the gray flocking.

As the shrink had mentioned, he'd spent a lot of time in the hobby shop, the scale vessels selling in Reno. But his finest work, a thirty-six-inch clipper ship named *Molly Bodden,* recently completed, hadn't been for sale. For kicks, he'd burnt it at a small private going-away ceremony—just himself attending—only yesterday, Sunday. She'd stood on the foredeck, hair on fire, body turning into thousands of tiny embers as he watched. She was screaming at him, hair straight up in the air and sizzling.

But he knew, just the same, that she was still alive, because on a cold, rainy Sunday the winter past he'd been looking at a magazine in the prison library and who should be smiling out at him *alive*: Molly Bodden. Fucking common thief. Knifer. Witch.

After seven-plus years in Paris, there she was, "bee-ootiful," selling her fine wares in St. Thomas, just like she said she would. Yorgi had carefully torn the pages out, taking them back to his cell, often looking at her smiling dinge face, hands shaking with rage.

"*Alive, alive, oh; alive, alive, oh; singing cockles and mussels— alive, alive, oh . . .*"

He could clearly remember the lounge music from the Irish group drifting into the Hilton casino that night in '79, the *tock* of the ivory roulette ball, Molly doing her body English . . .

And there'd been a whole lot of cell-bunk dreams about Molly during the long nights in Carson City. Sometimes she was slicing at him with a straight razor. Other times she was running away from him in empty Caesar's, Atlantic City, with the half-million briefcase. He could never catch her. Once, just once, she was in bed with him, laughing at him because he couldn't get it up.

Now he wanted to cup her bloody eyes in the palm of his hand before incinerating her. Well, that's what you did with witches and jumbis, *The Book of Bocor* said—you drove a stake through their miserable hearts and then burned them. Didn't you? Didn't you? He didn't need a stake. All he needed was a can of gasoline. He'd found a copy of *The Book of Bocor* in the prison library under "witches."

For fat Guido Malavasi, back in Oak Park, he had other plans. He hadn't dreamed about Guido very much.

Those plans aside, smiling widely, he reported to his parole officer in DuPage County twenty-four hours after arriving in Illinois, so ordered by the State of Nevada.

Molly's shop was down on Main Street, near Boolchand's, famous already in a year's time. She carried high styles, expensive jewelry and accessories; sold collections of Yamamoto, Jean-Paul Gaultier, Bylbos and Sonia Rykiel, as well as her own line of extravagant cotton polychromatics.

She swept around the shop like a long-stemmed tropic flower, sandals slithering, talking in a breezy West Indies dialect if the mood struck her, throwing in a little French or Italian now and then.

Molly's of St. Thomas was the label, the same exotic Molly Bodden who had danced at the Stardust back in '79, then at the Lido in Paris.

But she had not forgotten the Greek the whole time she had lived by the Seine. She had thought of him, wishing, hoping, praying he was dead.

His sister said, "Oh, Yorgos, we have so much to catch up on," holding his hand across the table.

Yorgi said yes, they did.

They were having dinner at Morgan's Crossing, on West Chicago, in Naperville, a homecoming celebration, Kathy insisting on taking him out.

"Okay, tell me about you an' Hajadaki," he said.

He'd asked about Hajadaki a hundred times in his collect calls to Kathy; she had never mentioned him in her letters after a while.

Kathy sighed. She was a little drunk and slurred her words. "I'll tell you the truth. He got married six years ago." He had never seen her drunk before.

"What?"

Yorgi said it so loud that people in the next tables looked up and over at the gray-bearded man. A shout! He rose halfway out of his chair, his good eye a hot drill.

She said "sssh" on top of her breath. "I didn't want to upset you."

"Upset me? Why, that son of a bitch! Did he do it because of what happened to me? Me goin' to prison? Didn't want to marry into our family? Brother a con?"

He was still loud.

Kathy said quietly, "I think he did it because he fell in love with another girl."

"He stop seein' you because of me?"

"I can't answer that, Yorgos, he just stopped and I have to tell myself it was because he fell out of love."

"He still at that PIP printing place?"

"He's the manager now."

"Well, I should stop by an' flat ask him." Grab his throat, break his arm, throw him into the lake.

"He has two children. It's long over, Yorgos."

"You datin' anyone else?"

"Not steady."

She'd aged, he'd seen right off, more than he expected. She was chubbier, though her face remained pretty, in his opinion. Round-faced, still pretty in a Greek way. But there was a sadness to it that had never been there, a look of loneliness.

"What do you do with yourself?"

There were little red dots beneath her nose. She'd visited that skin doctor again. Kathy was always fighting a mustache. Hair did run in the Stathos family. Their father had gorilla hide.

"Go to the movies and play solitaire."

He hadn't remembered dark circles under her eyes. They were there now. He hadn't remembered Kathy drinking hard liquor. That's what she was doing now. Vodka on the rocks.

Molly Bodden's fault. All her fault. Her's and Guido's.

Kathy was just another reason to whack them.

After they got home from Morgan's Crossing and went to bed, Kathy could hear voices coming from Yorgos's room. She heard his voice, and then there seemed to be another voice. Once, he shouted. And her brother had also started to hum, she noticed. He'd never done that before. She thought about going to Father Peter Potamianos, at St. Athanasious, and asking his advice.

2.

FRIDAY, YORGI WENT UP the walk of the two-story house on Linden Avenue, in Oak Park, and pushed the buzzer, then waited patiently, looking around, waiting for the voice of Guido Malavasi to come out of the tiny speaker by the door. He was wearing his old Borsalino.

Place hadn't changed much since 1979, Yorgi saw. Was that the same porch furniture? Yes, for chrissakes, it was. Waiting, he was making a noise in the back of his mouth like a choirmaster giving the pitch for "My Country Tis of Thee."

There was a security service emblem on the front door now, an embossed police badge on it. Yorgi had to laugh. A Malavasi with a rent-a-cop service?

"Who is it?" Guido finally said.

Well, the voice hadn't changed much in eight and a half years either, still high-pitched.

"Yorgi Greco."

The old name, when he was working for the family; when Tony was still alive. The good days, the exciting days.

"Be there in a minute."

Yorgi wondered if Guido still had all his blubber, those triple chins? What had happened since Tony died?

Yorgi had called Guido yesterday to say he was out of Carson City and that he'd like to talk. No, he didn't want his old numbers district back. Just talk a little while.

Okay, come in the morning, Guido had said. About nine.

So here he was, on Guido's porch. This neighborhood hadn't changed much, either. Always a quiet neighborhood. There was a lady out working on her flower bed about six houses down.

Chains rattled and keys turned, then the door opened, Guido filling it. No, he hadn't changed much, either. He still weighed three hundred and looked like he had an extra chin. Four now! Balder than Yorgi remembered.

"So they let you out," Guido said, not offering his pudgy, soft hand. "You look awful with that gray beard."

"I know how I look," said Yorgi, taking off his hat.

"I'm eating breakfast," said Guido, closing and locking the door, then turning to lumber down the dark hallway. "You want some coffee?"

"Okay," said Yorgi, walking behind Guido, thinking of an elephant's ass.

"You look awful," Guido repeated. "You sick out there?"

"Not often," Yorgi answered. Just older.

"Your new eye don't look too bad," said Guido.

"It matches," said Yorgi. And it wasn't new.

They went on into the kitchen. The house smelled stale. After smelling the antiseptics of Old Max and Medium Security for so long, Yorgi found it hard to accept any other air, even fresh air.

Guido filled a coffee cup for him. "Sit down," he said, motioning to a chair opposite the *sottocapo*, as Yorgi had known him. Was he now the *capo*, the big boss?

"First, I want to say how sorry I am that Tony died."

Guido just grunted.

Yorgi said, "Please give my condolences to your mother."

Guido grunted again.

"I never knew he had a heart condition," said Yorgi.

"Neither did he," said Guido.

"It *was* the heart, wasn't it?" said Yorgi.

Guido swallowed a mouthful of fried potatoes and said, "You think somebody shot him? He died in Peppitone's. Just slumped over. I was there."

"You the *capo* now?" Yorgi asked, studying the moon face, sipping his coffee.

Guido nodded.

"I didn't come here to ask for a job," Yorgi said.

Guido nodded again. "It's just as well. Tony gave your numbers district to Gaetano Profaci long ago. You do a dumb thing like kill

201

that guard in the Stardust parking lot . . ." Guido shrugged as if to say, I don't need somebody does dumb things.

Yorgi said he understood.

"But I'll help you get a job with another family," Guido said. "I'll call around."

Yorgi said, "I'd appreciate that, Guido. You know all the bad luck began with that girl, Molly Bodden. I think she's a witch. Me sent to prison, almost broke. Kathy loses her boyfriend. Tony has a heart attack and dies. I think it all began with her. She cast a spell."

But Yorgi knew that it really all began with Tony's fatso son sitting here in front of him, pigging as usual.

Guido was sopping up his eggs over-easy with white toast.

"Why didn't you ever call Kathy while I was in Nevada? Jus' to see how she was gettin' along? Your father did."

Guido was inserting the yellow dripping bread into his mouth, chewing noisily. He didn't answer the question about Kathy but did say, "I never believe much in good luck or bad luck."

"I never did, either, until you got me that date with Molly Bodden," said Yorgi. "Stake her at roulette, you said."

Guido's mouth was full, cheeks looking like he had a peach stuffed in each side. He frowned and swallowed. "That was a long time ago, Yorgi. You live in the past. Last time you and I had lunch, almost nine years ago, you were hung up on her."

Yorgi admitted that was true.

"You ever know a man named Floyd Cramer, same name as the piano player?" Yorgi asked, searching the pasty moon face.

Guido's eyes narrowed and he put his fork down. "No, I've never known a Floyd Cramer," said Guido slowly.

"You lie," said Yorgi, reaching behind him in one smooth movement, taking the silenced Beretta 9mm out of the pants band above his right hip pocket, firing it five times into Guido's ballooned gut, the face of Tony's only son dropping into the yellows of the last two eggs on his plate, coloring them red.

Guido Malavasi taken care of, promise to the late Floyd Cramer fulfilled, Molly Bodden was next.

Humming, Yorgi put the Borsalino back on his head and walked down the dark hallway, letting himself out of the house on Linden, seeing the woman down the street still working on her flower bed.

On sunny Saturday morning, when the Chicago papers and TV stations were devoting some space and time to the "gangland" slaying of Guido Malavasi, Oak Park police leisurely investigating, downtown cops glad it hadn't happened there, both thinking good-riddance, Yorgi was out cutting the lawn around the house on Glenwood Drive. Springtime in Illinois, after a mild winter. Tiny new leaves on the trees.

Shirtless, in shorts, wearing an old Cubs baseball cap, he looked like a taupe orangutan, following the noisy Honda around. New damp grass clippings sticking to his ankles, he would have been happy to cut all the other lawns on the block. It had been a long time. No guards with semiautomatic rifles; no Cyclone fencing and concertina wire.

About ten-thirty, he went inside the house, into the kitchen, seeing lifeless Kathy at the table in a pink robe, fingertips on the *Trib*. "You see this about Guido?"

"Heard it on TV while you were still asleep."

"Guido never liked you, did he?"

Yorgi said that was true. Never did. He was always jealous.

Kathy said, "I feel sorry for his mother, just the same."

"So do I."

"Shall we send her some flowers?" Kathy asked.

"Yeah, a big, big bouquet. Lotsa roses."

"Will you go to the funeral?"

Yorgi shook his head. Donati's would be swarming with cops and cameras. "Just the bouquet."

Kathy nodded.

She knew, he believed. Or at least she'd guessed that he'd gone to see Guido. But she'd never asked many questions about what he did and where he went. She wouldn't start now.

There was a glass of clear liquid, ice cubes in it, on the table near the *Trib*.

Booze, Yorgi suspected. So early in the day. All the more reason to get to the Caribbean and back home.

The girl at the travel agency on East Ogden was saying, "We can put you out nonstop Monday afternoon to Miami, with a connection to San Juan. But you'll have to overnight, connect Tuesday morning to Eastern's Metro for St. Thomas."

"Why can't I get out Sunday morning?" Yorgi asked.

The girl glanced at the computer screen again and shook her head. "Fully booked Sunday, same for Monday morning. Carnival time down there, you know."

"What's that?" Yorgi asked.

"Don't you read the travel sections?"

"Nope."

"Like Mardi Gras in New Orleans, like the big one they have in Rio. Fun time."

"Oh."

"That's the best we can do. Out of O'Hare Monday at three fifty-five."

"Okay. Where do I stay in San Juan?"

"I'd suggest the airport hotel. The first Metro takes off at nine. Let me check the bookings." She punched the computer and studied it. "I can get you on the noon Metro."

"Okay," said Yorgi.

"Which credit card?"

"Cash."

The girl laughed. "First one of those in a long time. Name, please."

"Frank Jennings. You spell Jennings like the TV guy." He used to watch Peter Jennings and the ABC Nightly News at Carson City on the portable Tony bought for him.

The girl nodded and went about completing the transaction. In less than ten minutes, Yorgi walked out of the travel agency, round-trip ticket to St. Thomas, returning Saturday, in his pocket. The parole officer wouldn't even know.

3.

HE PACKED LIGHTLY, some typical tourist clothes for an old skinny gray-bearded duffer in green pants, wearing a green porkpie; two long-sleeved shirts to hide the hair on his arms. The Beretta was carefully rolled up in wadded paper and duct tape, an extra X-acto, his favorite knife, with five blades, was underneath the shirts.

It took him a while to write his note:

> Dear Kathy,
>
> I know this is a surprise, but I have a little leftover out-of-town business to do. I'll be back Saturday. Don't worry about me.
>
> > Your loving brother,
> > Yorgos

He boarded the DC-10 for San Juan, sitting in no-smoking economy class, the Beretta safely down in the luggage compartment, checked through. There were still no X-ray machines for hold luggage.

Economy was customary for Yorgi. In that other life as Yorgi Greco his only luxury had been clothing, always first class. Smart blazers, gray slacks, leather tassels on his shoes, two-hundred-dollar hats.

The DC-10 arrowed on toward San Juan, above the clouds.

"That's where you were last night? With *him*?"

"Mama, I can sleep with whomever I want to sleep with. When and where I please. Last night, tonight, tomorrow night. I don't know why I have to say it, but I'm twenty-seven years old. I'm a big girl! I don't have to ask your permission." Molly knew that daughters had been saying the same thing for five thousand years and never winning.

"But Epp Watts is a black," said Chaktri, making a face.

"I keep saying he's no blacker than I am, and you married one."

"A mistake," said Chaktri, dark eyes angry.

They were in the kitchen of the big house in Estate Neltjeberg, across the island from Charlotte Amalie. Molly had her hands on her hips, facing her mother. Though she was sixty-one years old, there was still a kind of beauty in Chaktri's face.

She'd never told Molly why she chose to marry Tom Bodden, the Creole, instead of someone her own kind from Debal or Penal, places where all the East Indians lived. But from that day on, she was an outcast, lower than the lowest, worse than anyone from Mangalore who came to work the Trinidad canefields.

Molly thought her mother still suffered from being an outcast.

"Mama, I don't want to keep fighting about this. It upsets me. You have to understand you can't pick out my men."

Chaktri didn't back down. "He's the one who got you into all that trouble."

"That isn't so, Mama. I've said it again and again. Epp didn't get me into any trouble. I did that myself. *He tried to help me get out of trouble.*"

Chaktri closed her ears, as usual. "There are other nice men of our kind."

What kind was that? All the Hindus? Molly sighed. "I've had a long day. I'm going up to take a hot bath, then we'll have a quiet dinner."

Just the two of them shared the big house they had moved into only seven months earlier. Nedley, now twenty-two, was a senior at Florida State. Molly had provided money from Paris so Nedley could have a good education.

Chaktri Bodden also remembered Yorgos Stathos, the man who had sent her daughter running to France, but she seldom thought of him. In the last year, since Molly had returned, she had thought much more about the nigger Epp Watts and how to get rid of him.

Neither had Epp forgotten Yorgos Stathos, a.k.a. Joe Carlucci, Nikolas Katsanis. More often than Molly Bodden, Epp thought of Yorgos Stathos. Subconsciously, every time he took a step he thought of the goddamn Greek.

He and Detective Lieutenant Laburnum Hotchkiss came into Ben Bottle's this same early evening. Laburnum was on a year's leave of absence from the St. Thomas force, but had been recalled for Carnival week.

Conkie, Ben Bottle's bartender, went to work on their usuals: Laburnum, a Molson on the rocks, and Epp, white rum and guava juice, as near to a health drink as he could get, guava having low sodium and a hundred-percent Vitamin C.

Epp said, "Conkie, congratulate us. We found Johnny Freedman's boat out at Pelican Cay this afternoon." Nice Charlie was sitting by Epp's stool, a hundred and ten pounds of Rottweiler, tongue dripping. The *Suzy Dee* was safely back in her slip at the Yacht Haven Marina, minus a windscreen and with some 5.56mm Bullpup damage on the after-end of her main cabin.

"You did? Congratulations. I thought that boat'd be long an' gone by now." Conkie was from Red Wing, Minnesota, a low-breasted beanpole, on nights at Ben's the past two years.

"Should have been."

Laburnum said, "Guess who grabbed it?"

Conkie turned her long neck. "Couple of Puerto Ricans from Vieques. They are wild and crazy over there."

"Not even close. Couple of West German blondes 'bout your age." Conkie was thirty. "One's in the hospital with multiple facial wounds. Other one's in the jailhouse, *no sprechen zie English.*"

"You're kidding," she said, setting the drinks down. She hadn't been out of a low-vee blouse, short-shorts and sandals since arriving from Red Wing, recuperating from a divorce and too many blizzards. She was living with a black guy out near the college, which made her one of the crowd at Ben Bottle's, more or less. "They stole that big boat? By themselves?"

"Wasn't anyone else on board," Laburnum said.

"They were going to take it back to Germany?" She was astonished.

Epp said, "No, Conkie. No, no. It's my guess they were going out about fifty miles to pick up a quarter ton of high-grade coke, take it on north. The great Atlantic relay."

"Just the two girls?"

Laburnum nodded.

"A lot of money they'd get?"

"An awful lot," Epp said. "Two hundred fifty thousand."

Laburnum smiled. "But they'll go to the correctional institute for ladies in Miami. Lose their tans."

Conkie cocked her head over. "You know, I got to admire them. Come all the way over here just to do that."

Another customer slid up, and Conkie gave him her usual wide-mouthed Minnesota smile.

An old house near the foot or head of Droningen's Gade, depending on which way you come into Charlotte Amalie—airport or east end of the island—Ben's was at the foot of Bluebeard's Hill, mostly local, not appealing much to tourists unless they were looking for quaint spots. The first-floor bar tended to be raunchy, and upstairs Ben served whelks and bullfoot stew, conch fritters and kallaloo, opening at eleven and closing anywhere up to four A.M., depending on the bar trade.

Yorgi stared out at the clouds. The pilot had just said they were crossing over Florida, more than halfway to Puerto Rico.

In another vivid dream in Carson City, Molly Bodden had been a hooker, wearing short-shorts and a halter, in parrot colors.

They were in a tropical bar, with a big tank of all kinds of fish right behind them. Fish a couple of feet long like you saw in aquariums.

He remembered asking her why she was hooking when she'd swiped all of his money.

She'd just laughed and laughed and laughed, then turned around and dove into the tank, making faces at him with fish lips, mocking him.

He'd grabbed a bar stool to smash the glass, but suddenly the tank wasn't there.

He couldn't wait to see her. Couldn't wait.

Epp was now Marine Search, Inc., an insurance-company endeavor doing business from Grand Bahama Island all the way to Trinidad, listed in the Vitelco yellow pages between Investigations, Unlimited, in Old Tramway, Amalie, and Security Dogs, of St. Croix, Christiansted, theft always being a problem in the islands. By now, seven companies were paying him to trace floating boats, blown-up boats or otherwise sunken boats; then turn evidence of any malfeasance over to prosecutors, meanwhile holding up policy payments.

Epp gulped half the rum and guava, ordering another. He was wearing shorts and sandals, exposing painted toenails—a little fun for Carnival—and a faded T-shirt that said Sebastian's, a waterfront bar of yore. He had on prescription shades that lightened indoors and a long-billed khaki cap that had STPS—St. Thomas Power Squadron—on it in faded gold letters. Super Bowl ring on his left hand, he'd converted to being a boatman instead of a developer: now thirty-three years old, fitting nicely into the body of a retired AFC wide receiver. The knee that reminded "Fingers" Watts of Yorgos Stathos wasn't flexible, and he walked with a cane some of the time. Married and divorced, four-year-old son Jeff was up in Philly with his mother.

Laburnum Hotchkiss now had crinkly white around his temples, mustache milky too, striking touches against the cave black of his skin. "Big week for Molly, I guess," he said.

"Listen, she's had nothing but big weeks since she opened. Says she's looking for a million gross this year. She did almost two hundred thousand for what time she was open last year."

"That's what happens when you appeal to the rich," Laburnum said. "How are you getting along with the mother?"

"Chaktri?" Epp's laugh was low and sour. "She still blames me for what happened to Molly. Still does."

"How could she do that?"

"Getting dotty in her old age. Still has it in her head that everything bad happened after I persuaded Molly to go to the police."

Laburnum looked over at Epp's face. "She wouldn't have needed to go to the police if she hadn't gone out with the Greek in the first place."

Epp shrugged. "She had her reasons. Anyway, Chaktri thinks I'm below their class. That's the real problem. She wants Molly to get hooked up with one of the Boolchands or that Jireh guy who owns West Indies Linens. She wants a Hindu for Molly."

Laburnum scoffed, "Molly'll go with whom she wants to go."

"Don't dare tell that to Chaktri."

The Coast Guard had better things to do than chase stolen boats, and Epp had persuaded Laburnum to try being a partner. The job usually required more than one man. Ten months to go before his leave from the Department of Public Safety was over, Laburnum was trying to decide whether or not to retire on twenty and go home to Basse Terre on St. Kitts, a quieter place, or work permanently with Epp. He still went to the office several times a week to nose around.

Epp had stumbled into this boat-search business when a fan spotted him at the bar in the Hotel 1829 and they began talking about Joe Namath and Kenny Stabler and Roger Staubach, guys of Epp's times. After a while the Allstate exec said, "Epp, we could use someone like you down here. We just paid out a million seven for a steel Kong and Halvorsen. Hundred thirty feet, five thousand cruising range, helipad. Where do you hide that much boat?"

The Allstate exec said three percent of the appraised value plus expenses if he found the Kong and Halvorsen and got it into an American or friendly port. Even checking out rumors it was last seen in Havana harbor, Epp didn't find it. But he had found five others during the past fifteen months, making a nice hundred twenty-two thousand. He'd only had trouble twice. Once in Hurricane Hole at St. Martin and then at Nevis. That's why he'd bought a Valmet Bullpup. The bastards on the other side were using automatic rifles. Dope haulers just didn't care. He had also gotten a license for a standard-issue .38, four-inch barrel.

"It works like this," he had told Laburnum two months ago. "I get a call from Allstate or Lloyd's or New York Mutual saying a boat's been ripped off at Martinique or San Juan or Nassau. Or local. They give me particulars, fax me a photo and I'm off. If it's anywhere but here, say Nassau, I check around up there, check out the anchorages in the Bahamas. Go over to Miami, Fort Lauderdale. Usually someone's seen the boat. Or you get a guy who burns his Grand Banks, or blows it up for insurance, I hire an arson man."

"And you always get a percentage?"

"Each one is different. Less expensive boat we may get ten percent."

There was a low, hurt cry from across the room and Conkie said, "Oh, damn," as Laburnum and Epp looked over to a table in the corner. A big straw-hatted guy—big-shouldered, big-necked, ham-fisted—was sitting there with a dark-haired girl cradling her head in her arms. Her shoulders said she was crying.

Conkie said, "That's the second time he's slapped her. I told him he'd have to leave if he did it again. Damn rum punches. They've had four doubles."

He *was* a big one, Epp saw, looking steel-mill type rather than redneck cracker.

Conkie sighed. "Husbands and wives, the battle eternal, I should know," she said, coming out from behind the bar to go over and

211

request a swift departure. Evening star time, usually a mellow time at Ben Bottle's, there were less than a dozen patrons.

Epp heard Conkie ask the big man, quite nicely, to depart and then heard him reply, distinctly, for her to go to hell and mind her own business.

Epp said to Laburnum, "You're the arm o' the law here, you going to ask him to leave peacefully?"

Laburnum shook his head. "Nope. I'm off-duty. And I well know that the worst thing a cop can do is get into a male-female fight. Never worth it."

Epp said, "I'm disappointed in you. Conkie said the man hit her."

"Some deserve to be hit."

"You ever hit yours?"

"I've thought about it."

Epp shook his head. He had been in bars where customers picked on football players, actually wanted to fight a linebacker or a two-eighty-pound defensive guard. Crazy.

Conkie, knowing who was belly-up at the bar this night, reserve troops, said loudly, "You are not going to stay in here and keep slapping your wife. Do you understand that?" She was planted in front of the customer, hands on her hips, looking brave but so skinny she might blow away.

"Fuck off," the man said to Conkie, causing his wife to raise her head.

Epp saw that she was hurt. The right side of her face was red, blood leaking from the corner of her mouth.

Epp got up slowly, sighing just as loud as Conkie had sighed, saying to Lieutenant Hotchkiss, "Some police force we have here, off-duty or not."

Laburnum's grin widened. "You are so right."

Epp said, "I'm doin' this for Conkie."

Using his cane, he limped over to stand beside her and said politely in his best West Indian, so the customer would realize where he was on the globe (—do not screw around with the restless natives): "Mon, de nice ladee 'as osked yu to leave dis bar . . ."

Nice Charlie had padded over, too, and was sitting by Epp's shoes, loving eyes on Epp.

The customer, maybe from Gary, Indiana, or Wheeling, West Virginia, glared up at the high yellow with the prescription shades and STPS cap, ignoring N.C. Then he saw the painted toenails.

"Butt out, fag."

Wheeling was just drunk enough to be daring, Epp thought. He glanced over at Laburnum Hotchkiss, who was laughing heartily, enjoying this special moment at Ben Bottle's.

Epp shook his head again at what he had suddenly gotten into, laid his cane down, then grabbed two mugs from the adjoining table, spilling what was left of cold beer into Wheeling and Gary's ample lap, chopping expertly and swiftly with them on the table's edge, leaving in his hands jagged edges of thick glass.

Epp had encountered so much hand-to-hand combat on football fields that he earnestly tried to avoid it in retirement. He tried not to tackle or wrestle or punch *anyone* anymore. He never had a desire to be a hero, dating back to Bakersfield.

N.C. arose from his sitting position.

Hearing Laburnum guffawing over on his stool, breaking up, Epp said, laying it on thick, "Cop'n, leave peaceable 'less yu want to go home wit' haf a face . . ."

The big slag man stared at the glass knucks, as shining and wicked as crosscut blades, looked at the dog, and decided he'd had enough of Ben Bottle's after all. He jerked his wife up, hearing Epp say, "Easy, mon," and they staggered out of the door.

Conkie, watching them depart, said. "He'll probably beat her up on the way back to the hotel."

Epp looked over at his partner. "Yeh, you ought to tail them, Laburnum, find out where they're staying and send a car over."

"You do such a good job intimidating, Epp. That man'll remember you until he dies."

Conkie, coming down from fright, going behind the bar, said "You sure do a good job, Epp. I've never seen that one before. Glass knucks. What'll I do with them?"

213

Laburnum suggested hanging them over the bar, like baby booties. Something to talk about.

Epp went over to sit down again, N.C. padding behind, Conkie saying the next drink was on the house for everybody, Epp thinking what a lousy way to end a nice and profitable day, having no idea that Yorgos Stathos was coming to town.

4.

THE AIRPORT HOTEL at San Juan International was in the main terminal, built in the fifties, not on the periphery, and planes went right through it. Seven-forty-sevens and DC10s, landing and taking off, came through the walls.

Brain in a turmoil, rapid eye movement in his good one going off the chart, the other one staring straight at the ceiling, Yorgi was dreaming again, body jerking as if he were taking shock treatment.

He was running across the room with her, and he had her up in the air, kicking and clawing, screaming, one hand gripping the back of her neck, the other under her legs; as he got to the window he shot-putted her out.

Just as the glass shattered, a 747 whined by, the two sounds mingling, and Yorgi awakened, panting and in confusion. He sat up, breathing hard. Was that Molly or the college-girl hooker in Dallas he'd just thrown out? The room was so dim.

He didn't sleep for a while, listening to the jets.

He awakened early, thinking of Molly Bodden again, and went to the john. The next thing he did, even before brushing his teeth, was unwind the wrapping around the Beretta to check and load it.

Over in St. Thomas, across the blue water and coral reefs, festivities had begun the previous night at Carnival Village and the smell of crab and rice, chicken legs, roti and conch lingered in the cool air over the Fort Christian parking lot. Calypso and soca would start pouring out of the booths at eleven. Molly was probably still asleep.

Sitting naked on the bed, Yorgi wondered if she'd recognize him now. She wouldn't be able to see the metha-something eye behind the big dark glasses; couldn't see the cheek scar behind the thick

215

gray beard. Maybe the ears, those pie-crust leftovers from taking punches, she'd recognize. Maybe the hammered nose? The body she wouldn't know, with all the weight loss, twenty-five pounds of it.

Minutes ago, the bathroom mirror had told him he was naturally disguised as a grizzled, stringy old man, one of those baldies you could see in country-club locker rooms, towels around their waists and knobby knees, talking about the stock market and cholesterol.

She'd have to think about it a while to connect cleanshaven Joe Carlucci or Yorgos Stathos to this skinny old duffer about to arrive on her island.

How many times had she seen him? He sat with the gun on his lap and counted them: night she played roulette and cut his eye. Night in the desert when she'd shot him and robbed him. The snowy morning in Atlantic City when she'd led him into Caesar's. The day in court in Las Vegas. All more than eight years ago.

She'd seen him enough but never looking this way. She'd have to think quite a while to make the connection.

Because she still felt a lot of guilt over involving Epp, having his career destroyed, she'd only talked with him about Joe Carlucci on one occasion since returning to the island.

They had been in the single table alcove at the Hotel 1829, a table set aside for romantics, about four months after she came home last year, celebrating the opening of Molly's of St. Thomas. Local girl makes good. TV cameras were there when the lieutenant governor cut the big red ribbon across the door. Champagne and flowers.

"You know, just in the middle of it all this afternoon I turned around and there was a man looking at me, and I could have sworn for a second or two that it was *him*. My heart flew out of my mouth, Epp. I almost collapsed. But then I realized it wasn't him. I ran into the backroom to pull myself together. My heart was pounding. Same old thing."

"You still think of him?"

She nodded. "At the damndest times."

"I do, but in a different way. I get angry at myself that I can't move around the way I used to. Then I blame it on him. No reason for him to shoot me that day."

"For more than a year I was looking around at the faces in the front row. There I was at the Lido, knowing he was in prison, yet I was searching the audience. It was like I was back at the Stardust."

"You ever wonder about him getting out? I mean whether or not he'll come after you again?"

Her answer took a while. "Yes."

"He could have changed."

"But maybe he hasn't changed. He qualifies as the original jumbi."

"I have to confess something," Epp said. "I called Nishgo in December, asked him to find out if the Greek was still at Carson City, whether or not they had parole plans. He laughed about it, saying Stathos was a thousand scums in the past. But he called back the next day. Still in the pokey, he said, and the parole board didn't have him scheduled. I said, 'Let me know,' and Nishgo said, 'Get that out of your mind.'"

"Get what out of your mind?" Molly asked.

"Oh, I talked to him while I was still in the hospital and said I wanted to do a few things to Stathos."

"Do you still want to do them?"

"Every so often."

Molly nodded.

Epp said, "Well, let's not think about the son of a bitch tonight." He lifted his glass of Dom Perignon to say, "To the world's greatest dress designer and to the opening of her new shop."

Yet there were constant reminders to Molly, not the least of which was Epp moving along on his cane, housed in a magnificent body except for one part. And Molly had put it on her own mental calendar to call Nishgo, or Agostino, in a few months, check on the prisoner, see what his status was. If they said he'd probably be getting out in a year or so, she didn't know how she'd handle it. Go back to Paris? Still, she couldn't run all her life.

In January, on a trip to San Juan, she'd bought two Colt Ace .22 automatics and had been going to the pistol range at the old sub base twice a week ever since. One gun at home; the other in the big bag she always carried. The notion of self-defense involved more than the possibility of a visit from Joe Carlucci. She was now a wealthy woman on an island that was still mostly poor.

She hadn't told Epp about the guns.

One of the most spectacular views on St. Thomas, and there were several, was Molly Bodden's body, and Epp was happily observing it at sunrise. No coverlet was needed; the breeze blowing over the house on the hill was summer warm, smelling of wild ginger, jasmine and Pagoda tree.

Molly wasn't a long distance away, just arm's length, facing him on the king-sized bed, sleeping innocently, head resting on the right bicep, shining black hair fanned out, left arm loose across the rib cage, hiding just enough of her breasts to make a painter clap with joy. Epp always appreciated the light and shadow of her, the taut skin, glacial smooth curves, curly dark patch beneath her flat belly. All of it very watchable and lovely at dawn. It was mature beauty after the years in Paris.

Down at Ducey's flower stand on Torve Strade: "Well, I'll take a red rose for my Miss Slimness." Flown down from Miami.

"Epp, that'll be five dollah."

"Nevah mind."

He was courting again, divorce from the lady in Philadelphia two years behind, after five years of hell. Living down here he didn't see little Jeff too often. What do you do? The judge granted her custody. *He was courting again.*

"If Epp and Molly came down the outside aisles in that dining room at Frenchman's Reef, opposite each other, singing in duet like Brazzi and Mitzi Gaynor in *South Pacific*, the whole damn place would blow up, believe me," said Laburnum Hotchkiss.

Laburnum thought they were meant for each other.

For six months, Epp had been saying earnestly to her, "Marry me, Molly, marry me," and she kept answering, "I can't, Epp. I just can't. Not now."

Epp couldn't figure it out, except for old Chaktri. What the hell to do with Chaktri?

Light had begun to widen and Epp checked his watch. Six-ten Wednesday. Four days of Carnival left. Let her sleep another ten minutes and then caress her out of whatever warm, dark tunnel she was occupying.

Ten minutes had passed. It was time.

Epp took another long look at Miss Slimness and reached over to go roundy-roundy on a pink-brown nipple with his thumb.

Molly came out of her tunnel slowly, breathing deeply, as Epp watched. Eyes opened, then shut again. She rolled over on her back, sighing, still wanting sleep, still needing it.

Tongue came out, like lizard tongue, lick bottom lip, disappear quickly.

Epp laughed, thinking lizard.

He murmured, "Marnin' 'tis Tuesday." Like Molly, he spoke Indies when the mood struck him.

She *had* to wake up.

He was about four, he thought, when Papa and Thready took him to his first Carnival, in the late fifties, five years after it was revived. On a barge pulled by a tug with a lot of other St. Cruzians aboard. Memories, vague ones: sleeping in the sand for three nights, getting bug bites. Men in donkey hides. All the older people, including Papa and Thready, getting drunk. Wasn't any J'ouvert then, following the bands up the street. In the big parade back then there were "fungi" bands and "scratch bands" and "pan" bands. All smaller, all simpler. He thought he liked it better than now.

"Days o' Carnival always collide, always a little or a lot drunk, hard to tell today from yesterday," said Laburnum in another of his wisdoms. Going on too long now, he said. Actually started on Palm Sunday six weeks ago, but it was just fits and starts until the last two weeks. Well and good for the reverends at Frederik's Lutheran to remind the pews Sunday past that it had started with the Church of Rome and *Carne Vale*, "farewell to the flesh," a final Satanic fling before lenten. But what had begun in Trinidad in the middle 1800s had nothing to do with any Pope of Rome. It had to do with high times for freed slaves, rum and jig-jig. Since then, drumbeats and calypso kings called the faithful home to have fun, and it had nothing to do with the church.

Molly, eyes still closed, said, "I need another hour."

Epp knew she planned to close shop over the weekend, but cruise ships were coming in today at the West Indies Company Dock, tethered nose to tail, looking like great horizontal dead-white skyscrapers, with red stacks. *Daphne* at seven, *Sun Princess* and *Cunard Countess* at eight. Two more he couldn't remember. Five or six altogether. Three thousand tourists shuffling ashore, spending it. Visa and Mastercharge plates getting hot.

She had to get up.

"I'll go squeeze some oranges," he said, massaging her shoulders, working around the base of her long neck, then letting his plotting hands drift down to the nipples. They bloomed, almost instantly.

"Uhm," she replied, eyes opening again, head turned slightly toward him.

Dark eyes, always seeming to go behind his own, seeing what was there, or what wasn't there. Warm and gentle eyes. But he'd seen them go from amusement to rage in a flash. She could be electric.

"You need help down there today? I can stay in the backroom an' wrap."

Molly shook her head, still looking at him, examining him, maybe thinking what he was thinking. They'd come in late from the congressman's party, had gone to one other party before that. Tired, barely kissing, falling asleep quickly. She said, slowly and thoughtfully, "They all come to work the next three days they get a bonus." Work, of *any* kind, was always a problem during Carnival.

Epp shrugged, using his thumbs to gently stroke the swollen nipples. Then there was a responsive tug in his groin and he gorged, hard as he'd ever be.

Molly smiled lazily, reaching for him, saying, "Why don't we brush our teeth, swish some mouthwash, then you help me take a shower." They'd had some memorable showers. Miss Slimness got up on her hands and knees, a very erotic pose whether she knew it or not. More light and shadow. Make one helluva jigsaw puzzle.

Epp grinned. "Grand idea," he declared, following her off the bed and into the bathroom, which had a six-by-six sunken tub, with a sea view.

N.C. sat up, batting at the side of his head with a rear paw. Ancestor of the Hatzruden, droving dogs and boar hunters in the old country, N.C. was the perfect companion for Epp. But Epp wasn't quite sure he needed all that protection. Yet he liked the idea of a one-man dog. He'd gotten him shortly after returning to the islands.

Day had begun on the hill overlooking the sea.

The long view from Epp's house was almost as spectacular as the waterbed view of Molly Bodden. He'd designed the front of the three-bedroom house—one for a guest, another for his boy when Priscilla was kind enough to let little Jeff visit—with glass doors opening to the wraparound veranda. From the bathroom, living room, dining room, kitchen and master bedroom he could look down into Bovoni Bay and straight out to the Capella Islands; looking southeast he could see Cas Cay, Little St. James and part of big St. James. Even the office, where Epp kept the insurance company business, plus some game balls, photos and three scrap-books, had a tiny view. Sometimes low-flying clouds would smother the house, then lift to reveal blue sea clear to the horizon, sun dazzling it. The house was a gift to himself after Priscilla's divorce. Glass, metal and imported wood. You didn't build houses on St. Thomas out of banyan or Pink Piou or frangipani. Everything had to be barged in. Nice enough house, though, for a middle-aged retired football jock, now in the boat insurance business.

While Molly was dressing, Epp came in with the juice, and she said, "I do need some help, after all. Meet the noon Metro and bring a lady named Sarah Levy to the shop."

"Who's she?"

The juice went down in a gulp. "Writer for *Women's Wear Daily.* She wants all my secrets."

"Don't give 'em away, sell 'em."

"What she really wants is an excuse to come to Carnival. I doubt she'll even interview me. I met her in Paris at a fashion show two years ago."

"I be nice to her? Make sure you get a good story."

"Nice? However you choose. She's mid-forties, dumpy, and talks like she has a tin larynx."

Epp smiled. "I choose to be polite."

Molly sashayed across the room, smelling fresh and wonderful, tweaked his crotch, pecked a kiss and was gone.

Epp whistled for N.C. and the Hatzruden *hund* came skidding out of the living room, losing traction on the tiles, going sideways, automatically heading for the back door. He always looked so pitiful, so sad-eyed, almost collapsing when left behind. Dogs did get lonely, according to Barbara Woodhouse.

N.C. jumped into the seat of the red Safari as if he owned it.

Droningen's Gade, Queen Street, as the historical purists insisted, was sure to be like the runways at Yankee Stadium two minutes after a game was over. Cruise ships had begun dumping tourists ashore since before nine. They always descended on the shops in the old terra-cotta warehouses like hungry cattle at a feeding trough, grazing on free-ported Patek Phillipe and Huer watches, Wedgewood and Royal Doulton china, Mats Johansen and Waterford crystal, Greek gold by Ilias LaLounis.

Except to come down and see Molly once daily, Epp stayed well away from the restored brick-and-stone arches, the uncovered floors of Italian tile and Spanish marble and the glassy-eyed shoppers.

Getting lucky, he found a parking space at the Federal Building, telling N.C. to stay put, walking on across to Carnival Village. Ten-fifty A.M., plenty of time before the plane got in with Miss Levy.

He'd look around the Village, find Laburnum, combine breakfast with lunch.

Ah, *Carh-nee-vahl*, the way the West Indians said it, slowly, reaching way down for the long vowels, here it was in all its joyful craziness. You had to go with it. *Mon, yu dance, yu sing, yu drink.*

But Epp wasn't in the mood this morning, and didn't know why. For one thing, his knee ached. He'd tried to jog a little the previous day. More than that, a feeling of uncertainty. "Wata boilin' foh feesh an' feesh don' know," Thready would say. One didn't know what was in store.

The Village had the usual ride concessions and thirty or forty booths. Churches, one association or another; private sellers. Calypso singers and steel bands at night, competing with the ride noises. Nightly band tramps from Emancipation Park up to Market Square. Mos' people color o' coffee and all its shades, all talkin' at once. That was Carnival.

"Hey, Epp, how yu doin'?"

"Okay, mon."

"Accurate gonna win Friday?"

"Dat hoss needs a long, long res', Clemence," Epp said, with a laugh. Races Friday at Clinton Phipps Park. Accurate had won last year.

Among the heads he saw was the distinguished one belonging to Laburnum Hotchkiss, and he began working his way through the crowd toward it. Summoned back to temporary duty for Carnival, he was drifting around town, from place to place.

Epp finally got to him, saying, "You busy already?"

Laburnum muttered, "Along with the pickpockets," nodding off toward one of St. Thomas's finest holding a cuffed white kid. "American Express, don't leave home without it."

Laburnum was wearing a coat and tie, as usual. Naturalized a long time ago, pledging to Uncle Sam forever, that impeccable Thames accent had gotten him into trouble now and then. Uppity Limey black cop. But a superior one.

A lot of tourists thought the St. Thomas force was rinky-dink, but all the law enforcement people had been trained in Florida and

Quantico. The police mobile crime laboratory sitting out in the Department of Public Safety lot didn't come from Woolworth's and the detectives weren't mail order.

He had his choice of tender conch on a bed of peas and rice or conch with creole sauce. He took the peas and rice.

5.

AS THE METRO PROP-JET commuter droned at low altitude toward St. Thomas over sparkling blue waters and whitewashed reefs, Yorgi was again remembering that final humiliation on a morning the complete opposite of this one, when she'd led him into the pack of hard hats.

Thinking of the unheard laughter from Peppitone's and Bolla's, out on Rush Street, when they read stories about Yorgi Greco being hog-tied by construction workers, he felt a redness in his face this many years later. Laughter around the world, tough guy winding up on his ass, five plaster nails in his chest, wrapped in electric wire. Even Johnny Carson, his favorite, had his little joke about it, he'd heard.

He looked out at the water through the small window and began to hum, almost reaching the level of the engine noise. Soon, the passenger scrunched-up in the seat next to him studied Yorgi with alarm, moving his body away, leaning out into the narrow aisle.

Sharp left turn and Epp headed for the terminal, which didn't look much different than when Harry Truman was alive: jumbo three-story Quonset-type hangar, World War II camouflage still bleeding through. What had changed was the runway, lengthened out to sea to avoid a nasty hill to the east. Now, medium-sized jets could land.

Epp parked, not needing to tell N.C. to be vigilant, and went toward the porters. Even in high season, December to March, they had tough times. Most worked two jobs, when they worked at all, like a lot of other people on the island. The glitter was surface.

Hardeen said, "Afternoon, me chile, how tis? Gotta mawney-mon comin' in?"

Thirty-three birthdays passed, it was always satisfying to be called a child. "Who's foolin' who today? Indeed, I have. Money-woman."

Beacom laughed, saying, "I keep oskin' yu need a boy hep wit de wark. An assisss-tant carry de camera, open de dorr, mix de drinks." Hardeen and Beacom had the strangest idea about what he did for a living.

Epp laughed back. "Mon, I barely stay alive me-self." He began walking ahead, on past Hertz and Avis and the duty-free booze pickup stand, hearing Hardeen shout, "Tell de money-wohman 'bout my tour . . ." Hardeen had five kids.

"That I will," said Epp over his shoulder, moving steadily toward the other end of the terminal, moving with grace on a tall man's big feet, graceful even with the cane, sparkling white Panama on his head and red lacquer on his toenails, courtesy of Miss Suzy in the beauty parlor of Frenchman's Reef. He'd helped Miss Suzy collect infant support, better and quicker than the court. He'd just said, "Pay up, shit-heel." The rest of him was in cool white cotton, immaculate as a just-bathed nun. No gold chains around his neck. Only the Super Bowl ring for decoration. To get that off would take a hatchet and six strong men.

Going on outside, he stood in the shade while the little Metro settled to the runway, turning briskly back, parking to unload several hundred feet from the terminal entrance. Epp took a few steps out into the sun, shading his eyes, as the passengers got off, mostly in pairs, and began walking toward the old building.

Three unpaired men led the way: a pudgy black guy, a scrawny Latino-type with specs, and a gray-bearded tourist in a long-sleeved white shirt and pastel green slacks, green porkpie. Suddenly, there she was, dumpy and mid-forties, as Molly had said.

He stepped up, lifting his Panama, nodding lightly. "Miz Levy?"

She answered in nasal Brooklynese and Epp said he was Miz Bodden's driver, welcoming her to St. Thomas. Free rum and coconut-milk drink just inside the terminal, if that was her pleasure;

if she'd give him her baggage checks, he'd take care of that task, too. Miz Bodden was sorry she couldn't do the welcoming herself but six tour ships were in. . . . Prim little mouth pursed, Epp realized she was gawking at his toenails, and laughed. "Gives my feet some personality, at last." They'd been stepped on ever since high school. "You been here before?" He planned to let the lacquer die a natural death.

"A long time ago."

"We're at peak now. Carnival all this week. We'll go up in smoke Saturday night. Big fireworks show."

Miss Levy said, unsmiling, "I thought you'd be black. She said her driver . . ."

Epp grinned. "Oh, you're disappointed. I've got some crow in me but it doesn't show too much. Born in St. Croix . . ."

"You don't speak in a dialect."

Epp kept on grinning. "I do when I choose. Monkey know wha' tree toh clime . . ." Epp expected her to laugh, but she didn't.

Barely touching her elbow, the red-toed driver all in white steered her through the terminal. She didn't look happy.

At the baggage claim, Epp passed the checks to Hardeen, noticing the gray-bearded man standing off to the side, waiting for his luggage. Epp had the strange feeling he'd seen him somewhere before. But on second look, he was like all the other cold-country tourists, forehead pale from lack of sun. Guy in his fifties, come down from Boston for roas-a-time.

Reflect Our Pas' in a Super Mas'.

Epp gave Hardeen three dollars to carry the brown bag and briefcase over to the Safari, maybe a hundred feet, telling Nice Charlie to jump into the rear seat. "He doesn't have many fleas," Epp guaranteed.

Miss Levy said, "I'm riding with a dog?" Her frown was dark and stormy.

"'Fraid so," said Epp, smiling widely. "I take him ebrywhere I go. At which hotel are you staying?"

"Grand Wyndham."

New one on the other side of the island. First class.

"Molly said bring you by the shop first."
Miss Levy sighed.

Almost immediately, he'd recognized the man with the Panama on his head—that football player he'd shot in the knee in Atlantic City—the one the sports pages had moaned and groaned about. So he couldn't play for the Raiders anymore. So what. Well, he was in the wrong place at the wrong time. Tough potatoes. Yorgi looked away and walked on into the terminal, renting a Toyota under the name of Nikolas Katsanis while waiting for his luggage. That name had been out of circulation for a long while.

The girl at Budget asked where he'd be staying.

"Tropic Isles Villas."

Then she penciled in a route on the St. Thomas map—which included an ad for Molly's, he noted—to take him there: along the Charlotte Amalie waterfront, then on to the Bolongo Bay condos. They were recommended by the barber from Sicily.

The girl said, "You got here jus' in time. Carnival Village with all the booths an' rides an' music started yesterday. Comin' up is Brass-O-Rama, Food Fair, Calypso Tent and J'ouvert, when all the ban's tramp. Then the big parade Saturday. A lot o' activity, Mister Katsanis."

Yorgi nodded, humming softly.

He couldn't wait to get his first look at Molly Bodden after eight-plus years.

Grinding along in heavy stop-start traffic on Veteran's Drive, Epp said, "The faithful come back to the island for Carnival from everywhere—New York, Chicago, even London. Then we get a big crowd from St. Croix, St. John. Ebrybody come, have fun."

Miss Levy sat there as if she had concrete slurp in her arteries. So Epp decided to take it to her.

"Not much goin' on today, but day after tomorrow is Food Fair. You might like the bull-foot soup or kallaloo. That's jus' gumbo. Salt meat, feesh, coupla crabs, okra n' mixed greens. Lil' vinegar so it don' look slimy."

Epp glanced over. Miss Levy's face was still full of stone. "White folks not much into kallaloo. Now, souse you use the pig head not the feet."

That didn't raise her. "Mebbe you got a sweet tooth? Candied tamarind interest you? Tie-tie sugar cake? Boiya pasteries? Mango on the stick? Wash 'em down with maubi."

Miss Levy glanced back at Nice Charlie and shifted around in her seat.

"Tonight may be of interest to you. We got calypso—Mighty Sparrow up from Trinidad, Lord Kitchner, Beaugeste over from St. Croix. You ought to hear the Mighty Bird sing about his Yankee wife . . ."

Nothing interested Miss Levy.

"An' don't miss the Tobago Untouchables Sports Club band at J'ouvert jump-up . . ."

Miss Levy's head remained in the forward position, lips tight.

"Or somethin' unique take back New York like a loofah sponge, shaped like a big penis. Scrub yu back, wash de car . . ."

Light rain had begun to fall. Epp thought he'd take one more shot: "When it rains whilst de sun ee shinin' de Debbil ees beatin' ee wife wit a hambone . . ."

Epp let it go. To hell with her.

"Where's Molly's?" Yorgi asked a shill who stood hawking at the corner of Hibiscus Alley and Main.

"Mon, yu almost in it. Downg dere."

Yorgi walked past Boolchand's and there it was, the already famous Molly's; in the windows, skinny, angular, porcelain-faced mannequins with scarlet lips and black brows displaying haute couture at four hundred to two thousand per. Blue carpeting, white furniture. The store was crowded. Noisy with female voices.

He stood near the doorway, gray-bearded tourist, absinthe porkpie and absinthe slacks, white shoes, cheap camera hanging around his neck, and there she was: lavender pants and gauzy white top, bare midriff, just as beautiful, maybe more so, as when she was sitting in court. Her face had been drawn and severe that day in Vegas, he remembered, but still beautiful.

The shining hair was swept back and gathered with a bone at the nape of her neck. The years had ripened her. Just enough. She wasn't a teeny anymore. What was she now? Twenty-eight? Few more pounds on her frame, she was ripe on the vine, tropic fruit to be plucked and squashed.

As he looked at her, excitement flushed through him, a vision of her without eyes; another vision of her on fire, the flames turning the lavender to brown, the long hair rising and rippling into the air as if electrified. Her mouth in an oval, scream coming out shrill enough to break glass.

Standing there, he grinned beneath his beard. More than three thousand days and nights he'd been thinking about this very moment. Excitement tingled in his stomach. In the past, it had been all professional—a job to be done, like Jin Lee—but this time there was personal satisfaction; anticipation.

Well, sir, from what he could see, she'd done exactly what she said she was going to do. He wondered how much of his four hundred ninety-five thousand had gone into Molly's of St. Thomas. Why, he was a partner.

He turned, facing out to Main and the foot traffic as she approached a customer. She was far too busy to notice him. This was really something—man she cut, shot, robbed and sent to the slammer and she didn't know he was in her doorway. He had to contain himself from laughing. He wanted to roar.

"May I be of service?" he heard her saying.

"I'm just looking."

"For a wife, daughter?"

"Girlfriend," said the customer.

Yorgi heard Molly say, "Oh, it is so much fun to shop for girlfriends. Anything catches your eye, let me know."

She still had the same bullshit honey tongue he'd heard in Vegas. He turned back to take another look at her, hearing her say to a clerk, "That Yamamoto, the off-shoulder one with sequins, is perfect for your customer."

Ripe, lush, in her prime, all right.

He was tempted to take off the dark glasses and say, *Guess who?*

He watched a moment longer, then walked up Main. He had serious things to think about: *when* to take her, *where* to take her.

He went slowly down Palm Passage, between Main and the waterfront, old tourist looking at everything, Janine's and Louis Vuitton and Courrèges and Java Wraps, but not thinking about the goodies. *And after he took her, how to get off the island?* Change his looks for one thing. Shave the beard off. Get out of the funny-looking clothes he'd been wearing. Catch a plane.

He emerged into full brilliant sun on the waterfront and went east, moving along the tied-up interisland boats. But *when* and *where* had to be answered first. He passed old beat-up wooden hulls with hand-lettered names: *Santa Martina*, of Tortola, BVI. The *MV Isabel*, of Virgin Gorda, with a chalked board on its side—*Accepting Cargo for Tortola*. The *Monte Carlo*, of Santa Domingo; the *Clio*, of Christiansted, St. Croix, unloading vegetables. They were bow to stern along the waterfront, all of them barely seaworthy.

He kept looking at them, thinking if he could find the right boat . . .

You destroy a witch at midnight, according to that book he'd read in the prison library.

Epp had driven Miss Levy by the shop for a brief hello and then on to the Grand Wyndham, returning her back to Molly's at six. The tour ships had sailed and the doors were now closed. Main Street was calm and so was Molly. Though it had been a trying day, over fourteen thousand in sales, Molly looked relaxed and cool, sitting there in a white cane wingback, one lavender-covered leg carelessly over an armrest, fingers wrapped around an ice tea.

Epp was relaxed, too, sprawled down on the indigo carpeting, reading the airmail edition of the *Miami Herald*, shoulders against the chair, legs extended. Levy had said she preferred to do the interview in private, just the two of them, but Molly said, with a low laugh, that Epp was much more than a driver. Hadn't Levy ever heard of Epperson Watts, Jr., wide receiver for the Raiders when they were in Oakland?

Frankly, no, Levy said, with a distressed look at Epp. Anyway . . .

The tape recorder was running and Levy was saying, "You spent almost eight years in Paris?"

Molly nodded. "Just about."

"Dancing?"

"I did some modeling as well and the last two years over there I worked as an assistant to Yves Saint-Laurent."

"Before that, Vegas?"

Molly nodded again. "And a short time in Puerto Rico."

"Dancing?"

"Yes."

From across the street, Yorgi saw that all the lights were still on in Molly's; she was still there. He also saw the head of the guy, without his Panama, who was at the airport; another woman sat in a chair near Molly. If the man with the bad kneecap got in the way, he'd get whacked, too. Tough potatoes, as Tony Ox used to say.

"I looked at some old clippings in New York—you were involved with a Mafia figure in Vegas and Atlantic City."

"I was nineteen then. Do we have to talk about that?"

"I may mention it. A throwaway. Makes you more interesting, Molly. But is it true?"

"Unfortunately, yes."

"He went to prison, didn't he? Second-degree murder?"

"Yes."

Miss Levy smiled. "All right, when did you start making clothes?"

"Here on the island, when I was thirteen, fourteen . . ."

That's how it went until nearly eight o'clock. Epp had kept an ear open for a while and then closed it down when there was a lot of heavy talk about Yves Saint-Laurent and Christian LaCroix; the quality of cottons from a particular mill in North Carolina and how they took dyes.

When Miss Levy finally clicked the Sony to off, Epp said he'd drive her back to the Grand Wyndham, but she said she wanted to walk around town for a while; she'd get a cab back.

"That's a long way," Epp said. "Fifteen minutes."

She looked at the ex-Raider. "I know it is."

Epp shrugged. This was one honky lady he could do without.

Molly said, "It's been nice seeing you again, Miss Levy."

Levy said, "Sarah."

Why hadn't she said it before? Epp thought.

"Sarah. I hope you have a good story."

That brought a controlled smile. "That's why I came down here."

Epp unlocked the door for her, and on closing it, Miss Sarah Levy sauntering away, Epp said, "Some people deserve to be invited to an ass-kicking contest. She's invited to mine—left leg only."

Yorgi was still watching.

He couldn't decide whether to splash the gasoline on her and set her on fire, disfigure her, or burn her to a pile of ashes.

Leaving the lights on, as usual, persuasion not to break in, they closed the shop and Molly locked it, Epp glancing across the street to see the man in the green porkpie standing over there, looking into a window. Epp again had the damdest feeling, still vague and half-baked, that he'd seen Porkpie before. But where? When? Maybe a fan? Maybe someone he'd met after he hung up his cleats and was married to ballbuster Priscilla, a period he chose now to forget?

Yorgi turned and watched them go up Main, "grocery boy" of Atlantic City at her arm. He followed a half-block behind, in the shadows, as they passed the big parking lot on the right, which was now paved with booths and all kinds of rides, steel-band music rising from it. He crossed over to that side as they went into a small private parking lot.

Yorgi watched as she got into a blue Porsche with "Molly" on the license plate, and backed out.

Then the guy got into a Jeep Safari and backed out.

Taillights of both cars disappeared up Norre Gade.

Yorgi had seen what he wanted to see.

Ten minutes later, he was sitting at the Mafolie Green Bar, having a brandy and milk, thinking about the future, not the past. Check tomorrow to see where she parked. Maybe the same place? Slowly the pieces were coming together.

6.

IN THE MORNING, Yorgi drove the Tercel west, past the airport, to the end of Fortuna Road, as far as he could go that way, then went east along Crown Mountain, skirting town, taking Turpentine Run to Red Hook, just so he'd know how all these roads connected. With this bitch nothing had ever gone right. Nothing! Think ahead, figure everything out. She was probably trickier now than she'd been in Vegas and Atlantic City. Take his time, detail everything. Get her, finally.

At Red Hook, he parked at the St. John ferry dock. Though he'd never been around many, his business not being involved with ships, Yorgi had always liked waterfronts. They went with his hobby. There was a union client Tony Ox had in the Chicago port, and Yorgi liked to go down there, watch what was going on. If he hadn't been a collector and enforcer, Yorgi thought he might like to sail on the Great Lakes, those big ore boats. He'd missed his calling.

He walked on past a small, silent white steel-hulled ship, *Oil Hunter*, of Wilmington, Delaware, which looked like it had been tied up at Red Hook for quite a while. Rusty, it had a long afterdeck with a huge winch at the stern. The bridge and superstructure were well forward. No one on deck.

Having a sudden notion, Yorgi turned around and climbed the rail of *Oil Hunter*, reading a sign that had been taped to the lower cabin bulkhead. By order of the federal district court, the ship was to be auctioned off by a U.S. marshal to satisfy the IRS. In May. No wonder there wasn't anyone aboard. The lousy IRS owned it.

Exploring, Yorgi went around to the port side, the outboard side, trying the steel doors on the lower cabin. The middle one creaked open and he stepped inside as heat rushed out. Stifling in there and hard to see much, but a steep stairway led down into darkness. He'd need a flashlight when and if he came back with Molly.

Outside again, he closed the door. There was another little sign by the jamb, for information of bidders. *Length overall: 110 ft., Beam: 25; Gross tonnage: 177.* A very small ship. For geochemical and gas exploration, baseline and pollution surveys.

No one was exploring for oil now, but maybe the *Oil Hunter* had other uses.

About noon, when the business district was in high tide with visitors, he stood under the awning of H. Stern's Jewelers, in the Camille Pissaro Building on Main, waiting for Molly Bodden to come out and go for lunch, presuming she wouldn't brown-bag it or send out to Burger King. Molly, lately of Paris, was too uptown for that, he thought. She'd go for a fancy restaurant.

About one, out she came, wearing those loose, cool pants, yellow today, still with her midriff bare, large white hat on her head, popping eyes and absorbing wishes as she went west on Main, steps long and confident. A big cloth bag, in parrot colors, was in the crook of her right arm. Nothing had changed.

Wanting to know what she was up to for the next three days, he waited for another ten minutes to make sure she wasn't returning right away and then angled across the street. Going up to one of the clerks, saying he was Bert Stone from St. Louis, in town for Carnival, Yorgi also said he had a radio show back there. "Kind of a *This Is Your Life*. Remember that one?"

"Why, yes, I do," said the clerk to the gray-bearded man.

"I think your Molly Bodden would be perfect for it."

"Well, I do, too."

"Until I actually tape her, it's got to be a secret. You can't tell her."

"Oh, I won't, I promise," said the clerk, positively beaming at the radio man in the big shades.

The clerk couldn't have been more cooperative about Molly and mother Chaktri and the man who was in love with Molly, that former football star, Epp Watts—you *have* to interview him—and where they all lived. Molly was dancing in the big parade Saturday. She'd be dressed like Cleopatra. Wasn't that grand?

Yorgi said it was. Then he said, "Say, thanks a lot. I'll be in touch with you later. I want you on my program, too. Now, don't tell Molly."

"I promise not," said the clerk.

Yorgi then put a few more miles on his rental, visiting Molly's residence off Crown Mountain Road, pushing the bell just to make sure she lived there. Chaktri answered, and when Yorgi asked, "Molly Bodden live here?" the old lady stared, said, "Yes," then slammed the door. The clerk had said she was a little strange.

Then Yorgi spent twenty minutes downtown in a large room where members of the parade committee were at work. There'd been a steel-band committee, a market fair committee, a calypso tent committee. Seventeen in all. Except for fireworks Saturday night, the adult's parade was the finale. So that committee was frantic this Wednesday about four when Yorgi walked in.

Smiling widely behind his shades, teeth glistening, he said, "Hi, I'm Louie Cicero, from Chicago. I do a radio show back there, an' I'm here to tape all day tomorrow an' Saturday. Enough for three or four shows."

Everybody looked at the old man in the porkpie hat, but nobody asked for credentials. That was the least of their worries.

He said he knew about J'ouvert bands tramping through the streets at dawn, but he needed a lineup on the big parade. Saturday. The schedule.

"He'p yohself," said a committeeman, pushing across three legal-sized Xeroxed pages.

Yorgi saw that Molly Bodden was dancing in the streets with the "Egyptian Days Troupe," Position 26B.

The program was wrong. Molly would have already danced for him, a little private performance down in the *Oil Hunter*, her crematory.

Dinging into bottomless sleep, Epp's alarm rang at four-thirty in the cloudy morning, J'ouvert Day, band day. People like Hardeen say, Dance in de street marnin'. Tramp behind the ban's marnin'.

Jump-up time. Boogie an' rock all de way to de waterfront. Ebrybodee jam together. Bes' an' wildest party o' all is J'ouvert.

Others say, "Tis a mess now. Ban's don' start on time. Too many people crowdin' de street. Feet git mash . . ."

Epp unraveled out of bed reluctantly, let N.C. out to lift his leg and considered skipping J'ouvert, going back to bed, getting wrapped in that soft pit again.

Acting like an ancient doddery, he limped on into the bathroom, yawned and peed and finally decided to go anyway. Get his lazy ass moving; take a shower, wake up; get some juice.

A little after five he called Nice Charlie into the kitchen, explaining that it was going to be one mad scramble down there, no place for good dogs; he'd be back soon. J'ouvert was supposed to end by eight A.M., children's parade to follow it.

N.C.'s shoulders slumped as usual, and he lowered his head in dismay, obviously believing that they should always be inseparable, finally trotting off to his favorite spot the few times Epp left him behind, up against the exterior glass doors in the living room in the front of the house, where the road could be watched—the first sight of the Jeep Safari returning.

Going down the hill, Epp felt a sudden uneasiness, like one of Thready's bats had flown in and he'd foolishly gone after it with a broom, forecasting a bad day.

At the intersection of Bovoni, he went left for about a quarter mile in the thick darkness, half moon clouded over, just to see if any cars were parked along there; anyone in them having no legitimate business at hand. None in sight. Thieves were still asleep.

Then he turned back west to go on into Charlotte Amalie, figuring to park somewhere along Prindsessa Gade and walk down to Veteran's, where the bands would pass on flatbeds and in dumptrucks. Stay awhile, he thought; get in the mood again, be part of it; move his feet around a little, watch the crowds. Say hello. Listen to Eddie and The Movements play "Legal." Shake off this damned uneasiness. Then go have breakfast.

* * *

About ten, Yorgi went back to the variety store on the hill off Long Bay Road, bought another five-gallon gas container, filled it at the station up the street, then returned to the *Oil Hunter,* a ship for which he was having a growing affection. He'd flood the steel deck of that compartment Friday midnight. Then he returned to town.

Epp had a life raft for his boat repaired in San Juan and it was waiting at Eastern freight, so about eleven-thirty he drove in to pick it up.

The neoprene-nylon raft with its inflating carbon-dioxide cylinder was in a canister, and Epp flopped it into the backseat of the Safari, rolling away from the airport in a few minutes.

Traffic was heavy on Veteran's Drive approaching the waterfront, bumper to bumper, radio talking about Saturday, ". . . Almos' two t'ousand march, all de ban's, all de troupes, all de floupes, all de *mocko jumbies . . .*"

The only reason Epp was going to the parade was that Molly would be looking a lot like Cleopatra in "Egyptian Days Troupe," moving along just after the Starlites Steel Band. He'd seen the costume, a variation on what a young Liz Taylor wore. His wouldn't be the only eyes on Molly Bodden as she passed.

Hey, what do we have here? Graybeard without the green porkie, wearing a red-mesh baseball cap today, blue long-sleeve shirt, red pants, crossing in front of the truck ahead, those big shades on, carrying a paper bag in one hand, a five-gallon red plastic gas container in the other. Why did this guy bug him? Why did he think he knew him? Where had he seen him before?

Guy dressed really weird. Long-sleeved shirt in St. Thomas heat, covering his arms. Epp was tempted to stop the Safari, jump out and catch up, say, "Hey, don't I know you?" But with all the traffic . . .

Epp watched him for a moment in the rearview, then lost him.

Damn, that guy bugged him for one reason or another. But Carnival always drew some freaks and nuts.

* * *

Humming happily, Yorgi drove the Tercel out to Red Hook, parking in the ferry lot. One had just left for St. John, so there weren't many people around. He scouted a moment, looking for anyone who might think he was a suspicious character and call the police, then walked over to the *Oil Hunter.*

Seeing no one in the vicinity, he hurried aboard, going to the port side, opening the steel door, letting the day's pent-up metallic hot air flush out. The space off the main deck was labeled "Instrument Room," and there were empty mountings for equipment, but Yorgi was interested in what was below, taking one of the boxy battery lights out of the paperbag, shining it down the steep steel stairway.

Heels clanging on the treads, he went below, the beam of light showing him the staterooms with bunks, and a data-conference room so labeled. That was the one, he decided. A table and some chairs in there.

Make her dance up on the table, for a private audience of one, then tie her up in a chair. This time, really truss her. Not like the time in the desert.

Then talk to her for a while.

Tell her what it's like to have only one good eye.

This time really tell her.

Tell her what it was like to be humiliated before the whole world.

Tell her what it was like in Carson City, sleeping on a steel slab for a bunk, with a thin mattress, lights on twenty-four hours a day.

Tell her about his job, sweeping the fucking tiers six hours a day, three days a week.

Tell her everything, then do what he came to do—scrape her eyes out and burn her.

He placed the laundry line, the five gallons of gas, the large Jack-In-The-Box paper cup, the spare lantern under the conference table by a chair. Then he went up from the lower deck toward late afternoon light, humming.

He soon drove back to the Tropic Isle Villas, not too far away at Bolongo Bay.

7.

MOLLY USUALLY CLOSED PROMPTLY at six, but a Manhattan real estate lady vacationing at the Grand Wyndham, having spent thirty-two hundred on five dresses, had asked that one of them be ready for a party on this partying Friday night and Molly had said, "I'll do it myself. We aim to please."

The alterations and fitting ended successfully about six-twenty when the bats were gliding and swooping around the tamarind trees at Drake's Seat and Mountain Top. Streetlights were on. Eating and drinking time. Relax, enjoy.

Locking the doors for the weekend a moment before six-thirty, she started wearily toward her temporary parking space off Norre Gade. Tomorrow it would all be over, thank God, and Sunday she planned to do not a solitary thing. Absolutely nothing. Sleep late, soak in the tub, put a robe on, put her feet up, watch the rolling clouds on the Atlantic horizon.

A dinner date with Epp tonight, the parade in the morning, tomorrow night they'd watch the fireworks from the terrace of the 1829; but Sunday, absolutely nothing. She'd let her mother answer the phone, say she was off the island. Had gone to San Juan, Martinique. Anywhere.

She walked on past the post office and Carnival Village, hearing clanging ride noises and shouts, steel band thumping away, thinking of all the catch-up paperwork she'd have to do next week. She hated the record keeping.

Full night was rapidly covering Charlotte Amalie, making it magical. Lights twinkled over the dark hills.

The key was less than a half inch from the left-hand door of the Porsche when she felt the gun barrel in her back, and a voice said, "Let's take a walk," and she knew immediately who it was, sucking in a breath, a back-of-throat sound, a hollow "ugg." The icy terror of Las Vegas and the Nevada desert and Atlantic City again enveloped her, sending her heart pounding, draining her body of strength. The nightmare, the one she'd been unconsciously waiting for, maybe preparing for, had returned. As they circled the back of the Porsche, heading toward a white compact parked nearby, he spoke again. "Hello, Molly, know who I am?"

The best she could do was make her feet move, responding to the small circle of steel pushing into her spine.

"Your one-eyed ex-boyfriend."

She didn't attempt to look at him, didn't want to see him. Like the little girl in *Poltergeist II*, ". . . they're baa-ack!" Only it was ". . . he's baa-ack." The identical same instant feelings she'd had more than eight years ago.

"Arntcha gonna say hello?"

Don't talk to him, she told herself. Let him do all the talking.

"We're going for another drive," he said, "Only this time you're driving. Last time I drove, remember?"

She remembered, all right. The Tonopah. There was a different unhurried quality to his voice now. It almost sounded filtered. She kept her silence and walked, barely breathing, petrified as before.

In the red and yellow bag was the .22, and given any chance at all she'd empty it into his face. Lately, when going anywhere by herself at night, she'd always removed the safety, just in case. So the gun was ready to fire. Dangerous but . . .

They reached the Tercel and he ordered, "Slide in," the barrel moving from between the shoulder blades to her upper rib cage.

Suddenly, thinking of the gun, the lessons she'd taken, she tried to fight off the fear, replace it with calmness. That wasn't at all possible, but she tried to get her thoughts together. The instructor said that the mental attitude was always very important in target practice. Here was the real thing.

The bag was in her left hand and once she was inside the car it would be by her left leg. While her right hand was inserting the key into the ignition, the left hand would slip into the bag and come up firing. This was all déjà vu, except that it had been encountered before in the desert, just a different version.

As she touched the door handle, he said, "I'll take that bag."

Oh, God.

She turned toward him, thinking that she now had to speak, try to hang on to it. "There's nothing in it except makeup, Kleenex . . ." In the shadows, he seemed smaller than before. He was wearing a baseball cap and it was difficult to see beneath the bill, impossible to see his eyes.

"I'll take it," he repeated, reaching over to jerk it away from her.

She thought about twisting and lunging at him, but the gun dug into her ribs.

"Get in," he repeated.

Twice before she'd outsmarted him. Maybe she could do it again. She opened the door and slid across to the driver's side, the gun staying hard against her.

His door closing, she heard him saying, "Let's go to the ferry dock at Red Hook. I know the way, so don't try to pull anything." He passed her the ignition key.

She stalled in starting the car, playing for time to think. The bag was on the seat between them, upright, and she wondered if she could reach in there after she turned the ignition key.

"Let's go," he said, an edge now in his voice, jabbing her with the barrel.

Out of the corner of her eye as she turned the switch she saw him fishing around in the bag with his left hand. Then he said, "Meant for me, huh?" He was holding the .22.

She started the engine.

Ben Bottle's had its usual Friday-evening crowd of locals plus some patrons visiting for Carnival, noise level up in the higher decibels, and Conkie had her hands full, supplying the talking drinkers.

Epp came in around seven o'clock, Laburnum Hotchkiss arriving a few minutes later. Epp had in mind having a couple, talking to his erstwhile partner, then leaving around seven forty-five so he could go back to Bovoni Hill, shave and shower, get dressed and pick up Molly at eight forty-five. They had nine o'clock reservations at Fiddle Leaf, where Molly could exercise her French, order *côte de veau Valley D'Auge*, or some other Frog dish that Epp would forego. He'd likely take catch-o'-the-day.

Laburnum announced, "They're sending those two West German ladies off to Miami tomorrow afternoon. Want to go down and say *auf weidersehen?*"

"Why aren't they trying them here? They took the *Bertram* here," said Epp.

"Some jurisdictional thing. Open ocean."

Conkie brought the drinks, the Molson on the rocks for the detective, the rum and guava for Epp.

A booming voice came from the door, a shouted "Laburnum Hotchkiss," and then a big body, in khaki shorts and a tank top, feet in Birkenstocks, made it across to the bar in three steps, two heavy hairy arms hugging the lieutenant from behind.

He looked around and up, puzzled.

"Billy Bancroft," said the owner, identifying himself, giant of a man standing off now, grinning ear to ear.

"My God," said Laburnum, rising, "I didn't recognize you without the beard. It's been ten years or more."

"Just about ten. I haven't had a beard for five years. Skin problem. How've you been? You look well."

"Just fine," said Laburnum. "And you?" They shook hands.

"Fat an' happy as a dog with five tails." He appeared that way, grinning, bellied and bald. "You still a cop?"

"More or less. You still have that tuna boat?"

"Nope. Retired," said Billy, beaming.

"Meet Epperson Watts," said Laburnum, nodding his head Epp's way.

Another handshake.

Laburnum's friend ordered a beer.

". . . *didn't recognize you without the beard . . .*"

Rising, almost spilling his drink, Epp said, "Ohhhhhhh, Christ!"

The gray beard . . . green porkpie hat. The man in green pants on Main Street, the guy crossing in front of the truck with the gas container.

The Greek from Illinois!

Out of the slammer.

"Oh, Jesus Christ . . ."

"What's wrong with you, Epp?" said Laburnum.

Already on his way into the back room to use the phone, Epp didn't bother to answer. It was well after seven, she'd probably been long gone from the shop. But he'd try there first. He let the phone ring in Molly's a half-dozen times, then hung up, immediately dialing the house off Crown Mountain Road.

"Answer, dammit," he said.

It seemed forever and forever until he heard Chaktri's voice. "Yes?"

"Is Molly there?"

"No." Old Chaktri, a flat *no*.

"This is Epp. If she comes in, tell her to stay home. Tell her I think the Greek is here. She'll understand."

He hung up before Chaktri could reply, going by the bar, pausing long enough to say to Laburnum, "Don't go anywhere. I'll call you. Stay right here," moving on out toward the door into the darkness at a fast limp.

Laburnum shouted after him, "What the hell's wrong with you, Epp?"

"Just stay here," came floating back through the doorway.

Thinking Stathos might have her holed up at the shop . . . if that graybeard was for sure Stathos . . . Epp climbed into the Safari, backed out, taking off for Main Street, Nice Charlie almost falling off. Yeah, it was; he was kidding himself to hope differently. He was already doing fifty when he rounded the curve to go north up Frederiksberg Gade; he'd drop down to Norre Gade, check to see if the Porsche was still there, then go on to Main. Why in hell did he have to be hit over the head to recognize that ugly guy? He'd thought enough about him over the years. There'd been that nibbling of curiosity from the moment he'd first seen him at the airport. Why hadn't he gone up to say, "Don't I know you?" But that was all hindsight.

The distance from the parking lot on Norre Gade to Red Hook was approximately fifteen miles on an aerial route—the whole island was only thirty-two miles long—but the twisting and turning of Frenchman Bay Road, Bovoni and Red Hook Road made it a distance of about twenty miles. She was taking her time on those miles, the needle on the dashboard hovering between twenty-five and thirty, trying to think of some way to escape. For a moment, she considered speeding up, taking that sharp curve on Frenchman's Bay, near the Antilles School, closing her eyes and plunging off the road. But there was no guarantee that she wouldn't be killed or badly injured, no better off than she was now.

He seemed to be humming, a high-pitched purr.

She glanced over at him, forcing herself to do it: in the glow of the dash he looked twenty years older, even in profile. She couldn't see the scar or the false eye on his right side. He was staring straight ahead, seemingly lost in his own thoughts, the nasal drone matching the whir of the tires. The gun was still in her ribs.

The ferry dock at Red Hook?

Epp was calling from a public phone at the post office, saying to Laburnum Hotchkiss, who was still at Ben Bottle's, "I know this sounds crazy, but the guy I told you about a long time ago, the mob guy that shot me in the knee, he's here, I think, and he may have Molly. He swore he'd get her. Her car is still parked where she left it this morning. She's not home, not in the shop."

"Give me a description," said Laburnum.

Epp guessed at the height and weight of Yorgos Stathos, but pinned down the beard and wacky clothes exactly.

"You see him driving a car?"

"No, only walking. But I'm guessing he's got one."

"Okay, we'll check the agencies. They're all closed but we've got home phones. Meet me at the office. I'll put out a call to any units on the street. We'll find her, Epp."

Epp hung up, then dug his phone card out and placed a call to Walter Nishgo in Las Vegas. He wanted to know if they'd let the bastard out. Or was he seeing things? It was still afternoon back there.

Nishgo said, "Give me ten minutes. I've got to call Carson City. You really think you saw him?"

"He's grown some gray hair on his chin, but I think it's him."

"If it is, I'll guarantee he's violated parole. That alone'll put him back in the pokey."

Putting him back in the pokey was great, but where the hell was he right now, Epp was thinking. He gave Nishgo Laburnum's number, then got back into the Safari, trying to think of where the Greek might have taken Molly, and drove toward Public Safety, three minutes away.

It wasn't like Philly or any other big city where there were thousands of places to take someone and hide out. Abandoned factories, old warehouses, derelict apartments. None of those existed on the island. There were a few remote areas where four-wheel drive was needed—Sorgenfri, Stumpy Point and Bordeaux west of the Girl Scout Camp—but it wasn't likely he'd take her out there. Where in hell was she?

Laburnum beat Epp to his office by not more than two minutes and was asking Epp, "You have any idea what he wants to do with her? Kidnapping doesn't make much sense, does it? Ransom her?"

Epp took a deep breath. "He wants to torture her—cut her eyes out, then kill her. I told you that a long time ago. Same guy, the crazy Greek."

Laburnum looked at Epp with frowning disbelief. "Cut her eyes out?"

"That's what he said."

The phone rang and Laburnum listened for a few seconds, then said, "Las Vegas," looking over at Epp.

"Less than three weeks ago," he repeated.

"All right, you'll notify Illinois . . . Yes, we're looking for him now, whether he's the same man or not . . . Well, thanks for your help, Lieutenant."

Laburnum put the phone down, dark eyes full of concern for Molly. "He's out of Carson City, all right."

"The son of a bitch is here," said Epp. "I'm sure of it now."

Yorgi waited until the lights of the eight o'clock ferry to St. John faded away, and then Molly felt herself being herded out of the car and quickly across the lot, gun prodding her every step of the way. He'd bound her wrists with cord within moments after they'd pulled into the lot.

She thought, why was it that people were never around? He'd had that luck in the Stardust lot, had it at first in the snow in Atlantic City. His luck was holding out here. No one in sight.

There was a marina nearby, boat people always sitting on deck chatting this time of night; an Italian restaurant, Piccalo's, where she'd had dinner a dozen times, was always full Friday nights. Up on the hill off to their left was a mini-mart selling everything from suntan lotion and beach hats to Danish ham and charcoal. But no one in sight this night.

"Where are you taking me?" she asked, hearing the trembling fright in her voice.

He didn't answer, just shoved.

Maybe this was another act in the never-ending nightmare? Act III, The Greek and The Fashion Designer, Scene 1. Parking Lot At Red Hook. Another dream sequence.

The outline of a small ship was ahead, and there was nothing else out there except water and sky. There were no lights on it and Molly knew, at that moment, that he intended to take her aboard. She also guessed that he intended she'd never leave it alive. Curtain. No dream sequence.

At the gunwale, the side rail, more than three feet above dock level, she balked, knowing he'd have to help her over. Turning to him, fighting tears, she said, "Why don't you just do it here?"

"I have my reasons."

When she screamed, "Help!" his right fist slammed into her jaw and she collapsed backward over the railing, blacking out.

8.

THERE WERE TWENTY-ONE auto and Jeep rental agencies, from the biggies like Hertz, Avis and Budget, to the locals such as E-Z and Sun Island and Think Left, and they split the list, Epp and Laburnum and the female duty officer on the traffic desk each taking seven.

If it had been any other night except Friday or Saturday, any other night except during Carnival, most of the car-rental people would be at home. Who needed to watch limbo or the bottle dancers, hear steel bands? That was strictly for the tourists. But it *was* Friday and Carnival. Lot of private parties going on.

"This is the St. Thomas police department, is Debra there?"

"No, I t'ink she at Victor's." An elderly male voice, probably Debra's poppa. "Trouble wit her, mon?"

"No, not with her. We just need to talk to her about a vehicle. Victor her boyfriend?"

"No, de café."

"Okay, thank you."

Victor's was at the Sub Base, 774–9379. Laburnum dialed it.

Budget was the fourth agency on Epp's list and Lucy Poshek wasn't at home, either. She was at a party out on Brewer's Bay Road, past the college. Someone named Tom Ross. Epp looked him up and dialed. Twenty minutes had gone by. Jesus God. His mouth felt like it was coated with baking soda. He was sweating.

He could hear a lot of talking and laughing; Arrow's "Deadly" in the background, Alphonsus Cassell singing "Body Bounce":

Move it, move it . . .
Let your body bounce . . .
Bounce, bounce . . .
Don't stop . . .

Then an electric guitar wailing.

"This is Lucy Poshek."

"Lucy, this is Epp Watts, I'm calling from the police department. We're trying to trace a vehicle. You're with Budget?"

"Yes, I am."

"Did you people rent a car to a gray-bearded guy Tuesday or Wednesday. He was wearing a green porkpie hat . . ."

A few seconds passed. Then, tentatively, Lucy said, "I think I did. Tuesday. I had Wednesday off. If it's the same man, he had a foreign name. Greek, I think."

Epp covered the phone and said to Laburnum, "Maybe we hit."

"Can you remember the name?"

"Not right off-hand. I remember the gray beard and the green hat, big dark glasses."

"Lucy, somebody's life can be at stake. What kind of car was it?"

"A white Tercel, I think. But I'm not sure. I'd have to go look at the contract."

"Will you do that? You're not far from the airport."

"Okay."

"Thank you. We need the make of the car, color and license plate. Who rented it. Call 915 and ask for Lieutenant Hotchkiss. Quick as you can."

"All right."

"Deadly" had segued to "Hot Mix," Phonsie Cassell again on the vocals.

Molly recovered consciousness, keeping her eyes closed, feeling pain lancing up into her head. Had the car gone off the road? She felt dizzy and nauseated. She heard a humming sound and opened

251

her eyes, realizing she was in the bottom of that ship, in a chair, and the Greek was tying her up. The rope was already around her lap. The last thing she remembered was screaming at the rail and knew he must have hit her. Her jaw felt like it was broken.

The room was shadowy, one of those big boxy red plastic battery lights, with a handle on it, sitting on a table illuminating parts of it. The smell inside there was damp and foul, as if the air conditioner hadn't operated for a long time.

He was now wrapping the line tightly around her chest and noticed her head had lifted. He looked at her, shrugged, his false eye less than two feet from her face, and continued humming. Chaktri used to hum when she sewed in the tin-roofed house. There was a seamstress at the Lido who hummed. Molly didn't think they knew they were doing it, hands busy, thoughts somewhere else.

"Why are you tying me up?"

He ignored her and began reeving the line around her legs, binding them to the legs of the chair.

"I asked why you're tying me up?"

The only answer she got was the throaty humming.

She looked around and spotted the two five-gallon gasoline containers under the edge of the table. On top of it was an odd-looking knife, a large-sized Jack-In-The-Box cup, and a cigarette lighter.

She began to weep, softly, inwardly.

Lucy Poshek called Laburnum from the airport, saying, "I rented a 1986 white Tercel to a Nikolas Katsanis at twelve fifty-five on Tuesday, license plate PDB 184. He told me he was staying at the Tropic Isles Villas, the condos above Bolongo Bay . . ."

Writing it all down, Laburnum said, "Thank you, Ms. Poshek," always polite. He was bending over his desk and when he straightened up, putting the phone down, he keyed the intercom, requesting an all-island alert on the Tercel to all units. He ordered any unit on the road near Bolongo to go to the Tropic Isles Villas and wait. No sirens.

"I'm going with you," said Epp.

"Sorry. We've got no insurance to cover you. My rear end would be in a very tight sling."

"I'll follow you," said Epp.

"That I can't stop."

"Or won't," said Epp.

Laburnum went out the door and Epp followed.

She watched as he filled the paper cup with gasoline, putting it beside him as he sat down on the table, facing her. The acrid fumes added to the foul odor of the room, but she barely noticed them, looking at the fast-food cup.

He sat there, impassive.

She tested the laundry line, straining against it. There wasn't any slack at all. She was effectively trussed. He wasn't making the mistakes of the desert again.

The angle of the circular light beam partially lit his face, as if it were theatrically directed, one side in the dark, the other in a pale light, the false unblinking eye staring at her more than the good. He sat there for what seemed to her to be ten minutes, fifteen minutes, staring, saying nothing. She closed her eyes, hearing *their* breathing, a gentle lap of water up against the hull, gurgling sounds beneath them. She said, silently, *God, let it be quick. Please let it be quick.*

Finally, he spoke. "In the library in Carson City I read a book about witches—"

"I'm not a witch—"

"I read a book about witches and it said the only way to kill them was find a splinter, then drive it through the heart. After that burn them . . ."

"I'm no witch, there are no such things as witches . . ." Her voice went up.

"I decided not to bother with a splinter."

His voice was so detached that it didn't seem to be coming from his body.

Shaking her head back and forth, she said, "Please don't burn me, oh God, please don't—"

"Hey, look what you did to me. My eye . . . you shot me . . . you robbed me . . . you goddamn humiliated me . . . you got me sent to prison . . . you're a goddamn witch . . ." His voice was soft. He was still humming.

The Tropic Isles Villas were on Bovoni Road, down by the sea, eighty-five one- and two-bedroom condos with a resident manager and maid service. Epp could see the roof of the three-story building from his front patio. There wasn't much of a beach, and the coral-spiked bottom of the swimming area wasn't kind to bare feet. Nonetheless, there weren't many vacancies from October to May.

Three of the cream-colored, blue-striped S.T. squad cars were waiting in the parking lot of the Tropic Isles when Laburnum arrived, followed by Epp's Safari. It took a moment for Laburnum to brief the officers who had already checked for a white Tercel, PDB 184. Not in sight.

Yolando Castillo, the resident manager, was in her one-bedroom condo, watching Barbara Mandrell emcee Ringling Brothers and Barnum & Bailey Circus with Gunther Gebel-Williams and King Tusk, the world's largest pachyderm, when Laburnum knocked on her door, showing his badge, apologizing for interrupting her program, asking for the room number of Mr. Katsanis. Gunther Gebel-Williams was doing tricks with big cats.

Yolando looked out beyond Laburnum and saw four uniformed cops, Epp Watts standing in the background, and hurried over to her desk. She flipped through registration cards, then turned to say, "Three twenty. Is something wrong?"

Laburnum replied, "We think so. Now we need a key."

Yolando picked one off a board, saying, "This one opens all the third-floor apartments."

Laburnum thanked her kindly, suggesting she stay in her resident manager's abode.

The Tropic Isles condos had sea-facing balconies, and rear-door entrances off back balconies. Epp and Laburnum stood at the top of the third-floor stairway with number 320 ten doors away, Laburnum saying, "Epp, why don't you go back down to the parking lot and wait for us? This is police business now. I don't want you hurt."

Three of the cops, weapons drawn, were standing a few feet away; the fourth cop was down at the foot of the stairs, his gun also unholstered.

Epp said, "With all due respect, Laburnum, that's horseshit. That guy has my woman."

"That's all the more reason for you to stay out of the way. Frankly, you could fuck things up, get her shot, get me shot. You told me this man was mob, and crazy."

"Okay," said Epp, reluctantly. He didn't have a gun. "I'll stay here." To have gentleman Laburnum say "fuck" was sobering.

"That means right here," said Lieutenant Hotchkiss. "And if you hear shots, go down these stairs. Fast as you can. All right?"

"Yes, lieutenant." Like talking to papa.

Laburnum shook his head, took his .38 out and motioned to the cops to follow him, moving quickly along the rear balcony.

Epp watched them go, watched them stop at 320, two on either side of the door, heard Laburnum call out, "Mr. Katsanis . . . St. Thomas police"—What was this mister crap?—"if you're in there, open the door. If you have a firearm, put it down and raise your hands . . ."

Laburnum repeated himself, knocking hard on the door. Silence from 320.

A moment later, Epp saw Laburnum reach around to insert the key. Then they all went inside.

Epp waited a few minutes more, then limped to 320 just as Laburnum was coming out. "He's gone, everything stripped out except three Bic razors in the bathroom."

"What now?" Epp asked.

"We wait."

"For what?"

"For one of the units to find that Tercel. Seven cars are out. I'll leave one man here and go back to town."

"You just wait?" said Epp.

Laburnum said frostily, "We're not equipped with ESP, Epper-son. We don't have mystics to look into crystal balls and say that the Tercel is parked at the Fortuna Mill. I'm going back to the office and wait."

With that, he went past Epp and headed for the stairway.

"Be damned," said Epp, and followed Laburnum down to the parking lot. There, he shouted to the detective, "I'll find her."

Laburnum said calmly, "Let me know where," and climbed into his unmarked car.

Epp went home, turning on the police scanner, going to his office for the .38, then pacing around while the dry-voiced lady worked the cream-colored cars. They were searching by sectors, Blue Water Bible College out to David's Point on east, sweeping the island. Hearing the back-and-forth, Epp began to cool down. They were, it seemed, doing all they could.

"You know what it was like in there? You could get stabbed over a game of dominos."

He was still sitting on the table, the Jack-In-The-Box cup still by his leg, the little X-acto knife there, gleaming. He'd been rambling about one thing or another for more than an hour. His eye, the money she stole, Carson City.

Molly felt as if there were nothing inside her skin but a big throb. The tight laundry line had stopped circulation in her arms and legs. She'd asked once for him to loosen the lines but he'd ignored her.

"And if there was a stabbing or somebody got killed, there'd be a lock-down and everybody had to stay in the cells."

She wanted to faint.

"Once in Old Max I got in a fight with a guy and they put me in the hole for three weeks. They'd let me out into the yard with handcuffs on for an hour a day. Then I went back to the regular section."

Molly wanted to go to sleep and never wake up, just sleep away.

"What was life like? When I got up on days that I didn't sweep—

they made me sweep three days a week and I got good-behavior credits—I'd go to the hobby shop. Then I'd come back and write a letter to my sister, Kathy, or I'd watch TV. Sometimes I'd go out in the yard for a while. Then sleep and do the same thing the next day and the one after that and the one after that . . ."

Without opening her eyes, Molly said, "You make it sound like I did that to you. You did it to yourself by killing Bobby Chapman . . ."

"Hadn't been for you, I wouldn't have hit him . . ."

"I'm awful thirsty, is there anything I can drink?"

He laughed. "That's the least of your worries."

9.

A CAR SLOWLY CRUISING the St. John ferry lot, spotlight focusing on vehicle license plates, picked up PDB 184 on an '86 white Tercel and notified operations.

"Anyone in it?"

"Negative."

"Okay, stay there for backups. Remind you that the suspect is probably armed and dangerous. Repeat . . ."

Epp heard it all on the scanner and was out the door, carrying the .38, Nice Charlie bounding ahead, and into the Safari before the desk's "10-4" was transmitted.

He drove to Red Hook at sixty and seventy, peppermint-striped canvas top flapping in the wind, N.C. lurching around, trying to keep his balance as the Jeep squealed on curves, arriving before any other units and Laburnum.

The police car sat with its lights impaling the Tercel. Epp drove up alongside, recognizing the cop at the wheel, who said, "Hear he's got Miss Molly."

Epp said, "You know it. Where is he?"

"I've been lookin' roun'. 'Less he walked back to Compass Point, not many places he could go. I figure he's on that ship." The cop nodded toward the *Oil Hunter.*

Epp meshed gears, hearing the cop shout, "Don' go over dere . . ."

He stopped the Safari three feet away from the railing of the ship, jumped out and vaulted over, forgetting to favor the right leg, N.C. leaping behind him. He tried the doors on the starboard side, then went around to the port, finding the middle door cracked. Holding the .38 with his right hand, he eased it open with his left, teeth on edge as it squeaked on rusty hinges.

258

Nice Charlie was making chest noises, sniffing, as the door opened wide enough for Epp to squeeze through.

Faint light rose up the stairway, and Epp moved toward it, Nice Charlie suddenly tense, nervous. Short moans came out of him as he looked down the stairs, then at Epp, then down.

Molly is down there was what N.C. was saying.

Epp hesitated, but Nice Charlie didn't. He went down the stairway in a brown-black flash.

There was a shot and a yelp, Epp yelling, "Charlie, Charlie," as he went down the steel steps, feet banging, holding to the rail with his left hand, gun in his right, light dying away, a blackout as his feet touched the deck. Total darkness.

Suddenly, Molly screaming, "Whoever you are, he's got gasoline."

Then the Greek yelling, "A lot of it. I'll burn her alive if you don't go back up."

Epp heard whimpering and moved slowly toward the sound, feeling his way along, touching the cold steel bulkhead to his left, finally touching Nice Charlie with a foot. He knelt down, feeling for the wound, saying to Charlie, "Hang in." The dog was on its side, breathing heavily.

As he found the chest wound, warm blood on his fingers, Molly was saying, "He'll kill me . . ."

Stroking the dog, Epp tried to pierce the overpowering blackness in the direction of Molly's voice, but he might as well have been hooded.

A wisp of red flame, lighting the narrow passageway eerily, came from a room not ten feet from him. Then, the Greek's voice: "Listen to her. I've got a cup of gas in one hand, a cigarette lighter in the other."

The flame went out as suddenly as it had flared.

Then a stern Limey voice from above: "Epp, come up here."

"I will when I bring Molly up."

"Like hell you will," Yorgi shouted.

Laburnum called down again, "Epp, come up here. You're interfering. Use your head, for God's sakes."

"He's got gasoline."

"Enough to blow the ship up," Yorgi shouted.

Laburnum stepped out on the main deck to say to a detective sergeant, "Let's get a fire truck and ambulance here—no sirens— and call the chief at home, tell him we've got a hostage situation . . ."

Then he moved back inside the *Oil Hunter,* calling down to Epp. "Are you armed?"

"Yes."

"Come up, will you please? You can cause her death, Epp."

"Matter of opinion," he said, stroking Nice Charlie. "He already shot the dog. I'm staying here as long as she's in there."

The Greek's voice came out of the darkness. "You both'll die." Then silence.

The fire engine arrived from the Red Hook station a quarter of a mile away.

Laburnum said, "Epp, I'm going to use you as a go-between. Tell him who I am. Ask him why he wants to kill Molly."

Epp did as directed, relaying the long, rambling answer to Laburnum, who was saying to the detective sergeant, "Tell the fire people to rig out a hundred fifty feet of hose, then get enough engine pressure to knock a man down."

Laburnum heard "witches" from below and said, "Tell him he knows there are no such things as witches."

Epp did, then Laburnum said, "Tell him if he lets Molly go, doesn't harm her, we'll bargain for him."

Epp relayed that to Yorgi. Laughter came out of the data-conference room. "Bargain for me in Nevada?"

The question went up to Laburnum. "Tell him, yes, in Nevada."

"I'm not going back there," said Yorgi.

Epp took it on his own to reply, "That's up to you."

Laburnum said, "I can even get the governor to put in a word."

That wasn't an idle boast, and Epp transferred it.

Yorgi scoffed.

Laburnum's voice seemed to be closer when he said, "I can bring the governor down here, in person."

And suddenly, Laburnum was there in the darkness, someone else behind him, whispering, "We've got a hose with a hundred twenty pounds of pressure. You light him up, we'll hit him." He passed a police halogen flashlight, thirty thousand candlepower, to Epp, adding, "Don't get in the way of the nozzle. Let's go."

They inched toward the door of the data-conference room, Yorgi threatening, "I'll burn her, I'll burn her . . ."

As they reached the doorway, the cigarette lighter flared, and Epp lit him up with the halogen bulb, Yorgi standing there, blinded by the MagCharger. As he tossed the gas, the stream of water slammed into his chest, driving him back, over the table, lighter flying away. His feet went up and his head hit the steel wall. He slid down it out of sight.

Molly, drenched with the gas, was in shock as Epp moved past her to go behind the table, where Yorgi Stathos was stretched out, an inch of water swirling around him.

The sound of a single shot split the air in the hose-washed conference room, and Laburnum said, "Why did you do that?"

Epp said, "He was about to get up."

"About to get up?" Laburnum shook his head.

Laburnum had moved behind the table and was standing beside Epp, looking down. He said, "You shot him in the knee."

Epp said, "Did I?"

Suddenly Yorgi lunged upward, his left hand coming from behind his back with the Beretta in it, and Epp fired another shot—this time, between the eyes.

Epp moved back to Molly, telling her she was going to be okay, saying it again and again as he gently unwound the laundry line, telling her the Greek was dead.

261

The shadowy room was filling up with medics and firemen, and their lights turned it bright. Epp looked over his shoulder at them. "Someone take my dog to the vet."

Sedated, Molly spent the night in St. Thomas Hospital, Epp sitting beside her bed, dozing off and on until dawn.

At parade time, in the morning, she wasn't in the "Egyptian Days Troupe" in her Liz Taylor "Cleopatra" costume. The troupes and floupes, those with both walking members and floats, the mocko jumbies, the calypso kings and steel bands, the bamboola dancers, in a hundred different colors, wound through the streets of Charlotte Amalie without her.

But feeling a lot better, she was on the terrace of the Hotel 1829 that night to say good-bye to Carnival '87 with fireworks bursting over the harbor.

When the finale was beginning to boom with sprays and showers of whites and reds and yellows, detonating flowers, silver sunbursts, Epp said, "Molly, tell your goddamn mother you're moving in with me. Tell her she can go live in that tin-roof shack at Red Hook. Or she can go all the way back to Trinidad, if she wants. Just tell her to stay the hell out of our lives."

As a double explosion rocked the harbor, a rocket going high, then opening into a white fountain, Molly turned to say, "Okay."

Epp couldn't believe it.